Prudence, Indeed

Also by Anne Bernays: *Short Pleasures* · *The New York Ride*

Prudence, Indeed

by Anne Bernays

TRIDENT PRESS · NEW YORK · 1966

FOR

Joe, Susanna, Hester, Polly

"Prudence, indeed, will dictate that Governments long established should not be changed for light and transient causes."

THE DECLARATION OF INDEPENDENCE

Prudence, Indeed

1

NICK AND SOPHIE.

The thought of the coupling diverted her, causing her to shiver. Olympian Sophie, unengaged, peered down upon upper Madison Avenue and watched rush-hour cars and buses wedge themselves into immobility. Sophie Golderman lived in a cavernous, rent-controlled apartment five floors above Emile's Salon de Beauté. The doorways were arched, the window glass thin and silky, the floors shimmery and golden. Her friends, most of whom had never left the U.S.A., would say about the Golderman apartment, "This place reminds me of Europe." It was, in fact, very like a flat in the capital city of a foreign country. The only feature of the apartment that oppressed Sophie was the ceiling. So soaring were the walls that sometimes she felt she was in a snake pit and would entertain fantasies of trying, without success, to scale them and escape.

"He's a doctor, Daddy, like you."

"Like me. I thought you said he did research."

"Yes, he does, now, but he was in practice for almost five years. He gave it up to do research." She told her father where Nick worked.

"Cancer research," Dr. Golderman said, with a serious face.

"You ought to hear all the letters," Sophie said, happy to explain. "They sound like the New Deal."

"Maybe your boyfriend can give the human race a new deal, if he's as smart as you say he is."

"Oh, he is." She was radiant. She looked at her father's face for some sign, one way or the other, and saw nothing.

"Your mother should be home soon," Dr. Golderman said. He wanted a cigar, badly, but decided to wait until after his wife came home from her meeting.

"Well," he said to his daughter, "have a good time. You said he was divorced?" Her father pulled out the uneasy question with obvious reluctance.

"Yes," she answered carefully. "Nick has a son almost seven years old."

"Don't wait for your mother," he said. "Go on and meet the doctor. And have a good time."

"Thanks, Daddy. And for heaven's sake, don't let Mother wait up for me again. I'm twenty-five years old, remember?"

"Of course, of course," he said and almost shoved her out into the hall. He looked very lonely.

"Why do you still live with your mother and father?" Nick asked her later. It was their third meeting.

"Because it's cheaper, and besides I like them. And I don't have to do the cooking."

"You're a big girl," he said. "Do they know you've had affairs?"

"Do *you?*"

(2)

"I can only assume you have. I assume most healthy American girls of twenty-five have. You don't walk like a virgin."

She laughed. "How do virgins walk?"

"Pietistically and with their toes turned in," he said. "Well, *do* they know?"

"I can only assume they do," she said, teasing. "But it's not something we're apt to discuss over the meat loaf." Sophie looked at the dromedary his eyebrows made across the top of his face. She wanted him.

"My congratulations," he said, "for managing them so well."

"They're terribly good about it. They never ask. I never volunteer. That way we both avoid what might be disagreeable for everybody." She smiled at him. He took a pair of tiny scissors out of his pocket and began cutting a piece of lined paper.

"What are you doing?" she asked.

"You'll see, you lovely girl. You are a remarkably lovely woman." He cut in tiny little snips. A thousand voices shouted at her and she could not hear what they said; they were only a hum.

While cutting, Nick leaned across the table and kissed Sophie's chin. His lips felt powdery, not wet.

"The waiter's looking," she said. "Would you like me to move in with you?"

"Soon," he said. "And let the waiter look at love if he wants. It's a simple and rare enough pastime." He unfolded the paper. There danced a miniature boy and girl connected by a heart.

"Oh!" she said. "How marvelous. I don't see how you did it."

"They're for you." He gave the cutout to Sophie. It immediately became precious.

Nick broke his roll in half and ate it, butterless. A few crumbs dropped onto the linen cloth, and he brushed them to the side. She wondered how he felt about dust. "Tell me about your wife," she said.

(3)

"Who's asking?" he said. "The inquisitive Sophie or the psychologist Sophie?"

She smiled, embarrassed. "It's not the psychologist; she's off duty. In fact, she's home watching television or something equally mindless."

"Sydney, my wife, my ex-wife, as I prefer to think of her, is happier now than she ever was when we lived together. She's very fat and is married to a fat C.P.A. who bought her a suitably fat house in Montclair, New Jersey. She and the C.P.A. have two new children fifteen months apart, and she is, in her blissful suburban setting, sparkling like a polished gem. Sydney and I met when she was seventeen and owned the best pair of legs I'd ever seen. Her mind is as rigid as a two-day-old corpse."

"Sydney," Sophie said.

"Yes, her parents always wanted a boy, a common obsession. Nevertheless, her father had utterly ruined her for other men before she reached thirteen."

"But you married her."

"Her legs dazzled me," Nick said. "I'd much rather talk about you. Are you aware you're the first Jewish girl I've ever considered marrying?"

"Watch out," she said. "All your hair may fall out." Sophie shuddered as if someone had just dropped a cube of ice down the inside of her dress. If he mentioned marriage, then it was fair of her to consider it.

"It probably will anyway. You should see my mother: completely bald."

She giggled and could not stop. Finally she said, "Where are we going after dinner?"

"Would you like to go to a movie? There's a science-fiction thing over on Fifty-ninth Street, something about radioactive oatmeal. But you look and see if there's something else you'd rather see." He took the movie page, neatly sliced from *The New Yorker*, out of his jacket pocket.

"I've got to be home early," Sophie reminded him.

(4)

"Why? Does your mother wait up for you?"

"No. My first client comes in at eight. Which means I have to be there ten minutes before him."

"Why? Can't he wait?"

"I don't like to keep them waiting. Besides, he might start snooping around."

"Is he a kleptomaniac, this kid?"

"No. His mother hit and killed a little boy in her car about fifteen years ago, and she's never recovered. Her only child's got guilt by contagion. He's a sweet boy, really, but angry."

"Somehow I find it difficult to picture you sifting through other people's grime and solving their problems. You're much too young and rosy. You ought to be sitting by a swimming pool, tanning your tummy and inventing delicious recipes to cook for some lucky man."

"Or is it that you have a thing about women working?"

"Not at all," he said quickly. "Women are unsurpassed in precision work. They can accomplish little things with their little fingers which would drive men up the walls."

"I can't do anything with my little fingers," Sophie said.

"You work with that gorgeous Egyptian head of yours. And, I imagine, your heart."

"We are supposed to leave our hearts downstairs in the coatroom," she told him. "It's bad for the therapy."

He smiled at her, knowing it all beforehand.

"Why did you give up your practice?" she said. They were playing ping-pong and neither one wanted the ball.

"The lure of the laboratory." He pronounced it the British way. "The excitement of the unknown, the shape of the dark night, *und so weiter*. I simply want to discover and chart the islands that don't exist on any map."

"And what about the fame that comes along with the discoveries?"

"If it comes, it comes; if it doesn't, I can live without." He was direct, at least. She adored him for slicing away the tall grass. Up to now most of her friends had talked—and thought

(5)

—like rabbis. Ponderously they attacked ideas from all conceivable angles and then asserted original prejudices with renewed vigor.

She murmured, "You're not like any doctors I've ever known."

"You're damn right!"

At this time, about eight months before they were married, Sophie did not suspect that Nicholas Brean was not perfect.

"My parents would like you for dinner."

"Fried?"

"No, honestly. It's something we really ought to do. I think they suspect that you're more than a simple passing fancy."

"How do they want me? Maybe I should get a haircut."

"They would like us to come on Friday. I said yes." Sophie now lived with Nick, in his three rooms on East Fifty-first Street. She had told her parents she was staying with Mary Fein, recently divorced and afraid of the dark.

"Isn't there something special about your Friday dinner?"

"For them there is. They light candles and pull the curtains."

"Okay. I'll get two haircuts."

"You're a love," she said, standing quite still, waiting for him to unzip her dress and the rest of it.

In his apartment, living now with Nick, she was on an island of love; very little existed beyond it. She played at being Mrs. Brean and it was the most satisfying part she had ever tried. He often sat in his large armchair and watched closely while she performed various wifely acts: cooking, cleaning, making the bed, stocking the refrigerator. Dr. and Mrs. Golderman had not once phoned Mary Fein. The river Sophie had been energetically paddling up for years had suddenly calmed; the view across either bank and up ahead was absolutely breathtaking. "You are a magician," she said and sank into his double bed.

"By the way," he said, sinking after her, "how come they suspect anything if they think you're living with your friend

(6)

what's-her-name, the depressive?" He ignited the roots of her hair with his fingers.

"Who knows?" she said. "Let's not talk."

He did not get the haircut. Sophie was sure he chose to wear it longer than most men, and its length was not simply a matter of carelessness. This, along with the way he carried himself, and his very dark brows and lashes, made him seem theatrical, especially when you put him up against his paunchy or balding colleagues at the institute. He wore dark suits and light patternless ties. When Sophie picked him up at his office on Friday she saw him in uniform for the first time. His white coat, pressed stiff and belted across the back, was so long it made him look exactly like a Swiss doctor in a 1930's movie. Or as she imagined Dick Diver to look, without the pince-nez of course. The coat made a shifting noise. She recognized, in a flash, that at work, Nick was quite a different fellow.

"What are all those tubes and trays and dripping things?" Sophie asked. She was fearful of coming too close; they were lit with a fatal spark.

"That's my garden," he said. "I grow things."

He called to a girl in a large room across the hall. The girl looked up. Sophie thought she saw a flicker of irritation. "Yes?"

"The distilled water bottle is empty again. Will you please see that it's filled before you leave for the night? It ought not to be left till Monday."

"Yes. All right, Doctor," the girl said. She looked for Sophie's eyes and tried to send her a message, which Sophie did not receive, distracted as she was by Nick's hand against her bottom.

"Does she have teeny fingers?" Sophie whispered.

"I don't know. I've never noticed. Come on, let's get out of this place." He was impatient. He shrugged off and hung up the white coat, checked the contents of his office, kissed her cheek, and said, "You smell like lilacs."

"What did you discover today?" Sophie said as Nick led her through a maze of hallways and out onto the street. It was the wrong time to get anywhere. Cars, taxis, trucks, buses moved along, honking like condemned geese.

"Damn!" Nick said. "No cabs. I learned today that three months of investigation is one big black dead end. We're back where we started in November."

"Oh," she said stupidly. His work scared her on the one hand and dared her to hope on the other. Her questions were generally loaded with dread. "I'm sorry, you must be terribly disappointed."

"It's all in a day's work," he said. "What should I call your mother? My mother-in-law's name was Cornelia. Cornelia was on the board of governors of the W.C.T.U. Like a good little girl, Sydney always hid the bottles when Mama came to call. I had to stash my own behind the garbage cans in the back hall. It was a running game between me and Cornelia, who knew perfectly well what was going on—all that naughty tippling we did—but she played it cool because she didn't want to upset her daughter. Cornelia and I never really held a coherent conversation in all the time I was married to her daughter. She kept sparring with me, trying to nail me with some imaginary charge. All the same, there was something distinctly admirable about the old girl: she decided what kind of life she wanted to lead and she lived it that way, right down to her last diabetic day. As far as I knew she never experienced the joy of being trapped in an impenetrable alcoholic haze."

"I didn't know people like her existed anymore."

"Sophie dearest, people like Cornelia, thousands strong, are still lobbying to get Repeal repealed. They're like delayed adolescents, obsessed with trivia—antivivisectionists, Mc-Carthyites, Segregationists, Zionists—all alike."

"Listen, Dr. Brean, I don't care what you call my mother but I wouldn't advise you to air those particular views on Zionism. Not if you ever want to hold a coherent conversation with *my* mama. Two of her brothers are Zionists. One of them lives in Tel Aviv, as a matter of fact."

"Really, in a kibbutz?"

"Of course not. Tel Aviv is a large cosmopolitan city. Morris owns a couple of movie theaters—art theaters. Not everybody in Israel lives in a mud hut and has sun blisters on his shoulders." Some non-Jews—and she hadn't counted Nick among them till this moment—were really incredible. If they didn't know, they didn't even bother to find out; they just went on hugging their precious stereotypes. Like Chinese women's slant, and Negroes have enormous organs, and Jews are hairy. "Morris has so much hair on his chest they call him I. J. Fox," Sophie said, testing her theory.

"What? Oh, that's very funny," Nick said. He was preoccupied. He hated to wait for transportation, hated buses more. "We'll have to start walking," Nick said, disgusted. "Maybe we can pick up a cab on Lexington."

"I think we're going to be late," Sophie said.

"Do you want to call them?"

"No, let's take a chance." If they walked, it would take them close to an hour. "It's just that Daddy gets hungry early," she murmured, wondering why on earth she had promised her parents they would be there at six.

They were fifteen minutes late, which wasn't really so much, but the chopped liver had already gone gray on top. Sophie apologized and kissed her parents, a token greeting. A man who generally swung into a room in high gear, Nick Brean stood quietly on this occasion, tentative, like a child on his first day at school. And then, to top it off, he said "Pleased to meet you, ma'am" to Florence Golderman. Sophie nearly whooped. If he thought he was kidding Mrs. Golderman, he knew what he was about: Florence began to melt right away, just like the schmaltz in the liver. A moment—which mercifully passed— held Florence's kiss for Nick above his head before it flew away, unbestowed.

Slowly and carefully, so as not to appear to pry, Nick examined the apartment and its furnishings, weighing the value of each item (for his own reasons), like an insurance appraiser. The baby grand Knabe, which no one had played since Sophie gave up lessons at fifteen, wore a heavy brocaded Spanish shawl with fringes Nick could not resist fingering.

"You play, Doctor?" Florence said, eyes alight. "I'm afraid it may be a little out of tune."

"I used to play," Nick said modestly. "When I was in college I had a jazz combo. We played for the proms."

"Jazz? You don't play anything classical? Liszt? or Chopin?"

Nick smiled. "My Chopin is fairly rusty," he said. "But I'll do some practicing so I can play the 'Minute Waltz' for you next time."

Sitting on the shawl, like birds at rest, were pictures in silver frames: the Goldermans—both sides of the family. A bride with her train hobbling her ankles, a group of children seated in a compulsive arrangement, like cans of soup in a grocery, a bearded somebody with calm shoulders and frantic eyes, Sophie at five, Sophie at seventeen, just de-braced and smiling for the first time in years. Sophie watched as Nick took it all in, the whole dimly lighted, tasseled place. If, as Sophie suspected, it seemed to Nick that the Goldermans had not bought anything new since 1929, he was wrong; they had bought furniture and knickknacks well into the forties and even the fifties, but by then they were buying antiques.

Sophie saw her mother's hands trembling, a sure sign of anxiety. Nick, deliberately ignoring his hostess' self-consciousness, flattered her into relaxing. Sophie saw her father come out of the kitchen, chewing surreptitiously. He was wearing an entire suit for once—vest and all—and a blue shirt Sophie had given him. He looked polished all over. They know, Sophie thought, which would save words later. Between Sophie and her father, thoughts and feeling very rarely got lost. If her mother made her anxious, her father was reassuring. She liked him for what he did: he was one of the few doctors she knew who, from the day he had opened his office, treated all kinds of patients, all sizes, shapes, colors, ages. He almost never discussed his work at home because he sensed—correctly—that his wife was impatient with anonymous medical revelations. Whenever one of his patients died, Herbert Golderman would stand by the window with head bent and eyes closed and say a short Hebrew prayer for the repose of his soul.

Dr. Golderman held his hand out and met a gaze that said nothing. "I'm very pleased to meet you, Doctor," he told his guest. "What will you have to drink?" It was not their practice to have a drink before dinner.

"Will you join us, Daddy?" Sophie said.

"Certainly, certainly." Dr. Golderman carefully poured Scotch into a shot glass and then transferred the contents to tumblers three times, sliding ice cubes and pouring soda as precisely as if he were filling a hypodermic syringe. "Here's to you, Dr. Brean," he announced when he had passed the glasses out. "Cheers."

Florence was nervous about the soup. "Why don't you three bring your drinks into the dining room with you?"

"In a little while, Florence. The soup won't spoil."

"I'll tell Maisie to put it back in the pot." Florence went off to deliver her own message.

"Your mother got Maisie to stay and serve tonight," Dr. Golderman told Sophie, "so we could talk without her having to jump up all the time."

The soup—black bean with a tablespoon of sherry—had not spoiled. Neither had the roast chicken, the asparagus, the tomato and avocado salad, or the cherry cheesecake. Nick, who preferred meals with a lower fat content, said, "This is an elegant dinner, Mrs. Golderman."

"I taught Sophie how to cook," Mrs. Golderman said, beaming. "But she doesn't seem to care very much about it."

"Oh, I think she does fairly well. The other night she and Mrs. Fein cooked me a dinner almost as good as this one." Sophie coughed, meaning thank you.

During dessert Florence began to dictate Sophie's biography to Nick. Some of it was true. Nick's face remained expectant and bland. "Sophie hasn't brought many gentile boys home," Florence said, in a moment she would have called "straight-forward and honest" and Sophie would have called crude.

Nick took it well: he laughed. "I'm thirty-six, Mrs. Golderman. I have a son six years old. He's the boy you must be talking about."

Florence squinted in horror. "You're married? I didn't know that."

"I *was* married. My wife and I have been divorced nearly four years now. Robby lives in New Jersey with his mother and stepfather. Robby generally visits me one month every summer." Nick began to feel the first few flickers of real enjoyment.

Sophie, mashing the cheesecake with her fork and pretending to eat it, thought it odd that her father had not told her mother about Nick's marriage and divorce; usually he filled her in when it was important.

Persistently, Florence went after the details of Nick's personal history; Nick, amused, obliged. He was clearly beginning to enjoy himself, in spite of a sensation of having overeaten.

"My wife and I were simply incompatible. We found, soon after the wedding, that we had different natures, different values, different habits, different tastes," Nick said, lighting a cigarette. "For one thing, she wanted seven children." Sophie gasped.

"And how many did you want?" Florence asked, pushing a cut-glass ashtray toward Nick.

"Not that many."

"How many?" Florence pursued.

"Flo, really, doesn't the man deserve some privacy?" Dr. Golderman said.

"He doesn't mind saying, do you Dr. Brean?" Florence said.

"Not at all. I'm not sure exactly, but not more than three, certainly. Most women can't spread themselves thin enough to take decent care of more than three or possibly four children, depending on her circumstances. And by circumstances I'm not altogether sure whether I mean she has money to spare or a constitution like a horse."

"Well, there's certainly something in what you say," Florence said, not really having heard what he had said. "But don't you think children are rewarding?"

"I don't really know what you mean by 'rewarding'." There

was nothing in Nick's voice that could have made Florence feel he was being provocative. But Dr. Golderman's eyes narrowed.

"Rewarding, you know. They enrich your life; they make you feel young."

"I think it's a mistake," Nick said, "for parents to try to exist on a child's level. I think it's much better for everybody if the child is encouraged to grow up fast. Mind you, these are just my little theories. In practice I'm as bad a father as the next man."

Florence sighed, bobbing away on the swell of her fantasies. "You know, Dr. Brean, I wanted at least five more children but after Sophie was born something happened to me inside and the whole business was removed—all at once and practically before I knew what was happening. I remember lying in that awful bed in Mt. Sinai—the old building, the new one hadn't been built yet—and crying day and night for two weeks."

"Oh, Mama," Sophie burst out.

"Yes, at least five more," Florence went on, misunderstanding. She lapsed into silent nostalgia and was temporarily lost to the others.

Dr. Golderman, relieved at his wife's silence (unlike her, he believed there are some areas of human experience that ought to remain locked up), urged Nick to talk about his work.

In an instant Sophie realized that Nick was caught between describing it wholly—and obscurely—or oversimplifying, which might sound condescending. Nick chose the former and swam, with giant strokes, out to sea, leaving Herbert Golderman floundering and helpless, just at the large waves. Sophie, seeing her father bewildered, signaled Nick to stop.

Nick said, "You see, sir, what we're after?"

"Frankly, Doctor, you lost me back there." Sophie wondered if her father realized that he was no longer a scientist.

"I can show you what we're doing, perhaps, more easily than I can talk about it. If you'd like to come visit my lab, I'd be glad to show you around. All you have to do is call me the day before you want to come. Sometimes I'm not there."

"It sounds like very important work you're doing. Smack up

against the great mysteries of human life. I imagine it's exhilarating work." Dr. Golderman slid the gold ring off a cigar and chewed gently at the tip.

"It is exhilarating," Nick admitted. "Also discouraging." Sophie watched, entranced, as Nick pleased her parents, not questioning his mood, but under the spell of his incredible charm, enchanted by the fact that he seemed to have been composed by a more careful and lyric hand than usual; by now, deeply in love with a man whom other people talked of in terms of wonder, respect, and envy. He would come out of this evening a victor of sorts; the fact being that he could turn most human situations around to suit a private vision or image of them. It took most people a long time to question the impulses that made him do it.

Florence, back with the living, said, "What did your father do, Dr. Brean?"

"He manufactured chocolate-covered mints—pepper-, spear-, and assorted."

"Candy?" Florence, a secret candy-eater, was intrigued and a little appalled. She had expected a profession.

"Yes, it was quite good. Brean's Cremes. My father lost his business in the crash and fell permanently ill shortly after that. Mother went to work for a dentist. They live in New Jersey, not far from my ex-wife. They get on well and my son adores his grandparents, though I must say I can't see quite why. Mother is very frail and something of a hypochondriac."

Sophie guessed that the questions would stop after she had committed herself to Nick openly. It was just that Florence *had* to know. Her mother's anxious probing, her father's obvious resignation would not matter after she married Nick. Their concern made her twinge but when she was Mrs. Brean it would matter less than their panic when, at the age of four, she had slipped from a playground slide and fallen to the asphalt, breaking her little arm in two places.

"Nick has two brothers, Mama. They are in respectable professions. One is an academic architect who builds city halls and libraries, and the other is a lawyer."

(14)

"A tax lawyer," Nick added. "My father, who is under sedatives most of the time, has been rewarded by his two sons' application to the American principles of hard work and civic participation. He's not so sure about me because I abandoned the bedside. He seems to feel that I must surely have suffered some dehumanizing in the process. But then, you see, drugged as he is, he equates science with godlessness. He ought to know better: there are just as many atheists taking blood-pressure readings as there are those examining viruses. On the other hand, since he's convinced I will find the one way to eradicate cancer, he is, though tortured, essentially satisfied. He will die hoping I still may save him."

Dr. Golderman gulped audibly. "I don't quite understand your attitude, Nick." (It was the first time Dr. Golderman had used the name.) "I should think you would try to reassure your father, support him."

"You mean about his condition?"

"No. I mean about this process of dehumanization."

"How can I? Maybe he's right."

Florence was stunned. She had never heard talk like this in her own dining room. It made the cheesecake sit like a stone.

Sophie, who suspected that Nick had changed his strategy and was deliberately playing with her parents, wished he would stop. And yet she sat and listened without staying him; it might do them some good to be aware of ironies and contradictions; everything had always been laid out straight for her, so straight: black had always been represented as black, the same with white. And as for gray, you did not discuss it any more than you would wear a shirt that was not quite clean.

Florence went out to help Maisie clean up. Sophie, whose offer of help was violently rejected, sighed, and told herself that chasms between generations are not filled in when the younger marries but on the contrary, widen, while parents and children aware, at last, of irreconcilables, stand agape and watch the earth split them apart forever. Sophie really believed

(15)

this was the way it always happened, in spite of what she had read, been taught, absorbed, and, in fact, dispensed.

Sophie left Nick's bed at eight one Sunday morning to have breakfast with her parents and settle things, if possible. She brought with her a waxed envelope of Nova Scotia salmon and six fresh bagels. Her mother's eyes widened over the gift. "I got two whitefish yesterday but this is better; we'll have this. Look Herbie."

Herbert protested but accepted. Sophie looked at him and decided he'd already guessed she was living with Nick; his eyes apologized to her for this knowledge. "Come and sit with us, Sophie. Have a little breakfast."

"I'm not very hungry."

"Sit anyway," he told her. "Have you been losing weight?"

"A little, Daddy. Don't you think I look better this way?"

"You mustn't starve yourself," Herbert said, as a parent. "Does Nick like you so skinny?"

Sophie nodded, embarrassed.

The Golderman stomachs nudged the kitchen table, the same table Sophie had eaten the majority of her breakfasts from. Florence sliced the bagels in half and toasted them under the broiler. She put out some cream cheese, which slid around the hot dough. Dr. Golderman cut his salmon into neat thin strips and laid them over the cheese carefully, as if he were dressing a burned arm with gauze. He bit, chewed, and smiled. "Delicious."

Florence ate without speaking, hardly pausing between mouthfuls. Sophie watched her mother and guessed what was going on. Florence simply had never wanted to hold or handle anything unpleasant. (She'd had Sophie out of diapers before the age of two.) Between Sophie and her father stood Florence, an enchantress who could change rain into sunshine. For instance, Florence's Aunt Rosie, who everybody knew for a fact had been locked up in a state hospital from the age of sixteen, a hopeless paranoiac, had been transformed by Florence into "A consumptive, poor old thing. She's in a sanatorium, in Arizona." It wasn't dangerous, what Florence did; it was merely obstructive. Florence, Sophie guessed, was transforming her daughter's affair with Nick into something as acceptable as it was fantastic.

"Mama," she said, unable to resist accepting a sandwich, "Nick and I are going to be married."

Florence smiled. She did not believe it. "Let's talk about it," she suggested, just as she had when Sophie was a child and had proposed an impossible project like buying a cageful of homing pigeons. Florence did not ever want to seem unreasonable, even though she knew herself to be as tough as Charlie Chaplin's boot.

Herbert rose slowly, believing it, and said, "Let's all go into the other room and talk about it." He knew there was little left to talk about; he could read in his daughter's eyes that it was quite settled.

Florence sat on the couch and said, "He's godless. He said so himself."

"Mama, this is 1957. Those terms don't apply any more. Besides, he said his father thought he was godless—whatever that means. I'll bet you don't even know what it means."

"It means he has no soul." Florence Golderman's mind snapped shut like a venetian blind in a doctor's examining room. "All right," she sighed, her substantial shoulders heaving with imagined grief. "Marry him, don't listen to me." Florence blurred her eyes and squeezed a single tear from each one. She accomplished, by this display, almost as much as if she had collapsed.

Sophie sighed, too, and sat down. It was hopeless.

"A godless goy." There it was, out in the open.

"Mama, good heavens, you're not holding his Christianity against him? I always thought you were so liberal. Daddy, make her listen to reason."

"Hush, Sophie, don't start saying things you'll be sorry about later." He shrugged. "Your mother's got a right to her prejudices just as you do. Let her think what she thinks and believe what she believes. If you want to marry Dr. Brean, go

(17)

ahead. It's not your mother who's going to live with him, it's you. You don't need our consent." The doctor's head sagged.

They despise him, she thought. "But, Mama . . ." she said, looking at her father.

"Mama nothing. You're the bride!"

2

IN HER TRIUMPH, Sophie felt defeated. It was always easy when you were telling other people how to do something; so impossible when it was yourself. ("Some conflict is inevitable, Ruthie, the point is you must first make up your mind and then convince your mother that you are not acting simply to hurt her but because it's something *you* must do, your *own* decision, do you understand? It's your life, Ruth; you must live it *your* way, not hers." "Yes, but Miss Golderman, how do I really know what's best when *she's* always told me what's right and now she says . . ." and so on, hour after hour, trying to get them to read themselves through their own eyes, not their mothers' and fathers'.)

It had now become a matter of readjustment for Sophie to

be with her mother without fighting. The older woman's questions and objections had emerged, presenting themselves in a regular pattern like a clear signal of distress. It was evident that Florence had shifted completely from her initial warm response to Nick (when the current of his charm was turned on) to one of suspicion and woe. Although Sophie, as much as most people, understood a mother's hesitations, she was nevertheless tense and angry when shut up in the same room with Florence. They had endless discussions, which, as they grew more heated, centered more and more on trivia. How could Sophie keep from telling her mother that a wedding feast was repulsive to her; all that food displayed like plastic food and so much of it thrown out afterward? How could Florence resist telling Sophie she thought that Nick's long hair meant he was a homosexual?

One night, after one of these sessions, Herbert Golderman (who throughout was so pained that he remained silent) walked Sophie to the front door. He saw her hipbones as two round knobs sticking out under the wool of her skirt and thought to himself that Nick must be a fool. "I'll talk to your mother," he told her, recalling her plump cheeks of a few years back and wondering if she had grown vain in the meantime. "She'll probably come around and let you have it your way. She doesn't really want to force her preferences on you."

"I hope so."

"Don't look so sad, honey."

"I can't help it. These arguments." She sighed, "You don't look so jolly yourself."

"It's because I still think of you as a little girl. And you're not; you're a woman."

"And you think I'm making a mistake."

"I didn't say that." He looked past her right shoulder into the chilly hall. The elevator whined in its shaft, like a family of ghosts wailing to be released.

"Oh well, Daddy," she said, in an effort to seem cheered, "after we're married you'll change your mind about Nick. Nick is the most extraordinary man I've ever met. Did you know that many people consider him a genius?"

"That's nice, honey, but how is he as a father?"

When she told him, Nick said, "I never expected your parents to fall all over me. Now you think about it. Wouldn't it be strange, actually, if they had? All fathers want to hold onto their daughters in perpetuity. All mothers are envious of their daughters—for one reason or another—not the least of which is their dewy sexuality. Sophie, dear, you have a distinctly and predictably normal set of parents; the situation only *seems* complicated by the religious issue. It occurred to me that this is simply a convenient screen for your mother, who doesn't want you to marry *any*body. We'll all try to share you in the proper proportions."

As he said this, Sophie saw herself being shared by husband and parents—the husband getting the bottom half, naturally. But she knew she couldn't develop the joke. For what she hadn't told Nick—namely that her mother's medieval objections on grounds of religion hadn't touched her in the least while her father's basic mistrust of the Brean personality filled her with despair and introduced her to doubt—made joking impossible. For her, there seemed only one course left and that was to ignore their objections as irrelevant. Sophie Golderman was a woman, a girl, in the white heat of love, when her natural and naïve optimism, combined with fascinating new physical satisfactions, threw her normally clear judgment out of focus. The phenomenon was hardly worth a glance; in that state she was like a million others.

As Herbert predicted, Florence "came around." Her lithe, self-protective imagination eventually made out of this alliance of her daughter with the godless goy a marriage to be consummated in heaven, preferably a Jewish heaven. As far as Sophie was concerned, her mother came around too far. For one thing, Florence wanted them to be married by a rabbi. "By Dr.

Beckman," Florence said, looking at her prospective son-in-law with misguided certainty. Neither Nick nor Sophie allowed the look to faze them. In fact, Sophie brought out a laugh of sorts. "We can't have a rabbi, Mama; you couldn't find one who would be willing to marry us. Nick's an Episcopalian."

"You mean Dr. Beckman, the man who confirmed you, won't marry you? That's nonsense; I don't believe it."

"He has no choice, not unless Nick converted." How her mother could be so ignorant was still a matter of some fascination to Sophie.

"Well, Nick? What do you think?" Florence was still challenging, and her eyes were pleading.

"Florence," he said, in a tone generally reserved for his slowest students, "I'm sure you wouldn't want me to convert to another religion simply for the sake of one fifteen-minute wedding ceremony."

"No, of course I wouldn't dream of such a thing. But you might begin to believe it, afterwards."

Sophie began to giggle. Nick was momentarily confused by Florence's simpleminded solution. He looked at Sophie, smiling, and then he said, "Florence, I'm not sure I can explain it to your satisfaction but I'll try. Actually, the point is this: I'm biologically opposed to organized religion. It's like a sort of allergy with me. Any clergyman, any body of men and women who associate with each other in order to pray and plead, whether they're Christians, Jews, Buddhists, or whatever, distress me beyond words. I start to itch all over. You see, I think this kind of behavior is subversive to human energy. God knows, men make rare enough use of what little they have. The ministers of my parents' church sang us one lullaby; yours sing you another. But to me, they're identical. As a child I went to church regularly. It was a place for children. I think children should learn stories from the Bible; it's part of their heritage, like learning the Declaration of Independence by heart."

Florence's cheeks grew splotchy. "You don't believe in God," she whispered. Florence touched the horrendous implications with the tip of her mind, shuddering as if they would crawl up her leg.

"I believe," he said, "in order. And also in growth. If that helps, you might be able to consider them the same thing. *I* do."

Florence looked at her daughter. "Sophie?"

"Good heavens, Mother, what on earth are you making such a fuss about? You know perfectly well I haven't been to temple for eight years."

"Order?" Florence repeated, baffled.

Herbert Golderman, who had been listening from the sidelines, said, "Florence, why don't you just drop it. It's *their* wedding."

Florence was stymied. "I suppose," she said, "that I'm hopelessly old-fashioned." She looked as if she were going to give up and go into mourning for the person she once was.

"It's not that, Mama," Sophie said. "It's just that you don't know many people like Nick."

Florence said, "And maybe that's a good thing for me. When I was a young woman we looked for values. If we couldn't find them in one person, we looked somewhere else." She sighed.

"Mama, please. You can't talk like this; actually you know very little about Nick's values, if you must call them that. The fact that they're unfamiliar to you shouldn't turn you against them."

"Florence, maybe you ought to listen to Sophie; she may be right." Herbert Golderman wanted peace.

"I can listen, but I don't think I'll ever really understand," the woman said. "I don't think it's any good." She sighed deeply, and then, as if she were a jukebox, she abruptly changed the selection:

"The whole thing sounds more and more like a circus. No rabbi and now, Herbie, it seems your daughter isn't even going to dress like a bride."

"I *am* going to dress like a bride, Daddy, just not like a child bride."

"Child bride, who said anything about a child bride? You're twenty-six years old," Florence said.

"That's just what I'm trying to say. If I wear a short dress I'll feel more comfortable; I won't feel silly. I'll carry a bunch of flowers and wear a veil if you insist but no long dress, no train. Listen, Mama, this is the way Nick and I would prefer it." Sophie felt prickly from head to toe.

Herbert said, "Florence, let her have her way. Does it mean so much to you? Is it worth all this *tsurus?*" He was the one who seemed, to Sophie, to be most exhausted by the endless niggling.

Florence longed to have an orgy. Herbert, distracted by doubts, wished the ceremony canceled altogether (and therefore its form was irrelevant). Sophie had in mind a stylized abstraction of a wedding. Nick, though plagued by recurrent images of the beauty of a free life and an endless stream of beauties crawling into his bed, felt that the sooner the nonsense ended the sooner he could get back to work. Basically, none of them cared in the slightest about the details; onto the details, then, was piled, in disguise, the sum of all their various emotions, anxieties, and expectations. The discussions continued for weeks.

Florence, under pressure from all sides, agreed to a compromise: the ceremony would be performed by a municipal justice, a man whose faulty gallbladder had been diagnosed by Dr. Golderman. The guests, consisting of fifty-five assorted family and friends, would attend the service in the Golderman living room and drink champagne and devour six different kinds of hot and cold hors d'oeuvres, turkey breast, and chiffon cake off plates held while standing. Sophie and Nick would exchange plain gold rings and fly off to Jamaica the same night.

Nick's father was too sick to come to the wedding. His mother, teary and composed, arrived looking very much like a middle-aged version of Peter Pan, so wispy and insubstantial that Sophie wondered what kept her anchored to the floor. She was shy but affectionate and seemed to Sophie to be confused as to why she was there at all. Nick called his mother Sally.

Nick's two brothers, Ernest and Frank, came with their wives, chic and chilly in basic prints. They talked to virtually no one except each other. Neither one of these acted as best man, a part enacted by Nick's closest friend, a writer named Ellias Shantz. Intellectually, Ellie was a deviant, though perfectly clean in other respects; Nick's two brothers looked at him as if he were a blue-black fuzzy-wuzzy. For the ceremony Nick wore a dark blue suit and a silver tie, a shade that exactly matched his several silver hairs. On the way up to the Golderman apartment Nick had stopped to have his shoes shined in a sidewalk booth. Ellie, already slightly stoned from the vodka and orange juice the two men had been drinking with and since breakfast, kept asking Nick why he was buying the cow when milk was so cheap. Nick said, "She's too good to lose."

"Isn't that a backhanded reason? Just so some other guy won't get it," Ellie said, swaying slightly as they approached Sophie's building.

"Listen, Ellie, if I examine my motives too carefully I'll end up leaving her at the church. I mean to go through with this thing."

"It's your funeral. Remember what happened the last time. Besides, Sophie's much too good for you. She's only half-formed. Give the poor girl a break."

"Ellie, shut your mouth and come on. It's too late now."

They went up in the elevator, examining the rings.

Subdued, Sophie dressed for her part in the wedding in her own bedroom. In an access of propriety she had moved back home the week before. Propriety and something else too, something she could not afford to identify as sentiment, as it might have overwhelmed her. But during that week Sophie sensed things she had never bothered to notice before. For example, her father seemed to have become a man of extraordinary generosity, a quality that needed only someone to receive it. Florence—a woman whom Sophie, with her degree in clinical psychology from Columbia, her two years of analytical therapy, her obvious aptitude for sizing people up (or breaking them down in analyzable components) had always considered meager—emerged as more pathetic and thus more appealing than ever before. Most of all, Sophie was suddenly aware that even if her parents did not begin to understand her, at least they were completely wrapped up in her. On the night she became Mrs. Brean, they would each cry quietly.

Sophie looked at the short white dress she had bought at Lord & Taylor. It was vaguely old-fashioned and made of chiffon, fitted on top and swirling silently around her knees. She said to her expensively lingeried image looking back at her from the closet door, "Some virgin bride." The image sneered back at her.

Florence knocked and entered without waiting for Sophie's invitation. "Your Aunt Milly has to stand; she's livid." Florence's eyes showed the strain of having to be producer, director, public-relations man, and exhibitor all at once.

"Let her stand, then; it won't kill her."

"She has to sit; her veins are acting up."

"Not her veins, her vanity. Let her stand."

"Sophie, what's the matter with you?"

"Here, she can use my bathroom stool." Sophie was impatient with Aunt Milly's troubles. "Mama, I'm trying to get dressed. Where's Margo? Is Nick here yet?"

"I'd like to stay and help you but you know how outside help are; they never know where things are."

"OK, go on. Maybe Margo can help me finish up." She felt frightened, nervous, as if waiting for a plane that was overdue. Her air supply seemed to be cut off; her stomach had contracted into a tight, hard ball; her knee joints felt watery and she could not remain standing. A draft blew across her shoulders, and Sophie shuddered visibly. The shiver, witnessed by Florence, was a magic invitation to be a mother again.

For years Florence had been held at a serene arm's length, starting, Sophie figured, with the day that Sophie brought

Margo home with her; Margo, a girl she had whispered to in art history, detached, ironic Margo who was built on Nordic proportions except for spidery hands and feet which were thin and white. They had melted together in an exclusive society of two determined to keep out all aliens—and only they could decide who the aliens were. Florence, watching them, these weary twins of eighteen, instantly recognized that her days of influence and protection were numbered, if not over. It did not take even a particularly perceptive person to recognize that the two, Sophie and Margo, were now ready for the major leagues. For example, Florence believed that the two best holidays were Mother's Day and the Fourth of July. Sophie and Margo celebrated June 16.

"Bloomsday, what's that?"

"It's a made-up day, Mother. A memorial of sorts for Leopold Bloom."

"Who did you say?"

"Oh, Mama, good heavens. In the novel by James Joyce. *Ulysses*. Don't tell me you've never heard of *Ulysses?*"

"Of course I've heard of it. That's the obscene one."

"Oh Jesus!"

"Sophie, I'm sure Margo doesn't talk that way to her mother."

"I guess I do sometimes, Mrs. Golderman," Margo said, lighting a cigarette with languid sexuality, like Lauren Bacall. To Sophie she looked as if she were literally smoldering with creative magic. "We're both a little impatient, I guess."

Florence took this as apology. "I hope this isn't what you learn at Hunter College, you two. It seems to me there are more valuable things to learn than how not to get on with your parents." Florence filled her eyes with tears, though she knew it would do no good. She could only blame the inevitable, and hadn't she gone through some of this with her own mother?

"Would you like something to eat?" Florence said.

"No thanks, Mama, I just brought Margo back so we could leave our books somewhere."

"Where are you going?"

"Downtown. Don't wait up for me, Mama; I'll probably be back quite late."

"But I made a roast," Florence said.

Margo watched Sophie, amused. Sophie said, "Save me a piece."

Florence surrendered. "Have you got enough money?" At that moment Sophie became as precious and as unreachable to Florence as the children she had never had. She looked, to her mother, as beautiful as an Egyptian princess, as beautiful as Bathsheba was supposed to have been, as alluring as Hedy Lamar and Rita Hayworth. Her eyes filled again, this time involuntarily. She continued to worry over Sophie after the two girls had left the apartment, for years after that, but it was as if she were worrying about someone who lived at a considerable distance, such as Cleveland, Ohio, or San Francisco, California. It was unsatisfactory and the returns were too slim. Sophie remained with her family though they were all aware that she hated it. She helped her mother with the cooking, put in an appearance at family weddings and funerals, visited relatives when required, and even worked, during the summers, in the admitting office of her father's hospital. She was dutiful and dreamy, spent hours and hours, in bed and out, with one or two men with whom she imagined herself to be eternally in love, and decided on a career, with the help of a favorite teacher. Florence was grateful that Sophie was not pregnant like several of her more careless friends, but the mother never glimpsed *any*thing of what really went on behind the daughter's face with its dark eyes, its pretty little mouth, its smooth flat cheeks. She was slippery: you thought you had her in your grasp and she would slip away silently, perhaps even laughing to herself.

So when less than half an hour before Sophie became a married woman, Florence saw her daughter literally go cold with apprehension, she acted on this once-in-a-lifetime opportunity.

"Sophie, honey, what's the matter you're trembling."

"I guess I am," Sophie said.

"It's natural for a bride to be nervous," Florence said. "You should have seen me on my wedding day. I was shaking so hard my sister Helen had to fasten my garters for me. Your father was nervous too; the perspiration was streaming down his face as if someone had splashed him with a hose. Of course it was the middle of summer and the heat and humidity certainly contributed, but I still think a good part of it was just nerves. You're bound to be nervous; after all you have no idea what you're getting into."

The two women looked at each other, both uneasily aware of how inappropriate Florence's reassurances were, how neatly they had avoided the realities.

"I hope you're right," Sophie said, wishing her mother looked different. She stood there, encrusted from neck to ankle in stiff, ice-blue lace, a ghastly version of mother-of-the-bride, thrust awkwardly forward by a corset that was far too tight. A phallic-looking orchid dripped down over her left breast, and her hair, blackened and stiff from Emile's last-minute touch-up, sparkled with bits of bottled glitter. You should have taken me with you when you went shopping, Sophie thought with a genuine pang. I would have bought you something soft, like real velvet, something rosy and soft. I would have made you buy a pair of gorgeous dripping earrings with small blue stones. I would have burned that iron maiden you're wearing which makes you look like the whole Hadassah rolled into one fat sausage. I would have given Emile a good kick in the parts if I'd seen him with that stuff in his hands. And then she thought, as if changing her on the outside would make her any different underneath. But at least she'd be handsome instead of grotesque. Sophie said, "Mother, you look marvelous." The lie stuck in her mouth like a stale caramel.

"Thank you, darling. I wonder if I should have bought that hat Helen wanted me to get. It had two feathers curving over the side of the face. I couldn't decide and then I saw the price and that decided me. Still. . . ."

"No. You look fine this way." The way Florence looked was

not nearly so hard to accept as the fact that she was unaware of it. Sophie felt like weeping over the caricature.

And Florence, catching sight of herself in the mirror, suddenly recalled that it was *she* who ought to be answering the questions, not Sophie. But how could she, when she was not certain what the questions were nor from what pocket in her daughter's strange mind they originated.

"Sophie. Darling. Do you know what to do afterwards?" Florence looked away, confused by her own bravery.

"After what, Mama?"

"Well, you understand: after you and Nick go off for your honeymoon. Tonight, after it's all over."

"Yes, Mama, I think I do. I'm sure I do. It's all right; it will be all right. I read a book." Florence could not decide if her daughter were joking; contrary to all the signs, she had, in fact, almost convinced herself that Sophie was the last virgin bride in New York.

"Sophie, please remember," she said, still baffled, "if you ever need some feminine advice, something you don't feel like talking about to your friends, please come to me; I'm always available. And even if I can't give you any answers, we can have a good long talk. I used to go to your grandmother with my problems and I always felt better afterwards." Sophie, whose memory of her Grandmother Minnie was associated only with a shrill voice and an enema bag, winced again at her mother's rearrangement of history. She was troubled too by the coincidence of topic: from the moment she had opened her eyes that morning she had been thinking about the wedding night and how, instead of being unique, it would be one of a series, a marvelous series, but still hardly a surprise. She would have enjoyed a surprise. But you can't have it both ways, honey, she told herself; either you lose it or you keep it. "Mama," she said, "you better go back now; they need you out there."

"Kiss me first, Sophie, your last kiss."

"What on earth are you talking about?" Sophie would swear later that her mother was proposing a kiss of death. If she

(30)

hadn't been so frightened at that moment, she would have found her mother's spookiness decidedly funny. Sophie rose, and sidestepping the two outstretched ice-blue arms, touched her mother's cheek with her lips. It felt like kissing stale cake. "Mama, you're the limit," she said, wondering why she was still so nauseated. If she didn't get married in the next few minutes, she would call the whole thing off. Her mind scrambled frantically through the masses of literature she had crammed inside her head for her orals; prenuptial jitters were treated more as a joke than a symptom. But why did she feel as if she were going down for the third time? If her mother had been about to toss her a life ring (which might easily have been inferred from the older woman's blurry eyes, her anxious hands, and her hovering), Sophie would have opened her mouth, shut her eyes, and sunk to the depths anyway.

Sophie opened her mouth and took in a great gasp of Madison Avenue air-shaft air. "Did you say Nick *was* or *wasn't* here?"

Florence poked her head out of the bedroom door like a stage manager counting the house. "He just came in, honey. Thank God he's wearing a dark blue suit."

Nick and Sophie began their legal life together by flying to Jamaica for a three-week honeymoon. They swam, sun-bathed, walked, went to bed early every night, and, in general, learned very little they did not already know about one another. During their second week Sophie discovered that she had a persistent case of indigestion. Although she appealed to Nick (who, after all, possessed not only an M.D. but a Ph.D in biochemistry) to diagnose and prescribe, he told her, "Next time we're in the village we'll stop in at the drugstore and ask the druggist for something."

She laughed, "The druggist?"

"Certainly," he said. "He's undoubtedly got some sort of charcoal pills that he's been selling over the counter for the last forty years."

"But supposing I've got something serious?"

"You haven't."

"But I feel heavy, here." She put her hand to her chest.

"You feel glorious, there. I know." Nick rolled over on their common towel, his chest to the sun. He looked at her, hungry but satisfied.

Sophie was not reassured by Nick's offhand recommendation but she was determined not to let her stomach spoil her honeymoon. The dense greenness behind their strip of beach had startled Sophie at first. The place seemed swimming, shimmering in an intense green and yellow light alive with tiny insects and strange, hardly heard, hollow noises. It was as if the jungle—more African than Caribbean, Sophie thought— had only recently been cleared for habitation by humans and might, at any moment or while they were sleeping, become overgrown once more. She was not sure that if she took a walk by herself poisonous snakes would not do her in. Or black-eyed natives, accusing her for their poverty.

"Where did you go on your first honeymoon?"

"The St. Regis. We had one night. I slipped the manager a twenty but the son of a bitch put us in a room with only a single cot in it. He also forgot to tell me we'd have to clear out by six the next morning. At noon, I and two thousand other involuntary patriots left for San Francisco where we sat on our duffs for two weeks waiting for them to glue our carrier back together again. It was a great war. Aside from temporarily solving the problem of overpopulation, it suspended all normal amusements for five years, thereby ennobling the human race through sacrifice. You had a choice. You could turn celibate or homosexual or, like most American males, you took what you could find when and how you could find it—mostly on the run."

"What did you do?"

"A little of both, I guess."

"Homosexuality, too?"

"Nope. But I was lucky. Women find me irresistible." He rubbed her back to show her he wanted only Sophie.

"And what about the wives?"

"Same thing goes for them."

"I don't believe it," Sophie said, realizing that she sounded like an innocent.

"And why not: women, men, we're all human. I'm convinced that the variety of promiscuity has kept together as many marriages as it's destroyed." Having had the last word, Nick raised his knees and stretched his arms high over his head, pulling his ribs up and out and sucking his belly into his pelvic cave. A strip of fine hairs had, eighteen years before, crept up his middle and spread outwards like two black mittens, over and across his chest and his tiny hard nipples. He was thin and muscular, a man who deliberately kept his weight down and his muscle tone up by playing squash winters at the Harvard Club and tennis summers in East Hampton. Nick lifted his chin and gazed down his own length. "Pretty trim for a middle-aged gent, if I do say so."

"Middle-aged?" Sophie cried. "You're only ten years older than me!"

"And you're just a baby, right? Come on, baby, want a swimming lesson?" Nick leaned back and then rolled forward with one thrust of his smooth body. With a little hop he was on his tiptoes and reaching down for her hand.

"My God," she said, "you make *me* feel middle-aged."

"You still have a few good years left in you, Sophie. Just watch those chocolate bars."

3

ONCE BACK in New York Sophie practiced getting used to two things in her new life: her name and Ellie Shantz.

At the agency they gave her a black plastic name: *Mrs. Brean.* How odd it was, she thought, for a woman to take a new name at twenty-five just when she was getting used to the old one. Brean née Golderman was quite a jump. Was she no longer as "Jewish" as she had been? Would other people, under the impression that she was one of them, drop anti-Semitic pellets in her presence? And if they did, how would she react? Would she unsheath her righteous anger and annoyance and announce, brandishing it, "I am a Jew; you must take that back"?

"Nick?"

"What?" Nick sat in the molded armchair in their living-dining room reading a scientific journal and laughing every so often as if it were a comic novel. Vivaldi poured through his hi-fi equipment.

"Do you think it was a good idea for me to change my name at work?"

"Sure. Why not?"

"I don't know. Something bothers me about it. It's not a simple change like say from Smith to Jones. The Brean sort of reidentifies me."

"Are you an undercover Lucy Stoner?" he asked, misunderstanding. He looked at her as if she were a little mad. "You *are* married you know. You *are* reidentified. What are you really worried about? By the way," he said, "how's your indigestion?"

"It's better," she said, realizing for the first time that it had improved since their return. "And what do you mean, 'really worried about'? I'm not worried about anything. It's just that Brean hides the very thing Golderman shouts."

"And you can't decide which suits you. Is that it?"

"The kids I see," she said, ignoring the question, "are confused by the change. One little boy asked me yesterday if I was still the same lady I was before I got married, the same person, incidentally, he'd been coming in to talk to for the past eighteen months."

"Isn't that *his* problem, not yours?"

"Yes, of course it's his problem. But his problem is also mine."

"I don't see why."

Sophie gave up. It *was* her problem and she knew it. Maybe she had even communicated it to that little boy and the others too. Wherever she was—on the bus, on the subway, in the market, pushing the steel cart in front of her like a baby carriage, at the movies, cooking, any place at all—she was conscious of the band on her finger, as if it were much larger and heavier than it really was. She felt the same suppressed excitement when she was called Mrs. Brean as she did whenever she caught sight of Nick and he was unaware of being watched.

(35)

"We're having lamb chops for dinner," she said. "Would you like to eat soon?"

"Whenever you say," Nick told her, distracted by his journal.

Sophie wanted to turn down the music. "Would you like another drink?" she said.

"No thanks. How're you going to cook the chops?" Nick asked abruptly.

"Broil them, I guess."

"I mean what are you going to rub on them?"

"Salt and pepper?"

"Are we out of dried mint and cracked telicherry pepper? I was sure we had some."

"What kind of pepper?"

"Telicherry. It comes from India. It's the only way to flavor lamb chops; otherwise they taste like lanolin. I'm sure I bought some at Altman's just before we were married. Come on, I'll show you." Nick rose heavily, as if the most important thing in the world was to stay seated.

"My mother should see this," she said, looking to her husband for a smile of conspiracy.

"Your old lady could use a few pointers."

"You don't like her style of cooking, do you?"

"Do you really want to know?"

Sophie nodded. "Well," he said, settling his hips against the wooden counter and crossing his arms, "I don't find it either subtle or especially imaginative—like Chinese cooking for example. And in addition it's inexcusably greasy. Aside from esthetics, the rate of arterial disease in Jewish males is almost double that of the general population—with the possible exception of French and Italians. The direct consequence of too much cholesterol."

"Isn't that like a Tootsie Roll?" she teased.

"It's a fatty substance that accumulates on the arterial lining. It's the biggest discovered boost to heart disease since God and Freud created anxiety. By the way, do you know what Marilyn Monroe asked Arthur Miller when he brought her home to

Mama for a nice Jewish dinner: "What do they do with the rest of the matzo?"

Sophie was grateful Nick hadn't told that one to the Goldermans. Sophie tried to laugh. "Yes, I think I heard that in the eighth grade. Listen, Nick, is being married to a doctor going to be like diagnosing all the symptoms before they even show up?"

"Only if you're a hypochondriac. And remember, *you* asked me. Now watch me operate, please. I'm going to demonstrate how you braise the mint leaves before rubbing them on the meat—which, by the way, ought really to be warming to room temperature so you can time their cooking accurately."

Sophie did not object to being taught to cook all over again. She too found her mother's cooking both bland and greasy. She thought it a novelty for a groom to instruct his bride in the kitchen; in fact it enhanced him, making him more the *huomo universale* every woman dreamed of but few got. While most of Sophie's college classmates—those Julie Harrises, Katherine Anne Porters, and Claire Booth Luces—had married accountants who knew only figures, businessmen who knew only business, and doctors who knew only medicine, immensely fortunate Sophie had married Nick Brean, the man of a thousand parts.

Ellie Shantz was invited to dinner on a Friday night soon after the cooking lessons began. Sophie was attempting curried shrimp for the first time—the curry powder synthesized in a mortar and pestle instead of already mixed in a jar.

At first Sophie was diffident about Ellie. He did not have a job. He smoked pot from time to time. He had—if you believed him—a sex life bordering on the unbelievable. Most days he rose about noon and most nights he began writing around eleven, when he would politely ask anyone in his Horatio Street walk-up to leave so he could get some work done. He would sit down in front of his typewriter and play it lovingly, like an organ, for three or four hours, until the smoke-filtered light over lower Manhattan began to break up the black and blue sky. A publishing firm whose name he never mentioned had brought out a disastrous novel of Ellie's years before. Once he referred to it as "my paraplegic baby."

Ellie was thick and squat, like a comic-strip gorilla or a man who has something wrong with his legs. His attitudes toward absolutely everything (including Sophie's family which had flourished, not surprisingly, only two blocks from Ellie's in the old days) were so obvious from the moment Ellie opened his rather full-lipped mouth that there was no need, ever, to ask him to define himself; in one sense Ellie Shantz was a walking case book of the psychologically mobile. On the other hand, since he spent his only working hours writing words down, he was different from almost everyone else.

Sophie perceived that one of the reasons Nick and Ellie spent so much time together was that there existed no conceivable tie between the cultures that Nick produced and the culture that produced Ellie. The two men were opposite in almost every respect except the most vital: they existed on the same wave length.

I must be on it, too, Sophie thought, amused. She opened the door for her dinner guest. There was garlic on her fingertips.

Ellie had brought flowers. He shoved them toward her. "Here. I picked these for you at a funeral," he said, slogging past Sophie and heading for the kitchen cabinet with the bottles in it.

"Thanks," Sophie said, following Ellie and wondering where she could find a vase. "Whose?"

"I'm not sure," Ellie told her. "I couldn't see her face too good."

Nick came out of the bedroom. His sleeves were rolled just past his forearms and his shirt was open at the throat. It was a steaming hot night. The windows of the apartment gaped like wide-open mouths trying to suck in a gulp of air.

"I see we're out of tonic," Nick said to Sophie after greeting Ellie. "No house should ever be without lemons, garlic, onions, or quinine water."

"Or telicherry pepper. Where do we hide the vases?" Sophie said.

"Don't have any. Here, use this pitcher." Nick handed Sophie a pair of shears and a glass pitcher. "Now, how about the tonic?"

"I'll go down to the corner and get some," Sophie volunteered.

"No," Ellie said, "*I'll* go."

"Why should *you* go? You just got here," Nick said. "It won't take Sophie a minute."

"You trying to teach her a lesson, pal?" Ellie liked to push people, especially his friends, close to the cage where truth paced and growled.

Nick just laughed. "Sophie doesn't mind; do you, sweetie?"

"I'll be back in a flash," Sophie said, wondering if she ought to mind, and left the two men pouring out straight gin and easing themselves into a common mood.

The air on the street below seemed to have been heated in a furnace and then released slowly. Sophie passed people walking at a doleful pace, like undertakers' assistants, afraid to stir up the air. Sophie strained for the slightest suggestion of a breeze off the East River and sensed absolutely nothing. It seemed incredible to stay if you didn't have to. Only one summer in her whole life had she lived outside of the city for more than four days and that was at sixteen when she was a counselor at a camp for blind children. That, too, had had its steamy side: most of the kids were disturbed as well as sightless. Sophie thought, It's hair-raising how some mothers think that their disabled children are just the tiniest bit repulsive.

In August she and Nick would be going to East Hampton, into a house generously rented to them by Nick's brother, Ernest. Sophie had not seen the place but she understood that it hadn't a rug, its stove was less than a year old, and it was so close to the ocean that at night you thought the waves were breaking over the foot of your bed. Nick's son, Robby, would be there, a third party to keep her from getting bored. She felt two ways about Robby, having only met the boy once. He was Nick's son so she loved him. He was an intruder so she loathed him. Besides, he smirked instead of smiling. Was she afraid that Robby, too, might be just the tiniest bit repulsive?

"It's a real undies-clinger, eh?" Ellie said, greeting her at the door with the splits of tonic. "Isn't that a great line?"

"You made it up," Nick said, from deep in his favorite chair. Since there was no opportunity for the two men to compete, Nick was proud of his friend and tended to show him off, like a bright child.

"Nope, you're wrong. I saw it in the *Mirror*. Now that's what I call a sparkling gem of journalism. You know what the *Times* would say, don't you—Record Heat Forecast—and I say, down with the *Times!*"

"Well, it's dramatic, if nothing else," Sophie said. Her own cotton slip clung to her back like the label on a glass jar. "Excuse me, I've got to finish dinner." She was nervous about the curry; it stung her tongue and Nick had warned her that too much spice would kill the delicate flavors.

From the kitchen, where Sophie stood staring into the large, orange enamel saucepan, trying to work up sufficient nerve to taste the stuff again, she could hear Ellie telling Nick a joke about a mouse who preferred being shot up in a rocket to contracting an experimental case of cancer. Nick roared. Sophie watched. Nick laughed until his teeth, slightly tan at the roots, showed like a braying horse's. His head flew back and his mouth was wide and red and exploding from way back where the laughter started as a gurgle and ended as a full balloon.

"The era of the morbid joke has just been ushered in," Ellie explained. If Ellie said so it must be true, Sophie thought. It takes a kind of psychological bravado to laugh at cancer. Ellie went on, "I think it has something to do with Wernher Von Braun, our new culture hero, and the Supreme Court decision allowing the jigs to sleep with my sister."

Nick was slowing down. "Christ, that's good. I'll have to

remember to tell it at the shop." He raised his eyebrows at Sophie indicating he thought it time to get on with the food. He said, "Ellie, if I didn't know you better, I'd think you were almost ready to take on the enemy."

"*Feel the fog in my throat, the mist in my face?* You got the right idea, Nick, and the wrong man." Ellie grabbed a fistful of soggy popcorn and began tossing them, one by one, with easy accuracy, into his mouth. "Tell me, before I forget to ask, just who is the enemy? air pollutionists? young Republicans? the Chinese labor force? Who?"

"The enemy—as if you didn't know—are the people who don't even want *you* to sleep with their sister."

"Me? What's wrong with me? Hey, Sophie, is your husband on the verge of an action?"

Sophie said, "If he is, it's the first time *I've* heard of it. Though he *has* been acting sort of strange lately."

"You sure," Ellie said, "you're not one of your brothers? Ah, come on, which one is it? Ernest or Frank?"

"Listen," Nick said, pretending not to mind Ellie's ribbing. "Just because I've never been organized for any socially acceptable reason doesn't mean that I ought to be put under observation. If it weren't for your sluggish metabolism, Shantz, you might—you just might—consider doing it, too. So lay off, both of you."

"As I said, you got the wrong man. But I'm with you all the way, kid." Sophie watched as Nick elaborated and Ellie listened like a baseball player who has opened the wrong door and found himself at a poetry reading instead of a poker game. But it was time to go back to the kitchen and get on with the food.

She examined the recipe and it said cloves. She had forgotten the cloves. Before she was married there were never so many little things to worry about. "Damn," she whispered.

Ellie did not notice the absence of cloves. Actually, Ellie ate whatever was around, though his favorite was corned beef on club at Katz's. If Nick was aware of the missing ingredient, he said nothing about it to Sophie but cut his shrimp precisely in half with the edge of his fork, chewed until whatever was in his mouth had turned to mush, and swallowed with his lips tight together. No matter what it was or how much he enjoyed it, Nick always left two bites on his plate.

During dessert—apricots, cherries, and Tallegio cheese, Ellie said to his hostess, "Got any girls for me, doll? Gotta change my luck."

"Black?" Nick said.

"Any color."

"As a matter of fact," Sophie said, "I have a friend but I don't know if I want to entrust her to you."

"What do you mean?" Ellie pretended to look hurt. "I treat my girls like princesses, every damn one of them. What's her name? And is she rich?"

"Her name is Margo Silverstein. She paints. She also waits on table."

"Silver. Did you ever think about what those lovely Jewish names are saying to you: rose-in-bloom, silver-man, morgen-stern—that's morning star for those of you who need a trans-lation."

"How about Lipshitz?" Nick said. "Come off it, Ellie."

"An exceptional case, you have to agree. But no matter. Tell me more about this dame. How are her legs?"

"Ellie my friend, this Margo has pretty good legs, a great development, and, best of all, hungry eyes." Nick seemed pleased with his description.

"*And* she paints," Sophie added.

"Listen, doll. Paints? As far as I'm concerned she could be a housepainter. It's not her everlasting artistic soul I'm interested in. It's her availability."

"I'm not sure Margo's your type," Sophie said. "Margo prefers painters. She says they may act like slobs but she claims they're freer than other people. Ellie, for heaven's sake, don't tell me you don't remember Margo; she was at my wedding. She was my maid of honor."

"Oh, *that* one. Why didn't you say so before. The one with the melon breasts. I guess I was too stoned to talk to her. She's ripe; she's lovely. I'll take two of Margo Silverstein. And if she doesn't want me, I'll find me another painter. A rich one."

Sophie wanted to wait until Ellie had left, but when he was still sitting there at eleven thirty, smoking a long cigar and listening to Nick's hi-fi with his eyes closed and his short stubby fingers scratching negligently at the side of his face and over his scalp, she slipped into the kitchen and cleaned up. She had a client coming in at eight. Her eyes felt heavy. She needed about twice as much sleep as her husband. Often he sat up with a book or reports until after two in the morning.

Just before midnight, Ellie roused himself and got up to leave. His shirt was soaked through; he looked as if he had played three sets of tennis. He kissed Sophie as he left, a moist smudge on her cheek. "You're OK, kid," he said softly. "Nick did good. You just prove his good taste, though I never thought he'd marry one of us. Let me give you one hint: just don't put on weight like number one. I don't know if you ever saw her, but Sophie, this girl is what you call fat. I mean this babe is so fat she's got fat armpits. She was skinny when he married her, though, so watch out. And listen, doll, when you meet Nick's kid, take it easy. He's a little mishugana, hates to be told anything. But if you leave him alone at first, he'll come around eventually."

"Thanks, Ellie," Sophie said, leaning against the door. "And thanks for the flowers."

"It's OK. Thank Frank E. Campbell."

Ellie went home to Horatio Street to write Chapter 29 entitled, "Brother, an Earthlouse."

Sophie washed her face and brushed her teeth and got into one of her trousseau nightgowns. She called to Nick from the bathroom, "How does Ellie manage to pay the rent?"

"He's got patrons. Or rather, patronesses."

Sophie decided to think this over before talking about it again. She said, "Nick, do you realize a bride is a bride for a long time but a groom is only a groom for one day?"

"And?" Nick came up behind her and explored his bride.

"I don't know. It's just that I still feel so much like a bride. As if I were all thumbs."

"You forgot the cloves," Nick said.

"That's what I mean. But you didn't have to say so."

"You'll learn." Nick started to undress. He hung up his pants and put his shirt on a hanger. "Are you tired?"

"No," she lied.

"Good," he said. "Neither am I."

They managed to sweat out July, more or less immobile and in need of sleep. They spent a lot of time in deserted movie houses and restaurants where lethargic headwaiters gave them tables they would never have gotten near in December. Sophie had never seen so many movies in one month. Nick was willing to try just about anything except movies about psychopaths. One night toward the end of July they went to a revival of *Gone with the Wind.*

"This is the kind of picture palace my Uncle Morris owns in Tel Aviv," Sophie said, indicating an expanse of glass wall and rich chocolatey carpeting. "Only he's got a popcorn concession inside the lobby. This place here is too high class for popcorn."

"Is Uncle Morris' movie house air-conditioned?"

"Of course it's air-conditioned. And he's even got two separate bathrooms. That's unusual over there. They generally mix it up."

"Toilet paper?"

"I won't tell you," she said, standing aside while Nick bought tickets. And then, suddenly, Sophie recoiled from a shot of memory: soldiers lying over acres of ground in gangrenous technicolor, groaning, while behind, the guns of armies advancing on Atlanta rolled and boomed. Sadistic realism, which, when she had seen it first, hadn't rattled her nearly as much as the present memory.

"Come on," Nick said, steering her past the candy-vending machine discreetly hidden behind a swath of mocha curtain.

"I just remembered," Sophie said, "there are some pretty chilling scenes in this flick."

"I'll hold your hand," Nick told her.

"Listen, I've come to watch a movie," she said, smiling.

"OK, no necking."

Within a few minutes, Sophie realized that something extremely unpleasant was happening to her. Where, under other circumstances, the movie's headlong romanticism would have amused her, she had now become a part of every excruciating event on the screen; the story was speaking both to her and through her and Sophie Brean recognized in herself, for the first time, what she had so far recognized only in others: a state of acute anxiety. Her own heart, so preoccupied with passion for her new husband, the man whose collarless neck she would stare at when she opened her eyes for the rest of her life (or his), her heart now constricted and throbbed as if she were running up a mountain instead of sitting in a $1.80 plush seat that slid politely back and forth for late comers and early goers. Her hands grew cold. Those barbaric Yankees were coming for her, sure enough, after they had raped all the other females, bayoneted the babies, and pillaged Melanie's house. Besides, whatever was to become of poor Scarlett and all her beautiful dresses?

At last, trying to gain control over her fear, Sophie watched with horror as the nameless soldier was prepared for amputation; all at once she was convulsed—as he was—with panic. She clutched at Nick's arm, felt for his flesh beneath the cloth of his jacket, and dug her fingers in for dear life.

"Hey," he said, squirming. "Hey, you're hurting me."

"Nick," she whispered, urgently.

"What's the matter, Soph?" He had not looked at her.

"I can't watch any more." In the dark, she was ashamed. The soldier's screaming got louder.

"Cover your eyes," he whispered.

"No, I have to leave."

"Oh hell," he said. "Come on then; I'll get you some coffee."

They both rose and Nick led Sophie, clinging moistly to his

hand, up the carpeted ramp to the back of the orchestra. "What a baby I am," she said, more ashamed than ever. Only one other time had she ever been obliged to leave a movie and that was in *Snow White* when the Queen became the witch.

"Not at all," Nick said in a restrained tone. They went down a flight of stairs to the basement where a sad little woman with corkscrewed gray hair and a maid's uniform handed Sophie a cup of bitter cooling coffee which she poured out of a huge silver samovar. Sophie sat down and drank it like medicine. Nick smoked a cigarette and paced.

"Don't you want some coffee?" Sophie asked him. "It tastes like ipecac."

He shook his head and squinted in displeasure at a display of watercolors hung against the dark walls of the lounge. "Christ," he said, "what vile talent dredged this stuff from its unconscious?"

"Maybe that's why it's here. It's not exactly the Whitney." Sophie was still troubled, her inexplicable panic now mixed with violent shame, which, to face it bluntly, Nick wasn't making any easier for her. She was aware—again he made it perfectly obvious—that Nick resented being dragged away.

"What exactly were you afraid of?" he asked her, turning in disgust from an unbelievable lavender and orange lake view. He challenged her like a lawyer in court.

"I don't know. It just got a bit too bloody. I don't know."

"Maybe you ought to think about it," he suggested, exchanging the brief for a couch.

"Perhaps I will," Sophie said. "I don't like it any better than you do."

"It isn't a question of whether *I* like it or not; it's a question of attempting to discover why you reacted so violently to some actors playing a fictional, sentimental story on the screen— something you've seen once before, mind you."

"I told you," Sophie said, her voice rising in anxiety, "I don't *know* why; I just know I couldn't watch it any longer. I was going to scream if I sat there another minute."

He looked at her now as if she were in fact as odd as she

(46)

sounded. And the truth was, it was odd, for here she was a practicing psychologist who spent her days working just this kind of kink out of other people: children, for example, who refused to eat chocolate ice cream, or who couldn't ride in cars, who wore diapers to bed at the age of seven, or who set small fires in the living room whenever they had an opportunity. Sophie had an office, a desk, a cabinet full of suggestive toys, and a fairly good salary. So her behavior now was all the more puzzling—if not paradoxical; she should not, she felt, still be falling into this sort of uneducated trap.

"Well," he said, with a heartiness that seemed as absurd as the coffee dispenser now bent over a copy of the *Reader's Digest*, "well then, are you prepared to evacuate Atlanta yet?"

"You mean go back?"

"We can leave if you want."

"No. Oh no, of course we'll go back. I've got to see how the bloody business comes out." He was visibly relieved, like a child allowed five minutes more in the fun house.

During the remaining forty-five minutes of the picture, Sophie sat with Nick's arm across her shoulder—as if that would soften her ordeal. The fabric of his jacket scratched her neck, and her heart's beat continued too fast and hard. Sophie watched without really seeing, heard without really listening, and tried to concentrate on anything else instead.

"Is it cold out there at night?" she whispered.

"Out where?"

"The beach. East Hampton."

"Good heavens, Sophie, can't that wait till later?"

"Sorry."

When at last, Scarlett, disheartened but swollen with purpose, turned away from the audience and the lights above their heads brightened, it was with an enormous sense of relief that Sophie welcomed the blast of hot air that struck her in the face when they emerged from the theater. "Lovely," she murmured.

"Wasn't she?" Nick said. "The perfect piece. Everyman's dream: lady on the outside, nymph on the inside. Christ, it's hotter than when we went in three and a half hours ago. Next year, I'm going to get us an air conditioner for the bedroom, no more of this nightmare for me." He appeared to have forgotten Sophie's trouble.

A residue of panic clung to Sophie like good, strong perfume at the end of a long evening. It made her fingertips tingle and tightened her chest. "I wonder why it happened," she said softly. "It only happened once before when I was a very little girl."

"It wasn't the movie." Nick sailed out into the street and whistled for a cab that went racing by him.

"What do you mean it wasn't the movie?" She knew perfectly well it wasn't the movie but Nick's dogmatic tone irritated her intensely.

"Only that the movie provoked something in you. Whatever is bothering you was already there, waiting to be aroused. Like a sleeping dog, you might say."

"*You* might say. How come you know so much about my psyche? That's hardly your specialty."

"Oh, Sophie, come off it. You should know by now that everything is my specialty. How can you be aware of life and not want to find out what starts it in motion and keeps it running? How can you sit and watch things operate and not be eaten up with curiosity? People who ignore life—with the exception of their own tiny, precious orbits—are just as dead as their own ancestors."

"Well," she said, and then was quiet. All this was familiar to her. In fact, she had to admit that Nick's passion for inquisition was one of the things that had made him so spectacularly attractive in the first place.

"Curiosity will not kill any cat if he's careful," Nick went on as another taxi drew into their street, "and those who say it will are the same birds who think evolution is a communist plot and Freud is a pan-sexualist."

It wasn't what he said, Sophie thought, furious—it was the way he said it, the pedant. She wasn't his audience or his student; she was his wife.

"Say," Nick said later that night, as he reached out to turn off the bedside light, "did I mention that Will Graham wants me to go out to San Francisco and St. Louis and a couple of other towns and make some speeches?"

"What on earth for?"

"For goodwill. In case you're wondering, goodwill equals public relations, and in our case that means consolidating our convenient tax-free status in perpetuity and solidifying an image of public-minded benevolence."

"Why you?" Sophie said, running her toes up and down his leg. "I thought they knew you would rather be in your white coat puttering in your garden."

"Something about my front-man type personality," he said, as if he were kidding.

Sophie laughed.

"It's not such a joke," he said, sounding uncharacteristically hurt. "You've met most of the others. Can you see any of them wanting to charm the pants off the business and cultural leaders of St. Louis at the Union League?"

"Are you going?" Sophie said.

"I haven't made up my mind yet," he answered, and shut his eyes and immediately fell asleep.

At first, they were all alone except for Robby. It was more of a strain, Robby's being there, than Sophie had anticipated. She decided, within the first few minutes, that he was easily the most perverse child she had ever seen.

The boy was the kind of platinum blond she found hard to believe.

"I thought blondness was a recessive trait."

"Rob is a sport," Nick told her. "Even though his mother has blonde hair—at least she did the last time I saw her."

The boy looked briefly at his father. "Mom's still blonde," he said. Robby continued to dig a hole in the beach with a board he had picked up. Specks of sand flew up and bit Sophie's cheek.

Nick sat back on his elbows and looked out toward the

horizon. "What a fine sight," he said. "The edge of a continent." The waves were enormous and roared like a cageful of starving lions. Sophie moved out of range of her stepson. The line of his jaw was truly formidable.

"What's for lunch?" Robby said.

"Peanut butter and jelly sandwiches," Sophie said.

"Ugh," Robby said. It was the second day of his month with them.

Nick paid no attention. "Would you rather have a hot dog?" she said. "I think I have a package in the freezer."

"Yah, hot dogs are neat."

This child was prickly as a porcupine. Sophie sighed, predicting troubles ahead.

"You're starting third grade in September, aren't you, Rob?"

"Yah. The kids are all cruddy. So're the teachers."

"Rob ought to be in a special school or at least a group for exceptional children. But they don't happen to have one in his school," Nick said, returning. "I've urged his mother to send him to another school but she doesn't believe in setting him apart. She has the incredible notion that it will make him feel unrealistically superior. He *is* superior; he *should* have all the encouragement and challenge he can absorb. But Sydney has him in the local public school where the average intelligence quotient is approximately twenty points below Rob's—and this goes for the teachers as well as for the students. I've offered her more money than the settlement calls for just to send him to a private school, but she'd rather bring up a normal, average, mediocrity with a catcher's mitt for a head. Is it any wonder the boy is bored silly in school?"

Sophie was silent a moment longer, watching her husband grow indignant as his feelings of injustice were aroused. "What about having him skipped?" she said. "Surely they do *that?*" She wondered why they were talking about Robby as if he weren't a foot away from them, listening with the back of his neck.

"I've written his principal about it," Nick said, "and they *are considering* it. These days, however, there's so much emphasis on peer groups and chronological equality that no one gives a hoot in hell about an extraordinary brain that may be going to sleep. They tell me it'll take a convocation of the entire New Jersey Board of Education to get Robby skipped. By the time they've decided that it is or is not going to ruin his chances of becoming a father of real children with real, common, garden-variety minds, Rob will be ready for Harvard."

"Em Eye Tee," the boy said.

"Well," Sophie said, almost smiling. "Well," she said again, standing, "I'd better get up to the house and start boiling those hot dogs."

"Not hungry yet," Rob said, his head investigating his crater in the sand. Sophie was certain the child had not looked at her once, not all morning.

"Nick?" she said.

"What, honey?"

"Are *you* ready for lunch yet?" She needed his help; she could not keep it out of her voice. The boy was obviously getting to her long before she would get to him. And she knew well enough that hypersensitive children take hyperaccurate aim at their enemies.

"Sure," Nick said. "Come on, Rob, let's go on up and eat. I'm starved myself."

"In a minute. I'm busy."

"I'm going with Sophie, Rob. You can join us when you're ready."

Sophie bit into her lip.

"No use pushing the boy," Nick explained to her as they started up the footpath to the house, which sat spreading and comfortable on the dune like a fat lady. "He gets enough of that from his mother."

"Of course," Sophie said, annoyed. She found it almost impossible to tell Nick how she really felt about Rob; it was the first taboo subject in their marriage and it troubled her enough to keep her awake at night. "Besides," she said, reaching for Nick's hand, "we can be alone for a few minutes this way." They continued uphill, the tall grass stabbing her bare legs. "Nick?"

"What? You're awfully edgy today. What's eating you?"

She blurted: "Robby doesn't like me."

"How do you know?" She would remember with clarity that he had not said, "What makes you think so?" The difference was enormous.

"The way he acts. It's as simple as that. He acts as if he doesn't like me."

"Rob is that way with everyone at first. He's cautious—all bright children are."

"You mean suspicious."

"No. Cautious. He has to make certain first you're on his side. Give him time. Once he lets down his guard you'll be great friends. Besides, he's got a fascinating imagination and a pretty good idea what to do with it."

"Like his father."

"If you insist."

"I still think he doesn't like me."

"You know, you're beginning to sound like one of your own clients. Furthermore, this is one of the most idiotic conversations we've ever had. Let's talk about something else."

"OK. What?" But they had reached the house and Ellie was somehow there, on the deck, with a can of beer in his hand and a huge smile on his face. "Here's your hairy friend," he said, "just like I promised." He had, it turned out, walked from the bus stop a mile and a half down the road. In his suitcase was a salami for Sophie. Sophie looked at Nick for an explanation and found none. It was plain: Ellie had been invited without her knowledge. But she liked Ellie, more and more, in fact, as she got to know him better. She felt, sometimes (and with a tinge of guilt) that Ellie Shantz understood her better than her own husband did. She attributed this remarkable idea to their common Jewishness. But another set of dirty dishes to wash. And she discovered that Ellie left towels with mysterious smudges on them on the bathroom floor. How can he get so many women, she wondered later as she stuffed laundry into a bag and headed once more into town for the launderette where she would sit for forty soggy minutes reading an ancient copy of *Good Housekeeping*. Ellie stayed only three days, leaving at six-thirty Monday morning for an appointment he said he had with Harry Luce. Nick told her that was Ellie's standard line when he did not want anyone to know where he was. Ellie, Sophie realized, was better with Robby than either she or Nick; and while Ellie talked with Robby, Nick stared at his son with the same detached curiosity he exhibited when he made note of the progress of one of his experiments. The expression on Nick's face at these times struck Sophie with a lingering unpleasantness similar to an equivocal dream. The whole triangle, she, Nick, Rob, was a mess.

Because they brought the three of them into the closest physical contact, meals were especially trying for Sophie.

Nick was accustomed to two boiled eggs (three and a half minutes), English muffins, and English breakfast tea. He never deviated. Sophie's theory was that great men are compulsively repetitive eaters—same thing, day after day for lunch, at their desks. And always something slightly disagreeable, like under-cooked soft-boiled eggs, unsweetened yoghurt, prune juice, dry soda crackers—foods Sophie associated with being sick. Every morning Nick had that sort of breakfast and it gave Sophie a secret satisfaction, this acting out of the "wife of a great man" ritual, setting the stuff in front of him each morning. She herself ate whatever appealed to her: fruit, cheese, hot soup in winter, Irish oatmeal, sausages and waffles, anything. She based her menu on nothing more nor less than spontaneous appetite. Nick would stare at her plate with undisguised disgust but he never commented, just tapped his egg with the back of his spoon and brought the runny contents precisely to his lips.

She had enough on hand, in any case, to satisfy any first-class passenger on the *Queen Mary*. Or so she thought.

"What will it be this morning, Rob?" She looked at the boy with his perfectly ordinary striped blue and white pajamas, his hair tousled photogenically, rubbing the sleep out of his eyes with his knuckles, and thought, Under that clean pajama top beats a heart of rock.

"Whatcha got?" The little boy blinked at her, all rosy and sinister.

Sophie reeled off the list, waiting for Robby to stop her. She came to the end. "Well?" Nick hung over the stove, measuring tea into the pot.

"Got any grits?"

"Grits?"

"Hominy grits. Mom always gives me grits on Saturday morning."

"I'm afraid I'm fresh out of grits, Rob. How about some buckwheat cakes? They won't take a minute."

"Nah, too sweet."

"Then why don't you let me make you a cheese omelet?"

Robby made a vomiting sound. Sophie wanted to shake him violently, loosening at least a few teeth. Nick was absorbed in his tea-making and appeared oblivious to anything else.

They stood there, Sophie and Robby, he challenging, she determined to be affable; and then, not quite by accident, she saw in his eyes a look so mistrustful as to possess a purity of feeling she could never hope to equal.

One of us has got to go, she thought, and I don't see how it can be me. Baffled by her stepson, she again fell back on her husband. It wasn't what she would have chosen to do but she couldn't help it. "Nick," she said, quietly, "maybe you can find out what Rob would like for breakfast. *I* can't."

"Rob," he obliged, "what would you like? Sophie's got just about everything here."

"Nothing."

"OK, Son, nothing it is. Do you want to sit with me and Sophie while we have *our* breakfast?"

"Nah."

"Then why don't you go on down to the beach. I'll be down soon as I've finished. We'll see if we can get that kite in the air this morning. OK?"

The boy mumbled something and disappeared into the

(54)

bathroom, emerged in his trunks, and wandered out onto the deck and down the steps, and down to the beach.

Sophie sat for a good five minutes without opening her mouth—except to eat her toast and coffee. This morning she wanted a light breakfast, having lost her appetite. Then, gathering what she thought was initiative and found to be courage, she said, "Robby asked for grits because he was sure that was the one thing I didn't have."

Nick was startled. "How can you be so sure? It would be typical of his mother to give him hominy grits every damn Saturday; it would nourish what she considers to be Rob's Southern roots. Besides, how could Rob be so sure you didn't have grits? Sophie, sometimes you say things without thinking; in fact, it's getting to be quite a habit with you, this impulsiveness. You ought to think before you make that kind of statement."

Sophie, restrained by moral scrupulousness, had not mentioned to Nick that only the day before she had observed his son going through drawers and closets, snooping really, looking for something, opening letters he had no right to touch, even inspecting her bureau drawers. Watching him from the deck, she had thought it very odd that although he was apparently an accomplished snoop, he had been quite unaware of her. She wanted to tell Nick now, but something held her tongue. She would save it for sometime when it would not be so irrelevant.

"Well," she said, "then why wouldn't he eat anything else?"

"He wasn't hungry; he told you that."

"But he would have eaten the grits if I'd had them."

"Maybe not."

"*Why* are you defending him? He behaved terribly."

"I'm *not* defending him. Rob doesn't require defense. You, Sophie, are pushing him. He'll eat when he's good and ready; he'll be your friend when he's good and ready."

"I doubt it," she said, feeling as if she'd just swallowed Nick's soft-boiled egg. "And for once I'm talking professionally and not just as Robby's stepmother. The boy is deeply distrustful, not only of me—which might be expected at first—but of all grown-ups. He acts as if he thinks we're all out to do him dirt or worse. He's going to get into serious trouble if he doesn't get help soon." Into this indictment Sophie put all the psychic energy that her training and experience had equipped her with. She surprised her husband with her flat-voiced passion; she could tell as much from his expression.

Nick frowned. "Sophie," he said, "I think we'd better let this subject drop for the moment—at least until you've simmered down. I can't really blame you for feeling thwarted—after all one of woman's basic urges is the urge to feed her family—but you mustn't, you really mustn't start harboring this sort of resentment against a seven-year-old boy. My son! If it keeps up, it will only lead to more unpleasantness than I'd like to think about." His voice, too, had gone flat, an electronic voice.

"Oh honestly!" Sophie stood up and heaved her paper napkin at him but it only fluttered down over his teacup. Nick looked at her with a half-smile, irritating her to the soles of her feet. Sophie left the table and slammed into the bathroom where, shaking with unexpressed and unexpected rage, she abused her image in the mirror with several masculine obscenities; she meant them not for Nick, her husband, whom she chose to see as honestly struggling to be fair, but for the little monster she had inherited when she married his father. He was worse, far worse than a mother-in-law. Mothers-in-law could be sent to Florida.

Ellie Shantz appeared again the next day. Sophie understood then that he would probably be wandering, unannounced, in and out of her life for a long time. In his suitcase were six half-sour pickles reeking like a drunk. He said, "The goy pickles they sell out here are only good for stopping up holes in the floor."

He also left a bottle of blended whiskey on the kitchen counter.

"How's the kid doing?" he said to Sophie. He took off the same sports jacket he had worn to their house last New Year's

(56)

eve. It had a long, diagonal, permanent-looking crease from shoulder to hem.

"Whose car is that?" Sophie asked, looking out through the back-door screen, purposely not answering Ellie.

"A lady friend's. Pretty snazzy. If it was mine I'd paint it gold. How's J. Robert?"

"What do you mean, J. Robert? Is the J. for real or are you kidding as usual?"

"Sure it's for real. Didn't you know? The little bugger's named after Oppenheimer."

"Nick never told me that."

"Ah well, the omission is hardly of world-shaking significance."

"If you really want to know, J. Robert is, as you predicted, taking his sweet time with me. In fact, he hates me."

Ellie appreciated her: he began to laugh as if he'd heard one of his own jokes, laughing really at the bite of honesty that always appealed to him. His laughter grew as Nick walked into the house from the deck, trickling drops of the Atlantic over the red tile floor. "Ellie, you joker, what the hell's so funny?" He noticed the whiskey. "Thanks for the hooch, pal," he said, throwing an arm across Ellie's shoulder. "Get out of those clothes and I'll race you to the point."

"No, man, I didn't come out here to move fast like that. I came to sit on my tail. Where's Robby?"

"Under the house," Sophie said, noncommittally, "making a Gatling gun out of some old pipe he picked up in the dump."

"Clever kid," Nick said.

"Maybe you oughta send him to military school," Ellie said. "You know: end as a man."

They all laughed. "What's that Christ-awful smell?" Nick sniffed and made a face.

"Pickles—*your* pickles." Ellie produced the brown paper bag and stuck his nose in it, smiling. Sophie started to salivate.

"You know I don't eat those things. You and Sophie can have a pickle-eating contest."

"Contest, contest," Ellie said, pulling off his black string tie. He sat down and removed his loafers, which he shoved under the chair. Sophie noticed his feet for the first time; they were long and thin and pale, with long slim toenails, like a statue's feet. Nothing matched on Ellie; he appeared to have been composed of leftover parts. "Everything with you is 'Who wins.' Relax, man, take it easy."

Nick paid no attention. "I'm going to get dressed," he said. "Sophie, why don't you get Ellie a beer and open a couple of cans of salmon for salad. You'll find some capers in the icebox."

Ellie shrugged and sat down on the daybed. "What are you three doing for kicks these days?" he said.

"Oh heavens, Ellie," Sophie said, rummaging in the cabinets for the salmon. "All I want is peace and quiet. And you know something: we almost have it here. You know the routine: the ocean's perfect for swimming and listening to, there's no phone to answer, the nearest neighbor's a merciful mile and a half down the beach, Nick doesn't go hopping around playing golf, polo, or drag racing. It's . . ." She paused, waiting for him.

"It's the kid."

Sophie nodded. "I never believed I could actively dislike a child—until I met this one. And the irony is he has to be Nick's!"

"Are you sure the fact that he's also Sydney's doesn't have something to do with it?"

She was unfamiliar with this sober Ellie; it warmed her. "I honestly don't know. But even if it did have something to do with her, that doesn't change Rob. I've talked with plenty of disturbed kids, God knows, but I've never had to live with one before. Would you like to hear something creepy?"

Ellie nodded.

"Well, the other day I saw Robby swat a large spider and not quite kill it. Then he sat over it, giggling in the most hair-raising way, while it thrashed around. Then he poked a pencil at it and giggled some more, and when he got tired of that game he picked it up and dropped it in a glass of milk and just walked away, while it drowned slowly. I can just see him in eight or ten years, raping some little old lady and giggling while he's doing it, in that same spooky way. Ellie, that child needs help—and Nick won't do a thing to back me up. In fact he seems to think I have it in for Robby."

"Ah, Sophie, come on. Rob's got like a genius IQ so you've got to expect he's going to act like an oddball even before he opens his mouth. I told you six months ago, just give him a chance. If *he* thinks *you* think he's a case, he's gonna act spooky just to oblige. That kid digs things other kids don't. Listen, you've put him in a tough spot, don't forget that. Speak of the fiend."

Robby walked in from the deck, covered with wet sand. He carried cradled in his small, bony arms what looked to Sophie like an uncomfortably accurate imitation of a weapon. He pointed it at Ellie, making rat-tat-tat machine gun noises.

Ellie said, "How's the boy, how's old Sam Colt this morning? Here, let me look at that thing." Robby handed it to Ellie, who examined it. Rob said nothing but appeared to be covertly pleased.

Why can't *I* do that, Sophie said to herself. Because I don't know anything about guns, that's why. She felt her mouth go dry with annoyance.

Nick appeared from the bedroom, in shorts and a polo shirt, as neat and consonant as a four-color page in *Esquire*. He looked at Rob's gun and expressed his satisfaction with it, suggesting one improvement and then said, "I'm going for a short walk. Anyone want to come along?"

Sophie, longing for a few minutes alone with her husband, said, "What about lunch? By the way, the salmon must have swum away; I can't find it."

"I'll find it later," Nick said. "Just a short walk, I need some more exercise. Who's coming? Ellie? Rob?"

Ellie said, "Count me out; I'm going to flake off for a while." Robby said nothing at all. Sophie, in silent desperation, was ordering him to stay behind. Nick shrugged and strode out of the house on the sea side. Sophie ran after him.

The next moment she grabbed his hand and brought it to

her face. It smelled clean, like good soap. "I love you," she said.

"You're a funny one," Nick told her. "You're so jealous of me, you don't want anyone else to even talk to me, do you?"

"Oh, Nick that's not so."

"Never mind," he said. "You're still the lovely dark creature I married. Give me your hand again and we'll just be quiet."

During that walk—which Sophie recalled later as idyllic— Nick Brean met a painter friend on the beach and asked him and his girl to come by later that evening for a game of poker. They all played until two-thirty the next morning.

Soon summer was gone and Robby returned to his other home and Nick and Sophie moved back to the city, cooling slowly like a pie left on the window sill. Once more Nick was faced with the decision over the speaking tour. Dr. Graham, who possessed no weapon of persuasion other than persuasion (Nick was too valuable in the lab to risk losing over something like this), bought Nick lunch at various bewitching restaurants on the East Side and attempted to persuade him to sell the institute like Mary Pickford selling World War I bonds.

This was the first time Sophie had witnessed Nick trying to make up his mind. Amused but somewhat disturbed by the unfamiliar image his vacillation threw on her screen, she tried quite sincerely to help him.

"Why don't you want to go?" she asked, wishing that she could leave her job for a while and go with him, fly to cities she had never seen, have a fuss made over her.

"Because another interruption, that is, *my* being away from the lab, and from my staff, might throw my experiments way off keel. A matter of a few weeks may actually result in several months' delay. The way my work is set up, physically and technically, requires almost constant surveillance by the director—who just happens to be me."

"Then how can you *think* of leaving?"

"Because Will Graham asked me to. Apparently, I'm the only one close enough to both the administration and the actual research to make the kind of presentation—based on firsthand knowledge—that Will feels we're obliged to give."

"The *only* one? What about himself?"

"Will hasn't stepped inside the lab for two years."

"I'm sure that's not true. Besides, he must know what's going on, what you're trying to accomplish?"

"Well, certainly he does. It's his job to be informed about the work; he's the boss, after all. The fact is that Bill is too busy; he flies to Washington once or twice a week handling and angling for government grants. He doesn't feel he can take on another project now."

"Besides," Sophie said, smiling conspiratorily, "you have the nicest table manners and the best-cut suits at the institute."

Sophie misjudged utterly the effect of her teasing. Nick said, "That's the second time you've suggested that Will's asked me to do this because of what you consider to be a trival reason. I don't particularly want to hear you imply it again, Sophie. It's not only untrue but it makes you sound jealous and resentful—which you're not."

"All right," Sophie said, realizing that what burned her eyes were tears. "But," she went on, "*you* were the one who suggested it first. *You* said 'Can you see any of the others turning on the charm for St. Louis?'"

"You, of all people, should have known I was joking when I said that." He was very angry. "I don't want to talk about it any more."

Sophie did not know what to do with her hands. She finally put them to her face to cover the tears which fell involuntarily.

"I'm going," he said. "I just now decided."

4

NICK LEFT; Sophie discovered she was more alone now than she had been before she was married. The temptation to cry each evening as she stepped inside their twilit apartment, which could not have been but seemed dustier, almost musky like a long unused front parlor, was often too much; and she sniffed the tears back with determination like a child who has been punished but does not want to admit the hurt. It felt to Sophie, left for the first time, as if, God forbid, he would *never* come back.

She ate dinner with a book beside her plate and though she would not make much of the lonely meal, neither would she stoop to a TV dinner; they were entirely too melancholy, the idea being, as she saw it, that you did not have to think in order to live; just unwrap, heat, and insert.

His side of the bed was cold, the sheets as uninviting as a glass of water that has stood by the bed all night. In fact, she thought, I am like a widow and I hate it. She understood why maiden ladies were happier than widows: it wasn't what you didn't have but what you were unaccustomed to not having.

Sophie got to work early the day after she saw Nick off on the plane. The building was deserted. Sophie sat at her desk reading the *Times* and listening to the others arrive. Then she opened her desk and cleaned out five years' accumulation of bent paper clips, foreign stamps, advertising flyers, and old, unread memos, matches, and calendar fillers. What does a psychological counselor keep in her desk? The same things as any other woman: a towel, a few sheets of carbon paper, nail polish for runs, peanut butter cheese cracker crumbs, and old unread memos. She ought to have a baby sometime, Sophie thought, but the idea had as little relationship to a real infant as a three-day-old fetus does to the delinquent it may become. And it was an idea as lacking in thrills as the probability that one day she would own an automatic clothes dryer. If her mother and father had sacrificed certain tangibles to put her into this comfortable swivel chair—which also tipped backwards, just as the other Ph.D.s' did—she, Sophie, had sacrificed any number of other things, less tangible than money and thus more central. She was not prepared to give up this desk space yet, nor the gratification she got when her mind picked the right answer and formed a solution. She was not ready yet to stuff babies into dryers.

I could have been just like Margo, she thought. But after all, was that so terrible? One of Margo's earliest pictures— the suggestion of a cripple crumpled into the corner, not altogether successful because not quite easy in its harmony— hung on a wall in Sophie's office. Her recalcitrant clients were always gratified by the splintered crutch in Margo's painting.

To Sophie a new face was as exciting as a new equation is to a mathematician. She must solve it, take this sullen (smirky, evasive, hostile, blank, brutal) face, break it apart, and reassemble it. Solve it. (If you can. She thought bleakly of

Robby). Faces told more than they meant to. Often it was hard on her, especially the smirky ones and she would end the first fifty minutes feeling that her clothes had been ripped off.

The day after the day Nick left Sophie prepared herself for a new face. As she walked back from the women's lounge with a mug of instant coffee, she said "Hello" to Mrs. Magid, the psychometrist, "Good Morning" to Dr. Strauss, her boss, everybody's boss, and 'Hi" to several secretaries, shiny like pennies in their brand new junior fashions of supersaturated blues, greens, and reds. The secretaries earned a lot of money and took off a lot of time, spending it either in the lounge making up their faces or in the coffee shop downstairs making up stories about their bosses and their boyfriends.

Widowed Sophie lost her sadness the moment the new face, Stuart Prince's, walked into her office. She got up and shook hands with a boy and felt the grip of a man. "Sit down, Stuart," she said, indicating the ersatz Danish modern on the other side of her desk.

To deflect his intensity, Sophie adjusted something on the window blind. Then she too sat down, opposite the boy.

"Where's the couch?" he said. He was starting out with an evasive face; Sophie knew it might change abruptly.

"No couch. I'm not a psychoanalyst. I thought you would know that."

"Yeah," he said. He was well built, strong. His dark hair was brushed forward. Aesthete with delusions of athlete, she thought and then dismissed the diagnosis as unscientific.

"I guess," she went on, "that you know why you're here."

"All I know is I don't need to be here. All I need is to quit school and go to work. Simple. Easy as crapping."

She accepted his challenge. "It's your mother's idea, isn't it? She and your principal, Mr. Farrow. As I understand it, they think you're too smart to be a dropout. As simple as that."

"Yeah. They're just dying to have me stay in school. What for? I'm flunking most things anyway."

"You don't like school very much, do you?"

"Listen, lady, what kind of stupid half-assed question is that?

You know damn well I don't. Why are you wasting time asking me a question you know the answer to?" The boy fidgeted in his chair as if he were sitting on shards of glass.

"Whose time are we wasting, Stuart, yours or mine?"

"Yours *and* mine. Oh man."

"If you had a choice, Stuart," she said, "what kind of job would you get?"

"Christ, I dunno, sell bowling balls, just a job, just anything."

"You know, don't you, that any worthwhile work requires, at the very least, a high school education and you've only completed"—she looked down at his record—"half your junior year?"

"Christ, you cats all sound alike. Why does it matter to old Farrow if I finish or not? Why does it matter to you?" Evasive changed slowly but with a Jekyll-Hyde distinctness to hostile. At least his pump did not require extensive priming. They had made a start.

Stuart, silent for a minute or two, uncomfortable under Sophie's gaze, looked up at Margo's painting. "I can do better than that guy."

"That guy's a woman," she said, gently. "Do you like to paint?"

"Not any more. When I was a kid I did."

"Do you have any pictures you'd like to bring in to show me?"

"No."

"All right," she said. "You don't have to."

"You're damn right I don't have to."

"This is your time, Stuart, and you can do or say whatever you feel like here. I'm not here to judge you." It was one of the most difficult—and at the same time one of the most basic—points to get across. Most of them did not want to believe her. "I'd like to ask you a few more questions," she went on, "but you don't have to answer them if you don't feel like it; we'll get to them another day."

"Like what?" Hostile switched again—to suspicious.

"Well, for example, is there some way you think you could

(65)

work more easily? What I mean is do you think you're flunking because the work's too hard for you or is it because you can't seem to get down to any real studying?"

He looked up sharply at this and she saw a smile begin, then disappear inside a grimace. He wagged his head very slowly left to right and back again, trying to keep his lips pressed together, obviously in some distress. It was a moment before he managed to talk and when he did he was clearly baffled. "I don't know," he said. "I don't think the work's really that hard. I don't know."

She was encouraged. "Well, then, that means that you don't want to study. Why?"

"I don't want to because I want to quit school." He was on safer ground now. He wanted to quit school; therefore he did not need to study. Sophie's job, then, was to show him he had it all backwards: he could not study; therefore he wanted to quit school. Sophie looked at Stuart Prince's clouded face and felt an unfamiliar urge to draw her fingers across his cheek. It was suddenly very important for her to pull him back from the edge. Not that he would fall into insanity or anything nearly as dramatic as that. But into the static pool of conflict, indecision, and anxiety, the delight of all committed neurotics.

"Tell me about how it is at home when you are trying to do your homework. You know, do they make it rough for you? Do you have a place to spread out your books? Is the television set going?"

"I've got my own room."

"Is there a desk in it?" She tried hard to picture his apartment. His address, a long, hyphenated numeral, indicated a street in the Bronx, whose name she did not recognize. But she knew what the building would look like, its approximate vintage, the fire escape zigzagging mercilessly across the façade, a barrel-like water tower squatting undisguised on the roof, a short, cracked cement walk leading to a glass and ironwork front door which might or might not sport, like a banner, a name like Semiramis or Samson.

"Yeah, but I got my gear on it."

"What sort of gear?"

"What do you want to know for?"

"I'm interested in what you do, Stuart."

"Then you must have rocks in your head, lady." She left the mysterious gear and tried another approach.

"How does your father feel about your wanting to quit school?"

"The old man's gonna cut me outta his will." At this point Stuart exploded into a loud, nasty laugh.

"Is your father orthodox?"

"Are you kidding?"

"No, I'd really like to know."

"No, he's not. Mom's folks were and she tried to get Dad to be religious when she was but it didn't work very often. He'll go to temple with her holidays, times like that—when he's not working."

"What does your father do, Stuart?" This question was a lie; the answer lay in front of her, on Stuart's record.

"I don't feel like answering any more questions. This is a drag."

"You don't have to answer anything. I told you, this is *your* hour. In fact you don't have to come here at all; no one is going to force you." She wanted it to sink in. "You just *might* want to do something for yourself."

"There you go again. Now you sound like Rabbi Gatterman; you all sound alike. I'm satisfied with the way I am. Why does everybody want to poke their nose in my business? Why does everybody want me to be another cat?"

The interview was essentially over; he was not going to give way any more than he had already. It was too dangerous. "Next time," she said slowly, "if you come back, that is, next time you're going to see a woman named Mrs. Magid, down the hall from this office. She's going to give you some tests."

"What for?"

"They'll help me to help you."

"Here we go again," he said. "I'll see." He got up and left her office without closing the door. Sophie sat and absorbed the shock of his rudeness. For a seventeen-year-old, he had a remarkably coherent physical presence. Yearning for love and fighting it as if it were the whole German army.

It was standard procedure to talk to the parents; Sophie always did unless they flatly refused to come. At this point Sophie usually felt she was facing both her orals' examiners and two people she herself was about to liquidate. The situation put a strain on her confidence, but it was as essential a part of the job as attending to her own unconscious responses.

Mr. and Mrs. Prince, Joe and Pearl, took their son's hour the following week while Stuart did and undid Mrs. Magid's puzzles, completed pictures, interpreted smudges, sighed, grunted, and stared out the window. Mr. Prince resembled his son physically, but his face was void of questions; Sophie felt he had already made up his mind about everything in life that mattered to him; and the rest he would simply ignore. Mrs. Prince, pale, black-eyed, and white-skinned, an aging and unpretty Snow White, had a body like an economy size tube of something viscid, with spindly arms and skinny legs. She seemed, at first, to lack sufficient energy to direct anyone in any direction.

"I see you're a musician," Sophie said to Mr. Prince. She recrossed her legs; Mr. Prince was staring at her knees.

"No. I play the clarinet at Gail's. It's a midtown club. You've been there? People pay to drink and dance to the music; they *don't* listen."

Mrs. Prince started to talk, then changed her mind.

"Are you out most evenings?" Sophie said.

"Five out of seven," he answered.

"He gets home at 2:00 a.m." Mrs. Prince contributed her first words. "And sometimes Sundays there are bar mitzvahs." Could she care less?

"You have another child, a daughter?"

"Frances; she works downtown in an office. She runs some kind of accounting machine there. She's a smart girl; she's going to City College at night for her degree."

(68)

"She's no beauty," Mr. Prince interrupted, "but she's got brains."

"She's not so homely as all that," Mrs. Prince sighed to her husband, as if she were merely adding words to an eternal dispute. "A little on the plump side maybe but not ugly." Mrs. Prince turned back to Sophie. "She's got beautiful eyes. So deep. Like Stuart's."

Mr. Prince grunted. "One's an ugly duckling; the other's a no-good-nik. *She* can't see anything the way it really is."

"What exactly do you mean by 'no-good-nik,' Mr. Prince?"

"I mean he wants to leave school and be a beatnik. Hang around and not do anything; hang around with the other no-good-niks, maybe get into some kind of trouble. Probably taking dope, too."

"He tells me he wants to get a job."

"What kind of a job? Who would hire my son? What can he do with no education except sweep the garbage up. He can't even read a note of music. He's a bum."

"Mr. Prince, do you have any idea why your son is so bent on leaving school? His records indicate that he has a perfectly respectable, even better than average, intelligence and that when he was in elementary school he not only kept up with the rest of his class but got along very well with his teachers. What do *you* think happened to change this?" She was determined to get him involved if it killed her—or him.

Instead of answering, he shrugged. His wife looked miserable.

"Mrs. Prince, do you have any feelings about this?" Purposely vague, Sophie was determined to exploit feelings at this point.

Stuart's mother said, "Maybe we don't help him all we should. I don't know." She glanced uneasily at her husband.

"I know what you mean by 'help him,'" Joseph Prince burst in. "You mean you want to feed him, hold the spoon to his mouth like you did when he was five months old. Help him! You're not sure he can even wipe his bottom!"

Willing, for the moment, to forget that she was being

studied, Mrs. Prince answered her husband: "And *you* think that if he doesn't do everything, *everything*, by himself, it doesn't count; it can't be any good. You never even looked inside his school books, not even when he started bringing homework home in the third grade. You said he's gotta learn the hard way. Why? Why has he gotta learn the hard way? Can't his father help him a little bit? No—you said it would make him soft. Now look what you did." Mrs. Prince's vehemence surprised even Sophie.

"Stuart can learn the hard way, just like I learned the hard way. No one held *my* hand while I practiced three hours every single day. Do you know what my father did? He locked me in my room to practice and wouldn't open the door, even if I needed to go to the bathroom, until the time was up. And no supper, either, till I was finished."

"And look where it got you," his wife murmured. He shot her a glance of disdain.

Sophie said, "Are you certain that Stuart wouldn't profit from a little more support from his father?"

"Yes," Joseph said. Sophie knew he was lying. He was ready to punish his son for his own father's brutality. That was the way it usually went. Sophie sighed without noise. Mrs. Prince had fallen back, meanwhile, onto the soft mattress of her miseries.

"What are you going to do to Stuart? Analyze him?" Joseph's anger showered her as effectively as if he had been spitting.

"No, Mr. Prince, I'm not a psychoanalyst. Stuart and I are going to talk. We're going to try to discover why he wants to leave school and then see if he wants to change his mind."

"Besides," Joseph said, "even if I *did* try to help him" (he emphasized his words with an effective sacrcasm), "he wouldn't listen. He hates my guts." Sophie was considerably cheered: they were definitely getting somewhere now.

"How long has he hated you?"

"Always." Even Nick could not have been more certain.

"Mrs. Prince, do you agree? Does Stuart hate his father?"

"Of course not." (What did she expect?) "They may not see

eye to eye all the time—and Joe is away from the house a lot. Especially when Stuart was a little boy, he used to keep asking why his daddy went out so much; he couldn't understand it. But how can you say he hates you, Joe? Maybe sometimes he can't always find you but that's a very different thing."

"I don't see him trying to find me when I *am* home," Joseph said.

"Mr. Farrow says that if Stuart comes here enough times he'll stay in school." Mrs. Prince obviously wanted a prognosis.

"I can't promise, Mrs. Prince," Sophie said. "I've only seen your son once." Even if she knew, she wouldn't tell them yet; her profession entitled her to some degree of secrecy. "I *would* like to see the two of you again," she added.

"What for?" Mr. Prince's eyes were outraged.

"Well, we've found that one side of the story isn't enough. I'm sure, for instance, that there's a great deal you can tell me about Stuart that he can't, things about his childhood and so forth. His health, which I understand is not especially good." She looked at the mother when she said this. "And there's a favor I'd like to ask of you, Mr. Prince." The man's expression remained unpromising.

"I want to ask you to see if you can try to find out yourself—without resorting to anger or impatience—what it is Stuart is *really* after. Obviously, his threat to leave school is his way of asking for your help, even if he's not aware what he wants your help for. Perhaps, if you two had a long talk . . ."

"Man to man?" Mr. Prince interrupted Sophie. "That's movie stuff. It doesn't happen in real life. Kids today don't give a damn about what their fathers or mothers think. All they care about is drag racing, bad music, girls, and whether things are going their way. Their parents could drown in front of their eyes and they'd stand on the edge, laughing. Stuart's no better than the rest of his gang."

"Stuart does *not* belong to a gang. He's a good boy." Mrs. Prince was aroused. But as a defense counsel she was too transparent to do her client much good.

By the time fifty minutes had passed, Sophie had worked

(71)

Joseph and Pearl Prince into a rich emotional lather. No one, she reasoned, must mistake cause for blame; however, no one was going to get out of this confrontation unscratched.

Watching from her window, Sophie saw Stuart leave with his mother and father. He walked with them slowly, perhaps half a step behind, and dragged his toes like a child who doesn't at all mind if he scuffs his new shoes—and knows his mother will.

The results of the tests told Sophie nothing she did not suspect. But how gratifying it was to be reinforced by something as abstract as a Wechsler and a T.A.T. Now *that* was progress in science, she told herself. Yes, Stuart was no idiot. Yes, his notions about women were distorted if not self-contradictory; yes, he did not have much faith in support from the previous generation. Mrs. Magid said, "You know of course that this boy will never be a scholar."

Sophie said, "I rather thought so."

"He shows pronounced artistic tendencies—with an equally strong desire to repress them. He kept belittling his obvious talents."

"He's very vehement about that; I've heard him. I wonder why."

"What's the father?"

"A musician." They both smiled.

"That's that," Mrs. Magid said. "In spite of his diffidence I liked him. I hope he'll stay with you. There's something appealing about that boy that he can't hide, though God knows he makes a respectable attempt to. Why is it that the ones with built-in charm want to disguise it and the ones with nothing at all come at you with all the subtlety of a gorilla?"

"Listen, if things weren't the way they are," Sophie said, "you and I would be out of a job."

Stuart Prince's problems were not, by any stretch of the imagination unique. The overtones of danger sensed by Sophie at odd moments were not serious and would undoubtedly disappear in time; she predicted to herself that he would respond well to therapy. Then why, she asked herself, was she preoccupied with him? Why, for example, did she hear the echo of his provocative voice when she got back to her empty apartment and sat down with her lamb chop and bowl of soup? She could stop thinking about her other clients without any trouble: the children who used her office as a stage for their boiling emotions, the ones who threw things, and the ones who sat silently with only their thumbs for company. She had learned to turn them off, more or less, when she left the office. It was best for everyone that she could. But not Stuart; he pursued her, not unpleasantly, but like the aftertaste of brandy.

Nick wrote elegant letters to Sophie. In them was the sort of message the sender expects more than one person to read—a biographer as well as a wife. His salutations were extravagant, "My dearest darling Sophia," "My only love," "My sweet dark angel," and so on, no two alike. The body of the letters were little models of epistolary prose. It was apparent that he was enjoying success from unpredictable quarters. About his speech-making he wrote, in part:

> *My audiences are, quite surprisingly, not simply satisfied with verbal formulas. They insist on being served the hard facts—and a great many of these are not so palatable, as you know.*
>
> *Though great stretches of this country are populated by the insane and the ignorant, there are, huddled in cities, people, men and women and even children, who might someday be able to persuade the others to act without haste and prejudice—though by what miracle this propaganda will penetrate the thick skulls of the multitude I have no idea. All this, I grant you, is based on meager but most pervasive evidence. We shall see. I hope to be around another thirty years or so to watch which way it goes. I'm not afraid of bombs half as much as I am of the American tendency to exploit its thick-headed righteousness, its sentimental slavering over a God who looks and mumbles like Eisenhower, and the incredible and dangerous notion that being dead is pref-*

*erable to being red—whatever in God's name that really
means.*

*Serendipity strikes at every turn. You, Darling Sophia,
will no doubt laugh to hear that in the process of making
these little talks I have been approached by men who
want to take me away from Graham, just like stealing
the Cordon Bleu chef. One such man is the president of
a mammoth drug firm in Oakland. He thinks he has
crammed the answer to infertility into a tiny pink capsule
and wants me to join him (at more than double the salary
I'm now getting) as head of research and development,
principally, I suspect, to make damn certain there is no
repetition of what occurred fifteen or twenty years ago
when this company put on the market an improperly
tested female cathartic and forty women went stone
blind. As far as I know his is one of the few drug firms
that spends even more on research than they do on advertising—to their credit, though I can't really laud their
motives. I informed President X, during a most courtly
exchange, that I was convinced the world's difficulties
were the direct consequence of a disastrous and malig-
nant fecundity and that I could not, with Christian conscience, promote fertility. He said something about my
conscience having little or nothing to do with the hundreds of thousands of American women (I suspect he
very nearly said womanhood but couldn't locate the apt
form of the word) who could not now conceive, but by
that time he realized I was incorruptible and was willing
to say what he meant. Oakland's climate, aside from a
rather uncomfortable humidity in the morning, is idyllic.
You, hating the cold as you do, would find yourself in a
spring garden the year around.*

Nick's letters were so like him that Sophie could hear his
voice inside her own head, reading them aloud, performing
them. The days he was away moved as slowly as the days he
was there sped, as if decelerated by an erratic time machine.
The night he came home, Sophie took a cab early to the
airport to meet him, her heart pounding, her throat dry. She

stood in the drafty barrack waiting room watching the others who, like her, paced back and forth in the metallic chill. His plane approached on schedule and she drew up to the shoulder-high window and watched impatiently. Nick was not first off the plane; she fidgeted as one passenger after another descended the stairs and hurried into the building. At last she saw him and smiled without a thought but exultant. He wore a new hat, a fuzzy hat, moss green with a slim ribbon around the crown. Laughing, she let him pull her into his arms where he held her against his coat. Nick's powdery lips encountered her mouth and her cheeks as they stood beneath a loudspeaker which blared suddenly, announcing in high-pitched female noises the supremely irrelevant arrival of another plane from the West Coast. Sophie clung to her husband like a lost child, found again. "Oh, Nick, I missed you terribly. I didn't think it was going to be so bad. Please don't leave again." She was a little reckless with the truth.

"Never?" he said, looking into her face.

"At least not for the next ten years. Hey, where did you get the snazzy lid?"

"In San Francisco. Like it?"

"You look as if you should be refereeing a polo match."

"Doesn't do for a scientist?"

"Oh, why not? I'm just loaded with prejudices. *Yes* it suits you fine. It brings out the green in your cheeks."

They found a cab. Sophie sat close to her husband and held his hand, rubbing shoulders. "Tell me what other ways a scientist should look?" Nick said to her as they drove toward the city, along the expressway, past the bay, and toward the subdued blur of violet city lights.

"Well," she said, "first of all he should have a long, matted beard, bristling with bits of his breakfast, and a stiff wing collar; then he should be wearing one blue and one black sock and pince-nez on a silver chain. He ought to have a slight paunch and a wild, fanatic look in his eyes. Mad, you know."

Nick laughed. "We all *are* a bit mad. I thought you knew

that. Someone made a study not long ago and the conclusion was: all scientists are a bit mad—especially those engaged in research—the pure scientists."

But he was not so pure any more, Sophie thought. Not with that hat on his head. It was an operator's hat. And was a bit mad better than neurotic? She wondered. As they lay in bed later Sophie said, "What about a baby? I started to think about it while you were away."

Nick said, "I'll leave it up to you."

"Why me? Why not the both of us?"

"You're the one who has to carry it for nine months, change it, offer it the tit, tuck in the blankets, and bolster the infant ego. Also leave your job."

"Listen, you sound as if you were talking to that man who offered you that fat job in Oakland. What have you got against babies?"

"I have nothing at all against babies. It's just that *you're* the one whose life will change most radically so *you* ought to make the decision."

"I've never heard of anything like this before."

"What are you getting so teary about? If you consider it carefully, you'll realize it's actually the sanest possible stance for me. Fathers get off pretty easy in our society. Look, they're away from home most of the time the child is awake. Mothers carry by far the greatest physical and emotional burdens. Therefore, you might even say it was a cruelty for some men to keep pollenating their wives without bothering to find out how many kids they really want or can manage."

"Most women (excepting good Catholics of course) *do* want the children they have."

"Do you really believe that, Sophia?"

"Well, if they don't, it isn't because the husband forces them. It's because of what's euphemistically known as an accident."

"And I contend the majority of accidents are caused by husbands who can't wait."

"We're at an impasse, Nick. In any case, I want to think

about it a little while longer. I don't think I'm quite ready yet myself."

"You're the mama," he said. He sounded pleased.

He's odd, she thought, and realized that often she had no idea what crouched beneath his words. And then—at the precise moment he found and held what in love and passion he searched for in her approximately three times each week— Sophie saw the face of Stuart Prince as he had denied her entrance into his life on his first visit. Then she, too, dropped down into the blue mist and they fell asleep, not together, not separate.

"Who *is* this boy?" Nick said.

"His name, I told you, is Stuart Prince."

"What's so damn important about him?"

"I'm simply trying to keep him from dropping out of school."

"If you gave half the concern to the atrocities taking place this minute in Mississippi, for instance, that you give to this one coddled adolescent, maybe I'd understand your incredible attitude."

"Nick, that's not fair, it's an unfair argument. Of course I'm concerned about Stuart; it's my job to be concerned. As for the atrocities, you've taken them on and I applaud you for it. But you can't equate Stuart's problems with the suffering of an entire race and you can't blame me for not doing what you're doing just because you'd feel better if I did. Life doesn't work like that. Besides, Stuart is not so important, as you put it. I'm just trying to keep him in school."

"Maybe he doesn't belong there."

"He does."

"How do you know?"

"Because I've talked to him alone for over fifteen hours. Besides, his test results indicate an unusual, not to say highly imaginative view of the world."

"The tests, eh? And I suppose he has an IQ of 139."

"No." Sophie's throat tightened up. "He's in the normal-bright range."

"God only knows what you people would do if you didn't have your tests to consult. You're aware, of course, that these psychometric tests are exactly as reliable in the long run as the majority of psychological theories."

"You seem to know more about my work than I do."

"Not at all. That's nonsense and you know it. I'm not saying what you apparently would prefer me to say. All I'm concerned with is what appears to be a holy mission over this kid, Stuart. Didn't you once tell me you were supposed to leave your emotions in the cloakroom, that in your work all patients were endowed with equal significance?"

"Nick, it's obvious I can't make you understand—or that you don't want to understand. Let's just drop it for a while, OK?"

"The lady lacks conviction," Nick said, disgustingly singsong.

Sophie could easily have held a pillow over his face until he stopped breathing but as it happened they were driving a rented car to New Canaan to join Ellie Shantz at the well-appointed house of one of his preferred patronesses.

Sophie saw Stuart Prince in her office at the agency once a week Thursday afternoons at four-twenty.

The boy was coming around; there was no doubt of this in her mind, though some lingered in his.

"You Jewish?" he asked, early in the game.

"Yes," she said. "Why do you ask?"

"Because you look Jewish but your name isn't."

"Dr. Brean is not Jewish."

The light outside the window slivered in the cold.

Stuart studied her as a horse of a different color. "What are your kids—half-breeds?"

"I don't have any children, Stuart. Would you like to talk about being Jewish?"

"Now you sound like my old lady. Always Jewish this and Jewish that. She wanted to keep us kosher, like her old lady,

(78)

but Dad said nothing doing. He doesn't go for that stuff. He says it's stupid."

"And how do you feel about it?"

"Who cares?"

"You."

A twitch caught his lips and played with them. He furrowed his forehead in the effort to keep quiet and not betray himself.

"Didn't you once get violently ill, throw up at temple, and have to be taken home?"

"How did you know that?"

"And since then you've had trouble with your stomach. It's been over five years now and it hasn't gotten any better. You even stayed behind one year in school because you missed so much being sick." She was putting it to him; she was taking advantage of the advantages permitted her.

"I said 'how did you know that?' I'll bet Mom told you. She's been dragging me around to clinics and doctors and they all tell her the same thing: they can't find anything wrong with me."

"If there's nothing wrong with you, then why do you feel sick so often?"

"Something I ate."

"Do you *really* believe that? Stuart, your stomach is one reason you're here talking to me right now. Do the others in your family—Frances, your parents—do they get sick when you do?"

"No. But they're different from me."

"Different how?"

"They got steel stomachs. Besides, it's not bad enough to talk about."

"According to your mother" (all right, why shouldn't he know?) "these attacks, or whatever we decide to call them, get so bad that you can't even speak while you're having one. Is she always around when you get sick?"

"Why can't she stay out of my fucking life!" Stuart gasped at his own violence. He dropped his shoulders and put his hands over his face. Motionless, he sighed then, like an animal in the final throes.

Sophie waited patiently, content with what she had accomplished.

"Why do you suppose you got sick that first time in temple?" she said at last, pressing her advantage.

"I don't know." He would not lift his face. She was touched by the sight of his hair. Soft and silky, it grew forward on his skull, uncombed but not quite in a tangle, thick, a wave here and there. She wanted to reach out and stroke it. She clasped her hands together in her lap, joining the fingers of one hand with the other.

"Can you think about it? We might discover something worth knowing if you do."

"I don't know."

"Try."

"Mrs. Brean," he said. He raised his excellent eyes, swimming in unshed tears. "How long have you been married?"

"I don't think that's really important," she said, taking her cue from the book and all her teachers and Dr. Strauss and her knowledge of what was correct.

"Balls."

"Good-bye, Stuart. I'll see you next Thursday."

He escaped from her office without another word.

He was coming around but it was slow work. The so-sensitive, she thought, are also the so-guilty. The boors, the clods, and the lunkheads go through life doing terrible things, ingeniously destructive and cruel things and never feel it, sleep all night, eat like horses, no stomachaches, dizzy spells, backaches, or fatigue. It is people like Stuart who build mountains of sin from petty, imagined molehills.

And, at the same time, Sophie began to have dreams about giving birth to a baby, the hospital procedures, the nurses, the quick, sharp, silent movements. Still puzzled by Nick's casual response to such an important question, she hoped she might become pregnant by accident and thus remove herself from the safety and danger of a decision. She was not as careful as she might have been, and an element of uncertainty entered her life hidden from everyone—even her husband, especially her husband.

"Mr. Prince, did you find an opportunity to talk with your son?" Five months after his first visit the patient's father looked exactly the way he had the first time Sophie saw him. Some people, she thought, repeat themselves endlessly, varying almost not at all from day to day and year to year, unaffected by what goes on beyond them with the exception of time. The man's gestures, expressions, the sloppy way he sat in the chair, his shoes, the unshaven area just under his chin, his little and his large animosities: identical.

"No. I tried but each time I started, that no-good kid had something better to do."

Again, as at the first visit, Pearl began to talk and then changed her mind.

This time Sophie pounced. "What were you about to say, Mrs. Prince?"

"I didn't see him." The woman opened her mouth and then snapped it shut, like a turtle's.

"I don't understand . . . ?"

"I didn't see him try to talk to Stuart, not once."

Sophie had a vision of father and son, living in the same three rooms, swimming by one another, silent fish in a large, cloudy bowl.

"When you were out shopping one Sunday morning, I tried."

"And what did you accomplish, Mr. Prince?"

"Nothing. He said he had something else to do. So, I did what any sane man would do: I gave up. I mean how long can you bang your head against the wall before you give up? The wall isn't gonna come down."

"When Stuart was a little boy, Mr. Prince, did you take him out? Did you go places with him?"

"Sure I did. I took him to the Bronx Zoo, some concerts, kid's concerts at Carnegie Hall Saturday mornings, but he didn't like them much; he used to wiggle in the seat; he couldn't sit still."

"Do you know what, if anything, he prefers to music?"

Mr. Prince stared at her as if she had just asked him to strip.

Mrs. Prince substituted for her husband. "He used to draw beautiful pictures. In the second grade his teacher said he should be an artist when he grows up."

"Yes?"

"But he stopped."

"Have you any idea why?"

"He thought it was sissy or something. Maybe something the children, other boys, said to him at school; I'm not sure."

Softening the words somewhat, she fed them like food strained for a baby, the news that Stuart was suffering from a case of too much mother and not enough father. "A boy needs a father as a model," she said. "If his father is unavailable, he will either find a substitute or somehow lose out and be unsure of who he is."

Mr. Prince denied, Mrs. Prince denied; it was apparently too much at one time. Incredulous hostility for Sophie altered their features. She had chutzpa, this young Jewish girl with the goy name, and who did she think she was, telling them such things? It was all there in their faces. But at least she noted that they were sharing a feeling; Sophie felt a faint hope that in this conspiracy they might help one another.

Stuart came back. By now there was no question in Sophie's mind that he would continue with her just as he would continue at school, his obligations to both projects originating in the same impulse, even if he was not yet aware of its nature. "Mrs. Brean," Dr. Strauss said to her, "I trust that you're not allowing yourself to get involved with this boy, Stuart Prince— that is, of course, over and above what is required by the treatment." She knew he hated jargon and would rather die than accuse her of an unsound countertransference.

(82)

"Of course, Dr. Strauss," she said. "Everything's going along splendidly. We couldn't be more pleased with his progress."

"Your reports," he went on inexorably, "indicate a slight emotional bias on your part, a bias perhaps that you yourself are not aware of. You realize, naturally, that you are not helping him if you don't handle the relationship properly."

Dr. Strauss wore pinstripe suits and a spotted handkerchief. He was often seen at theater openings, especially benefits for the United Jewish Appeal and UNESCO. He had plucked his wife, Ellin, from the teaching staff of a private progressive school, transplanted her from the devitalized soil of West Ninth Street to the fertile ground of Fifth Avenue and Eighty-third Street. Still, she shopped at Ohrbach's; Sophie had run into her at the nightgown counter where she was inspecting something black. Smiling confidently at Sophie, Ellin Strauss had suggested they visit over coffee, which Sophie refused. "I've got a client in half an hour, unfortunately, so I've got to get back."

"Some other time, then. And Martin and I want you and your husband over for dinner very soon." Sophie figured Ellin Strauss to be at least six years her junior and at least fifteen years Dr. Strauss'. Well, she seemed happy enough and she was inspecting something black.

Sophie watched the stripes on Dr. Strauss' jacket and did tricks with her eyes so that they danced back and forth across his chest and disciplined stomach.

"Yes, I'm aware of the possible consequences. I'll try to be even more careful."

"Otherwise," he said, stirring his coffee into a small whirl-pool, "we'll have to pass him on to one of the others."

5

"I CAN'T SEEM TO GET PREGNANT," Sophie said to Nick.

"How long have you been trying?"

"Three months."

He laughed. "That's nothing at all. Women have been known to have intercourse for ten years before conceiving. Why don't we try again? Right now."

"But what's the matter with me? Look at all the silly girls who sleep with a boy once and get knocked up."

"The chances of that happening are statistically minute—which forces you to conclude that these silly girls, as you put it, are sleeping with silly boys day and night, all the time. A woman is fertile only about forty-eight hours out of each month, give or take several hours. The point about these girls is that obviously they're not aware their fertile two or three

(84)

days are any different than all the other days of the month—
the idiots. A woman old enough to get laid should be old
enough to know when she's ovulating and stay away from
it."

"*I* don't know."

"You should. How can you expect to get pregnant without
having this absolutely basic item of information about your
own body?"

"I'm sure most women don't know; they simply go ahead
and get pregnant."

"My God, Sophie, what amazes me is that you can call
yourself a counselor and give help to silly girls who go and get
themselves knocked up and be so totally ignorant about sex
and cycles."

He was quite right—as usual. It was a lapse she herself was
unable to fathom. Perhaps, she thought, she had forgotten
something learned along the way. The next day she went to
the agency's library and read up on sex and cycles, something
most girls know at fifteen.

Nevertheless nothing happened. And the edge was taken off
both the pleasure of her work and the delight of her love.
Perhaps, she thought, the honeymoon is now officially over.

With Stuart Prince, she was on much firmer ground. The
problem was to get him to differentiate between women.
Together they were working hard on it.

"I'm not your mother, Stuart."

"I never said you were."

"But you act as if you expected me to tell you what to
do—and what not to do. That's not what I'm here for." She
pasted this formula on the client, as she had done countless
times before. The words were printed on an endless roll of
tape.

"Listen, Mrs. Brean, why should I believe what you tell me?
Why should I think you're any straighter with me than any
other grown-up is? Except for my old man who doesn't bother

to hide what he thinks of me. You're just going to force me to finish school because *they* want me to and they told you to. So why should I believe anything you say?"

His logic was, after all, impeccable. He could see with absolute clarity that her goal was the same as his mother's and never mind about the means.

"If I told you, Stuart, that I don't care if you don't finish school as long as you're doing what you really want to do—whatever that is—would you believe me then?"

"Oh shit, you're all the same."

"Who's all the same?"

"Women!"

"How are we the same?"

"Pretending to let a person alone but all the time watching him like a hawk, sneaking up on him, going through his things when he's at school, going through his gear, and warning him about chicks." The final item was so out of place on Stuart's list of grievances that it caught Sophie off guard.

"She warns you about girls?" Sophie asked, trying to keep her face steady.

"Yes, to listen to her, they've all got dirty minds with dirty thoughts, didn't you know?" The sound of his sarcasm was so like his own father's that again Sophie was startled. The dam seemed to be breaking all at once.

"Did your mother tell you that?"

"Sure she did; she always does. That and a whole lot of other crap about life."

"But you really believe her."

"No I don't. It's a lot of crap."

Sophie played out the line. "Stuart," she said, "if you had your choice, which would you rather do: play an instrument or paint? or maybe write?" Now he bit.

"Who said anything about painting?"

"*You* did, the very first time you came here. Don't you remember?"

"That kind of stuff is faggoty." He had raised his voice.

"Would you like to know what I did after that first time here? I went home and ripped up all my old pictures. They're lousy." He had done it to wound her, she was sure. Sophie was not so sure he would do the same thing now.

"What is this gear you keep talking about?"

"I'm building a steam-driven generator, if you really want to know. But what do you want to know for? You're just like my mother. Asking questions and then pretending you're not interested in the answers. Get off my back, lady."

The "lady" hurt.

Nick and Sophie had dinner with the Goldermans about three times a month. Florence never had got tuned in to her son-in-law's wavelength. Now the older woman began to see incisions in the marriage.

"Sophie," Florence to Nick, "when are you and Nick going to give me a grandson?"

"Florence, for heaven's sake, we can do without such questions. They'll have a baby when they're ready. Don't rush them. You always want to rush things." Herbert was cross.

"This is no rush, Herbie; it's almost two years. What are they waiting for? A million dollars to fall into their laps?"

"Florence, it's *their* business." Sophie's father was an infrequent censor. When he was, he was emphatic and economical. Florence ducked her head over the baked grapefruit, scooping the sections out as if each one represented a frustration she had never got over.

Encouraged to go on, Florence said, "Why don't you then?"

"Shall we ask God?" Nick said softly.

Sophie felt he should not tease her mother so obscurely. "Shall we ask Sophie?" she said. She helped her mother clear for the next course, a veal stew.

Florence said, "It's got rosemary in it. I hope you like it; it's the first time I've tried this particular herb. And now, Sophie, I'll ask. I don't see any reason for me to beat around the bush."

She gave her son-in-law the same look she would have given Martin Bormann.

"And I won't beat around the bush either, Mama. We're doing the best we can. And now can we change the subject?"

"What doctor are you going to?" Florence asked.

"Why should I be seeing a doctor? I'm not sick. Besides, I see a doctor every day of my life—except when he's off making a speech somewhere."

"Florence," Herbert said, sharply, "why don't you let Sophie alone. She doesn't want to talk about it and I can't say I blame her."

As if he hadn't spoken, Florence said, "You need to see a doctor because you can't have a baby."

"I never said I couldn't have a baby, Mama." The piece of meat she had just swallowed felt like a bullet in her throat. "I never said that. I don't see how you can infer such a thing!"

"Florence," Nick said, trying to soothe the older woman, who had worked herself into a small but vicious panic, like a threatened terrier, "I'll take Sophie to a doctor if she hasn't conceived in another several months. After all, Herb, you know how these things are—some women conceive if a man just looks at them. With others, it may take years. Both have the same kind of babies and are equally good or bad mothers."

Dr. Golderman agreed. "Of course," he said. "And Florence knows that, too. She's just a little bit anxious to have grand-children now. You can't blame her for that. It's hard to be perfectly sensible about something you want so much." His fondness for an emotional woman like Florence was very appealing to Sophie and made her mother's silliness even harder to take.

Somewhat reassured, Florence heaped a second helping of stew on Nick's plate before he could refuse. In a way, it was her revenge. Dr. Golderman said to Nick, "Sophie tells me you're getting to be quite the public speaker, Nick. Half the time you're away somewhere, raising money and spreading the gospel of charity for health; and when you're not doing that you're cooking up those demonstrations for colored people.

Tell me, Nick, how do you manage to do all that and get your own work done?"

Though Stuart Prince remained in school because he did not know what else to do, Sophie had won a victory of sorts.

"So," Martin Strauss said, "I see you have succeeded in keeping the boy from joining the dejected army of dropouts. Good for you, Mrs. Brean."

"He's staying chiefly because he feels it is the lesser of two evils. It's hardly a positive decision on his part."

"We can't discount the fact that he made the *right* decision though, can we?" The others sitting around the polished mahogany conference table listened glibly as the dialogue between Sophie and Dr. Strauss threatened to become an uneasy debate.

Mrs. Magid said, "The boy shows a healthy tendency to make the most of his defenses. It seems to me he also has the equipment (though he hasn't exploited it yet) to free his creative energy—which is substantial. It's his motivation that's weak."

Sophie said, "So far he hasn't demonstrated any motivation at all to me."

"You believe, then, that his treatment ought to continue? Remember the waiting list is growing every day." Dr. Strauss was not an unfair man; he simply, like a good retail grocer, liked to see a healthy turnover.

"Yes, I do." Under the table, Sophie's hand grew cold and wet as if she were holding a damp washcloth between her palms.

"You show a rather special interest in this boy."

"He has an impossible situation at home." (She would be damned if she would say "life situation.") "His father pays less attention to him than he does to the family cat. Mr. Prince is a bitter man who can't help inflicting the poison of his own professional and emotional disappointments on his family, particularly his son. We knew this when Stuart first came to us and nothing has happened since to alter the situation, as the father is almost totally out of reach. I won't admit failure with Stuart but his father is another story. He won't even try. My own feeling is that he has failed to give his son a model for life. The mother, on the other hand, is out to smother her son with concern and protection against life's little shocks. It's absolutely vital that Stuart" (it was a slip; she ought to have said "the boy" this time) "learn how to counteract a destructive emotional environment."

Harry Steiner, next office to Sophie, said, "Maybe Mr. Prince needs you more than Stuart does."

Sophie showed Dr. Steiner her teeth to indicate she appreciated the joke. "The boy is still terribly angry," she said, playing her final card. "I don't see how we can possibly dismiss him now."

"Well, we can't spend all morning on one case," Dr. Strauss said, closing Stuart up inside his manila folder. "I'll accept your recommendation, Sophie, and allow him to continue treatment here. However, I think I should remind you again that the countertransference *must* be destroyed at the proper time."

Her colleagues stared at Sophie in embarrassed horror, as if she had in fact been directly accused.

Her wanting a baby became less a desire and more an established fact.

Nick insisted, at last, that she see a doctor. "When was the last time you had a Pap smear?" he asked her.

"I've never had one," she said. "After all I'm not even thirty."

"It doesn't matter. You ought to have one. Who's your gynecologist?"

"His name is Frank Gottlieb. A bit smooth but cute."

"I never heard of him."

"You wouldn't. He's a colleague of Daddy's at the hospital." That seemed to satisfy Nick who, it appeared, somewhat to Sophie's surprise, respected his father-in-law's judgment on medical matters.

"OK. Please, Sophie, make an appointment with your Dr. Gottlieb."

"Maybe."

"Why do you say maybe? Look, Soph, if you don't go see him you can't come complaining to me about not conceiving. You've got to have an examination. Sometimes they do a simple thing like cauterize the cervix or blow out your Fallopian tubes and that's all it takes. Besides, you ought to have that smear taken."

"Those things sound ghastly. What do they do after they blow out your tubes—change your tires?"

He laughed. "Go see for yourself."

She was extremely nervous about the appointment. Although Nick offered to come with her—it was on a Saturday morning—she refused, feeling that his presence might be more a constraint than a support; she preferred to be alone so she could savor her anxieties in private.

Sophie arrived at the doctor's office early; for once the subway train had reached the platform at the same time she had and she was rushed uptown in the almost empty train at a hurtling speed. The car rocked back and forth, slipping past stations and growling like a monster while Sophie hugged herself. Dr. Gottlieb's waiting room was immense, large enough for a public meeting or a buffet for a hundred people. In its center stood a great mahogany dining-room table across which lay, in neat rows, like the dummy's hand in bridge, copies of the *National Geographic, Holiday, Parents' Magazine, Yachting,* and a throwaway from a diaper service. A receptionist with pendulous, motherly breasts under a violet sweater greeted her by name and showed her where to sit. Sophie took another chair, an armchair so upright she felt she was being thrown forward. Her insides began to pulsate so she got up and grabbed a copy of *Holiday* and sat again, this time on a couch.

A pregnant patient looked up at her from her knitting. The girl appeared to be very young and in her eighth month. She was working on a small yellow sweater with an air of heroically achieved complaisance. Sophie noticed that the girl wore a pair of support stockings and that underneath the stockings, on both her legs, crawled little, purple, wormlike lumps.

Sophie shuddered. Her insides throbbed and glowed; her hands felt like cold rubber gloves. Her throat was dry; her impatience to get it over with was acute.

Noises issued from down the hall; a patient sailed into the room, picked up her coat, and left, beaming.

"Mrs. Beaver?" The pregnant girl heaved to her swollen feet, nodding to the nurse, and walked past unpregnant Sophie as if Sophie were invisible.

The issue of *Holiday*—dedicated to the rites and joys of southern hospitality—was not quite funny enough to distract Sophie. Phones rang, and a couple of new patients came in, one with a small restless boy. Time went by. Sophie discovered that she had to go to the bathroom.

The receptionist said, "Please leave a specimen of urine for the doctor." Sophie did not know where to put the beer-glass beaker and finally left it on the windowsill against a pane of pebbled glass. The bathroom's equipment was huge, as if designed for giants, and included a bathtub filled with drug samples in colored boxes.

As she emerged, the receptionist pounced on her. "Did you leave a specimen?"

Sophie said, "Yes, I put it on the windowsill." She felt about seven years old.

"Dr. Gottlieb will see you now."

The man rose, shaking hands, as Sophie entered. Small, neat, trim, he looked a little like Frank Sinatra. His desk was as large as everything else in the suite.

"How are you, Mrs. Brean?" he said, slipping back behind his desk. He pretended not to recall that he had fitted her for a diaphragm two years before she got married.

"I'm fine, Dr. Gottlieb," she said, sitting down uneasily, as if she might be required to get up unexpectedly.

"Well," he said, inspecting his forty-three year old hands and picking up his gold-trimmed Parker 51, "and what can I do for

(92)

you?" He poised the pen for a frontal attack on her record, which lay spread in front of him on the desk.

"Two things," she said. "The first is a checkup. My husband —he's a doctor in research—wants me to have a smear taken. Though there's nothing wrong with me, I'm certain. And then—" Sophie paused, wondering how to put it.

"Yes?" he asked. Sophie could tell he'd been to his barber within the last day or so; the sideburns along his polished pink ears were as precise as Japanese makeup.

"I, we want a baby and. . . ."

"And you can't seem to get one started? Is that it? It may surprise you to learn," he said, launching into a lecture, "that this is one of the commonest stories told in this office. I had a woman in here yesterday who had been trying unsuccessfully to conceive for seven years and now is well—and quite normally I may add—into her fourth month. You musn't worry or allow yourself to get discouraged so early in the game. You have many fertile years ahead of you." He checked her record to make sure he had not misjudged her age. "Now, how about answering a few questions." The pen pushed on and on, advancing without difficulty until Sophie's privacy lay ravished. Then the doctor sprang to his feet.

"Now," he announced with an enthusiasm Sophie hoped she was misinterpreting, "let's have a look!" He buzzed a box on his desk. "Miss Spider will help you get ready."

Miss Spider, a grandmotherly type with pink plastic glasses and tight white curls, appeared at the door, and, leading Sophie into the examination room, instructed her in the ritual she already knew.

"Please void your bladder and leave it for me to examine."

"I did," Sophie said, "before. The receptionist knows." The lack of communication between the two ladies confused her and increased the feeling of unreality connected with all such impersonal and intimate appointments. In and out of small cubicles, dress, undress, open wide, or move closer. It won't hurt, it won't take long, hold your breath, let's look in here, now turn over—these were the proddings and puncturings, this was the investigation of a body only you had a right to possess and submitted to only for some compelling reason.

Undressed, partially covered by something white and crinkled, Sophie waited again, sitting on a scrap of paper towel, her clothes hung discreetly behind a screen, staring down at the tiny bows on her pretty high-heeled shoes. She inspected the doctor's certificates and diplomas. They had been issued to him by medical schools whose Jewish quotas had been so infamously low that he was obliged to be a genius. It was some comfort to her, although she realized, with a fresh shock, that she disliked him; his fake heartiness probably shielded, she thought, a repulsive lack of affect.

At that moment Frank Gottlieb slipped in through the door with Miss Spider a foot or two behind him. Together they propped her in position until she was virtually pinned to the narrow table. Sophie studied the ceiling and tried to pretend she was somewhere else, anywhere else, but the effort was too much. She closed her eyes.

Dr. Gottlieb began to do an incredible variety of things to her, without uttering a word. She opened her eyes and watched the top of his head, his brow furrowing and unfurrowing with the effort. She heard him distinctly; something clicked, something breathed and sucked, and the nurse rose with a slide. There were a couple of clanks.

"Now, Mrs. Brean," he announced, "I'm going to cauterize your cervix with this electric rod. You have a slight cervicitis —and I want to clear it up. It won't hurt while I'm doing it, but you may notice a twinge or two after I've finished." Sophie tightened as if she had been pinched.

"Please relax and take a deep breath," he ordered.

Sophie was aware, then, of a sizzling noise—it couldn't be anything else—and a foul, pungent smell. She watched, horrified, as a thin white thread of smoke emerged from beneath the sheet over the valley of her knees, rose and disappeared among the diplomas. She felt herself willingly letting go and slipping backwards into a cold black hole. But the next moment she was revived by a pain so intense that her entire body

(94)

was instantly covered with icy perspiration. She suppressed a cry only with difficulty.

"Take another deep breath," Dr. Gottlieb commanded, dropping his instruments into a tray with a clean clatter.

Stunned, Sophie stared at Miss Spider, whose smile seemed to indicate a dilemma between admiration for the doctor's skill and sympathy for the patient's pain.

"That's all now," the sleek otter of a man said. "You can get dressed. When you're ready, come back into my office and I'll talk with you there." He vanished.

Miss Spider approached and peeled Sophie off the table. She pitched forward and nearly fell over her own feet. The woman held on to her arm with tight fingers. Sophie's legs felt like cooked spaghetti.

"You'll be all right in a minute or two, dear. It's an unpleasant surprise the first time."

Sophie smiled wanly. "Why didn't he warn me?"

"Some women seem to mind it more than others," Miss Spider said. "Dr. Gottlieb told you it might be uncomfortable."

"That's right, he did," Sophie said, remembering.

"You just get your clothes back on now," the nurse told her. "And then go right on into the doctor's office. He'll want to talk with you." They seemed to be rushing her down the line.

Distracted and in a hurry, Sophie ran a stocking and cursed. She got into her proper blue suit and fumbled with the clasp of her beads, gave up, and stuffed them into her purse.

As it turned out, what Dr. Gottlieb had to tell her was an anticlimax.

"Apart from your cervicitis—which cauterizing should clear up—I can't find any indication of even the slightest organic anomaly. In other words, I don't see any reason why you should not conceive tomorrow. Incidentally, Mrs. Brean, in a great many cases cauterization facilitates conception. We're not quite certain why, except that the passageway is somewhat cleared for traffic after the scar tissue heals. It does appear to work."

"The smear?" Sophie asked.

"Oh, that's just a routine precaution. In your case, I'm quite certain the results will be negative. We'll let you know by mail, however, in about ten days."

He appeared so pleased with them both, she thought he might get up and give her a kiss to show how pleased he was that no anomalies existed. "Remember," he said as he showed her the door, "it's important not to tense up over this; if you're anxious, your chances of conception may diminish. Pregnancy and birth are two of the most natural life situations. Now, go home and don't come back until you have either missed two periods or nothing has happened in six months."

Still shaky, Sophie rode the subway downtown. "We're back where we started," she said to herself, pessimism blackening her future like a *D* in a final exam.

That night, in her sleep, Sophie hemorrhaged, a great wet gush, over a cup. She sat up soaking and terrified.

"My God, Nick," she shrieked, "look at me, look at the bed." She was trembling.

"Didn't Gottlieb warn you this might happen?"

Sophie shook her head.

"Well," he said, "he should have. Now, go change your nightgown and get a mattress pad or something to put over this lake and let's get some sleep."

"I don't understand," Sophie said, not moving, still stunned by what had happened. "If this is normal, why didn't he tell me? My God, where does it all come from?" Her insides seemed suddenly more than simply mysterious; now they were definitely threatening her.

"It's a perfectly normal reaction to trauma," Nick told her, shifting so that he would not get blood on his pajamas. "Delayed, perhaps, but normal. He ought to have told you so you wouldn't have panicked this way. Now please do go get something to cover this with, Sophie, and go back to sleep; you're not dying."

After Sophie mopped up, she got back in bed and lay there, wishing Nick had been even a *little* sympathetic.

Sophie was determined not to be discouraged. She tried, in

fact, to push what she considered to be a major impediment to perfect happiness as far down in her consciousness as she could, knowing all too well that the doctor was right: the more anxious she was, the less chance she had. It was with dismay and impatience that she discovered how little control she had over her own emotions.

Life bubbled merrily, obliviously, around Sophie while she stewed and waited. There was, for one thing, the question of Ellie and Margo. The match, grown into a connection of sorts, amused Nick. Sophie remained wary.

"Margo appears to like Ellie very much," Sophie said, walking in the front door to find her husband home before her. "What's that smell?"

"A roast," he said. "I thought we could have a good chunk of red meat for a change instead of slops."

"What slops?" she said, feeling her muscles tighten.

"Casseroles. Good enough for kids but not for grown men. Come here and give us a kiss."

Sophie was too angry; she swept by him into the bedroom. "I talked to Margo on the telephone today. She and Ellie are living together."

"Good," Nick said. "That's what the world needs—a little more intimacy. If there were more screwing there'd be fewer wars."

"Oh, Nick, really. Margo's looking for a husband." Sophie changed into slacks and an old sweater.

"So you say. I don't happen to believe it. I think she's looking for the same thing Ellie is: a neat, comfortable, terminable friendship. Otherwise she wouldn't have picked Ellie. All you have to do is take one look at the man to realize he's single for life."

"Women want children."

"Again, so you say. Margo doesn't want children; she wants paintings."

"Can't she want both?" There was a familiarity about this conversation that made Sophie weary just to think of it.

"Not sincerely. One thing has to yield to the other. Just look at you, for instance: you're perfectly agreeable to interrupting your work for the sake of a child. I don't think Margo is. Aren't those slacks getting a little tight?"

"Not that I've noticed. Margo's case is entirely different. Margo paints; she doesn't even have to leave the house. She can have it both ways."

"Look, Soph, apparently Margo doesn't want to spread around the energy she puts into her paintings. Otherwise she *would* have. How old is Margo, twenty-eight, twenty-nine? Old enough to have made up her mind."

"She's not so old. And she might be changing."

"Listen, why don't you just let Margo go ahead and live with Ellie without worrying about her precious psyche or whatever it is you *are* worried about. She's a big girl and Ellie is a very good man for her; they're a lot alike; why do you always feel compelled to marry people up?"

"She's poor." Sophie felt defeated.

"Then Ellie's going to drop her, probably sooner than later. He can't afford to screw a poor girl indefinitely."

"I'm going to tell Margo."

"Good heavens, deary, don't you suppose she understands all that? You're so naïve even your closest friend won't tell you. You're just like your old lady, in fact. Margo doesn't need to grow up; you do!"

Sophie kept her client, a little girl named Robin who wet her bed regularly three or four times a week, a few minutes past the hour, because things were going so well. Robin had built a Stonehenge with chunky wooden blocks and had then sat in the middle of it, declaring she was a camel and never had to drink any water. It was the first time in ten visits that Robin had told her anything at all.

"I'm sorry I kept you waiting," she said to Margo, slipping into her coat.

"That's all right," Margo said. "I went to sleep. Ellie sat me upright until 3:00 A.M. reading me a new chapter of his novel."

"Any good?"

"I can't honestly say. It's funny but is it good? It's about this scientist, see, who's a Boston Brahman, and lives on Louisburg Square, who discovers the key to life in his little home laboratory in the basement and starts grinding out human beings; only all of them are bearded, garlicky Jewish intellectuals in long mohair coats and he's in this conflict, see, whether to turn them loose on society or keep them locked up. He's fond of them because they're his but he's also a little appalled."

Sophie laughed. "You know, Margo, Ellie has never let me or Nick see a word of this book."

"You forget that I'm cooking his meals, buying his food, washing his socks. I gotta get paid somehow. Where should we go?"

They decided on a basement off Madison Avenue where all the food tasted as if it had been converted from powder or paste but they gave you a glass of wine, gratis, to apologize.

Sophie looked hard at her oldest friend. She had put on weight, which showed as a slight puffiness in her cheeks and a softening of her jawline. Her hair, always full and wavy, seemed to be glowing with tiny red highlights which might or might not come out of a bottle; still, it did not matter—they were beautiful. Margo was wearing a knitted cotton turtleneck shirt, Ellie's, and her nipples showed through like gumdrops. Her skirt creased across her lap and the seam down her flanks gapped in several places. Her face was uncharacteristically flushed.

"What on earth have you been cooking for Ellie, chicken tettrazzini and lobster thermidor?"

Now Margo laughed. "Mostly pot roast and pan-fried potatoes. The man has simple tastes, you might say. I've got to stop eating so much, though. I'm getting grotesque." She patted her stomach, not unhappily.

"Aside from the food, Mrs. Lincoln, is everything else OK?"

"Couldn't be better," Margo said, studying the menu.

"Are you getting any work done?" Sophie persisted.

"Some. Not much."

In silence they ate their powdered eggs disguised as omelets and Boston lettuce smeared with cooking oil. Margo buttered a large roll and gnawed at it, hungry and appeased. Then she asked the waitress for another glass of wine.

"That will be sixty cents additional."

"Skip it," she told the woman. "Just some coffee." Margo made a face signifying disgust. "This place is the end. They say all the society ladies come here when they're feeling sexy. Listen, Sophie, is it true that Nick is giving up research for public relations?"

"Is that what Ellie says? Well, he's not altogether wrong though Nick hasn't quite abandoned his lab. It's just that he's been giving a lot of speeches recently, for the institute. He's trying to make up the work he's missed in the lab by staying late three or four nights a week, but apparently it's not going very well—most of his staff has left by that hour and he really needs them around. I think he's trying to find the right spot for himself. Maybe the trouble is that he does everything too well. It isn't right somehow that the man born for research should also be such a genius at selling the product."

"You can imagine, of course, that Ellie's not altogether sympathetic." Margo threw this out like a wad of paper but it hit Sophie like a stone.

"What do you mean?"

"Ellie thinks Nick shouldn't mix business with pleasure."

"*Ellie* does it." Sophie said, watching, fascinated, as Margo swept a mound of crumbs onto the floor.

"I'm a slob," Margo said.

"I said, 'Ellie does,'" Sophie said again.

"Ellie's different," Margo announced. "Ellie's an outsider. He sees things; he isn't required to *do* anything. And Nick is."

"And Ellie thinks that Nick's speech-making is pleasure? That just proves how little he knows about it. Look, Margo, I'm just as nuts about Ellie Shantz as you are—maybe more— but I'm not going to consult him about my career, my love life, or how much to give the mailman at Christmas. He's great when it comes to in-laws, stepsons, and book reviews. And that's about it."

"I think you're wrong about Ellie," Margo said. "He makes such a joke of everything it's hard to realize how serious he is sometimes—and how accurate."

"You would think I was wrong, wouldn't you?" Sophie said, laughing, to break the tension. "By the way, Margo, what would you do if Ellie asked you to marry him?"

"Spend a week at Riggs and think about it," Margo said. "He doesn't wash his feet. It's a very important consideration." Sophie could read nothing in Margo's eyes. She was sure Margo was as fertile as a mouse.

"Just please don't get knocked up," Sophie said. "Abortions are so expensive." They stood outside the restaurant before parting.

"Oh well," Margo said, "I know the address of a nice accommodating medical student who'll do it for one hundred green men." And Sophie realized with a pang of envy and revulsion that Margo, from personal experience, knew exactly how his office was furnished and the color of his ceiling.

Stuart Prince was completing his senior year, though not with what Sophie would have called enthusiasm. She was, however, resigned to letting him slip away.

Their meetings now gave her so much to go on that she could have thrown some overboard.

"My father says lousy things about you."

She did not ask him to specify, trusting it would come.

"Don't you want to know what he says?"

"Only if you want to tell me."

Still she waited, her mouth shut tight. As far as she was concerned, Joseph Prince was the end, a flop as a man. He was rigid and self-justifying, and he projected obsessively. She hadn't really got more than an inch or two closer to the man since the very first time he had showed her his resentful face or rather since he had boasted that his son hated him. A musician too; it was enough to make her give up her faith in art.

"I guess I don't."

"I imagine that he tells you something like this: I am in

league with your school principal against you. You should not trust me because I'm young and inexperienced. He might also be suggesting that there is something wrong with me because I work, and decent Jewish women stay home, wash socks, and have babies." This was somewhat more than she intended to say and Stuart's flush, his dip of the head, told her that somewhere she had struck ore—perhaps even gold.

"Do we have to talk about it? I don't listen to half the crap he hands out anyway."

"Do you think a father and his son ought to listen to each other?"

"Yeah, I suppose so. My old man's really in squaresville. If and when he makes an appearance he's either reading the paper or flaking off. Or else he might be practicing on his fiddle. Ever try to outshout a G string?"

"It's a fairly effective barrier," Sophie admitted. And still she couldn't fault the man for practicing.

"Amy says you're neat, though. She says she's glad I come here. I didn't want to tell her at first." Stuart shifted in his chair, crossed his legs like a man. "Mom got mad at Amy on Monday; I can't bring her around any more. Mom called Amy a sleep-easy."

"But you do sleep with Amy, don't you?" The boy was nineteen after all.

"Sure I do. What do you think we do, play post office? We both know how to be careful. Amy doesn't sleep with any other cats. I'm the only one. She doesn't even see any of the other cats."

"Tell me more about Amy. What do you two talk about?"

"Mostly me and her." He laughed, inappropriately. "And how we're gonna live."

"And how *are* you going to live?"

"Away. Simple. One bed, one table, two chairs. No crap. What do you need a pile of junk for—to show off to the neighbors?"

"Babies?"

"I can't think that far ahead," he said.

"What does Amy look like?" Sophie found she was more than professionally curious.

"Blonde. Not at all like Mom. You know why Mom hates her? Not because we screw but because Amy's a shiksa. You'd think Amy had the clap or something, the way Mom looked at her on Monday. Amy just took it like a man and kept her mouth shut. My mom really knows how to make a guy feel like shit."

Sophie thought he might be learning what to do with his anger.

"What are you going to do next year?" Sophie asked, afraid of the answer. "You're going to have to start thinking seriously about it very soon," she added.

"Yeah, I know." He seemed discouraged. His eyes, fixed on her desk, were intense. They held the sort of intensity Sophie had seen in only a few adults. If the intensity did not reflect, within a short time, both action and passion, Sophie would be surprised.

"I. . . ."

"Yes?" Nick would have appreciated this suspense.

"I've applied for a scholarship to art school." He named a good one. Inside Sophie's breast a sigh of relief swelled and ebbed.

"And supposing you don't get it?"

"Commercial work," he said, disgusted. "But I've got a pretty good chance."

"Has your stomach been all right recently? You haven't mentioned it," she asked, tying up loose ends.

"It's been swell," he said. "You people really fix things up don't you? You suck a guy in here, you drag him in when he's down and then you brainwash him to a fare-thee-well. You chase away all the naughty little troubles and give him a new face. To you, life is babies and a regular salary. The way I see it, all that is some square's wet dream. I know damn well—and you ought to know by now for Christ's sake—that I'm never going to *be* or *act* the way you and Mr. Farrow and my mom and that lady down the hall with the hairy chin think I ought to be. Maybe you got me to finish high school but I'm not like you people. I'm somewhere else. Me and Amy, we're both different." His passion spewed over her like foam.

"And you," he went on with fire, "with your soft ladylike voice and your silent black eyes, what's in it for *you*, taking a cat and changing him. Where's your charge?"

She spun in a circle of true anger. "I'm not here for a charge, as you put it. This is my job. I see other people besides you, Stuart."

"Yeah, I know all about it. Little Mrs. Fix-it." He was no longer a child talking to her; she *had* fixed him.

"Do you realize how angry you are?"

"I'm not angry." He paused and started to smile. "Yes, I am angry, I don't know why I denied it. I'm sore because you act so frigging superior—your nails are so clean, your collars are so pressed, your breasts are so ladylike and concealed. Why do you always wear black and dark colors?"

She was vulnerable. "I don't always wear dark colors," she said. "Those are the ones you choose to remember."

"Yes, I remember them."

"And you *don't* remember the others."

"No."

He seemed to be getting the last word. She felt washed-out, as if she were recovering from the flu. "You won't be coming here after the second week in June," she told him.

"I figured," he said.

"You still have a way to go," she reminded him. "Do you think you can manage all right without me?"

"I kind of have to, don't I?" His face told her what she ought to have known all along: he dreaded the separation.

"You can always come back from time to time. . . ."

He broke in on her. "For a grease job, a thousand-mile checkup, and a little confidential chat. You want to keep me straight real bad, don't you?"

"For talking about things." Sometimes Sophie despised the flat things she was obliged to say. "That is, if you feel you need to."

"Well, I guess I ought to thank you." There was no heart in it. His eyes went to her bosom.

"You don't have to."

"You just keep right on saying sentences that don't mean anything. Now what does *that* mean?"

"Is it too simple for you to understand?" she demanded. "Nobody is going to force you or even ask you to say 'thank you.' This isn't an academy for good manners. Gratitude has nothing to do with our relationship." In her own ears she sounded repulsively like her own husband, pontificating.

"There you did it again. Listen, Mrs. fancy Brean, if a doctor puts a cast on my broken leg, shouldn't I thank him? I should just get up on my crutches and hobble out—screw you, doc? It's OK with you if we act normal with our families and our friends, but the minute we try to act normal here, with you superior beings, we get our nuts cut off. Oh, no, you mustn't say 'thank you'; that would spoil the hothouse relationship, the dead dead relationship. We're all under glass—you, too, Mrs. Brean; I'm not the only one." He sighed heavily and closed his eyes a moment. "If I want to thank you," he said, just above a whisper, "I'll thank you. If I don't, I won't."

The boy always presented her with a perfect little tearose of nonanalytic logic. It was getting progressively more difficult to argue back. She made a stab at it nonetheless: "Aren't you aware yet, after all this time, that ordinary, everyday habits and manners simply don't apply here, between you and me, Stuart?" It was her turn to sigh; she couldn't help it.

"And aren't *you* aware," he answered, "that maybe there are some things you'll never be able to shove in through my thick skull? The hour's up, isn't it? I have to go and pick up this cat's car. My cousin's. Amy and I are going to drive out to Jersey and shack up in a motel. I'll send you a postcard from the boardwalk."

April was particularly difficult for Sophie as certain events tampered with the rules she had made for herself and abided by for most of her life: Nick was away for two three-day periods and that was always disagreeable (though in an odd way, very restful); her mother went into the hospital for a close examination of her lungs, giving them all several days of nail-biting and guilt and revealing nothing more than congestion from smoking; a candle dripped all over a new silk dress and the cleaner said "Throw it out, lady—them spots are permanent"; and Ellie showed up for a drink hauling behind him, like a pet on a chain, a female who wasn't Margo and who wore a kumquat shaped (and sized) topaz on her left hand. Her name was Diane and she pronounced the *i* as *ee*.

"What do you do, Diane?" Nick said, handing her a drink of rye and water, and bending over her bosom for a look.

"She's a dancer," Ellie answered. "She comes from Lake Forest originally, don't you, honey?"

"Yes, doll," Deeane said, "but I like it ever so much better here. It's ever so much more alive." Sophie wondered why she did not say "aleeve." Diane scratched her leg. The noise set Sophie's teeth on edge. The girl kept scratching herself deliciously, the sure sign of a narcissist. Sophie went into the kitchen for cheese and crackers.

Diane wanted to hear all about the doctor's fascinating research work.

When Sophie came back with the tray she found Ellie had moved over to the couch. "Sit down next to me Sophia and let's schmoose a little." Sophie sat back and raised her eyebrows toward Diane.

"When are you guys going to produce something worth-while?" Ellie said, ignoring her signal.

"I assume you mean a baby?" He nodded and crammed two saltines into his mouth.

"You mean you, Ellie Shantz, think children are worth-while?"

"For other people, for marrieds. They help keep the vital juices flowing. Also once in a while a kid will say something that will knock you on your ear."

"Like J. Robert," she whispered maliciously.

"Exactly," he said.

"Well, Ellie dear, I'll tell you: I seem to be having a little trouble in that department."

"It isn't anything serious, is it?"

"No, you don't understand." Sophie did not want to talk about it, but Ellie—one way or another—always got his answers. "We've been trying for awhile," she said. "Nothing seems to happen."

"Have you let a *real* doctor look at you?"

"Yes."

"And?"

"He says there's nothing wrong with me. Ellie, please let's just leave it at that. Discussing it makes me squirm. And you know all about what angst does to the soma."

"Come on, kid, you believe that crap? You think it's all in your mind? Don't try to sell that brand of eyewash to Ellie; I'm not buying."

He looked so much the man she always imagined she would end up with. Definitely not overlaundered, with a tiny smudge of oil on either side of his tumid nose and crescents of grime under his fingernails. His hair, uncut for weeks, stood out from his scalp in dark curls, clusters, and clumps like Dylan Thomas'. His blue shirt was fringed at the neck and cuffs and missing one button to button down. Now Sophie noticed for the first time that for Ellie, he was in rather formal dress.

"Where are you off to all dolled up?" she said.

"Diane's dancing later, in this grade C musical. I got to sit in the audience and watch her."

"I'm sure it'll kill you."

"It's a drag. Except for her thighs. You ought to take a look at this chick's thighs."

"I believe you, Ellie. What happened to Margo?"

"The inevitable parting of the ways." Sophie thought, for a moment, that he had said waves, and she giggled. Ellie pretended to look inconsolable. "Dear girl," he said, "leave us not talk about it; it makes me *ängstlich*." He bent across the tiny gap between them and placed a damp smudge of a kiss on her cheek. "You know why I keep switching from chick to

chick?" he murmured. " 'Cause I'm looking for you and I can't
find her."

J. Robert was not required by law to spend more than a
month each summer with Nick. His mother, Sydney, discouraged him in various open and covert ways from seeing his
father at all, although she knew better than to forbid him
altogether. Sophie was privately delighted by the arrangement,
for when Robby was around she was apt to find niggling faults
with Nick, which in turn caused her, out of guilt, to hate
herself; it was not a happy situation.

Sophie was surprised when Robby called Nick one Wednesday night around nine o'clock. Sophie answered the telephone.

"Hello, this is Robert. May I speak with Dad?"

"Hi, Robby. Sure, I'll go get Nick." She called to him softly,
"Nick, it's for you. Robby."

Nick took the phone, giving her a shrug of curiosity. "Hello,
Robby. What can I do for you?" He drew Sophie to him with
his free arm and held her about her waist, nudging her neck as
he talked.

"What did he want?" Sophie said, after he had hung up.

"He wants me to take him to the circus on Saturday."

"We promised the Grahams we'd go with them to New
Canaan; don't you remember?"

"Oh, Will and Nancy can do a much better job of house-
hunting without us along; real estate agents always bring out
the worst in me."

"And what's that?" she asked.

"You don't really want to know, do you? Come on, honey,
get on the phone and call Nancy and tell her I've got an
ingrown toenail or something and can't make it. I promised
Robby I'd get tickets for the two of us."

"Two of you. Aren't I invited?"

"Nope, this is a father and son deal. I'll take you next year if
you really want to see the clowns."

"It's not that; it's just that it seems so exclusive this way.
Don't you agree it would be a good idea if Robby came to

terms with the fact that you're remarried? I'm certain he's accepted his stepfather with less trouble than he's accepted me. After all, he's spent parts of two summers with me. If you don't include me it looks as if you and he were in league to deny my existence. It would be bad enough if he liked me, but distrusting me the way he does, if he doesn't accept me as part of your life now, he'll never get used to me."

"Sophie," Nick said, pushing her away from him without realizing it, "you're just babbling. Look, naturally he accepts his new father more easily than you. He lives with the man, after all. And the idea that we want to deny your existence is so ludicrous that it doesn't merit an answer. Sophie, I don't understand you; whenever Robby comes up, you turn paranoid. I don't quite know what we're going to do about this; it's an issue which we've simply got to try and straighten out."

"We *can* straighten it out," Sophie said, trying to contain her agitation, "by your not aggravating a situation that is destructive enough already. I think it's fine for you to spend an afternoon with Robby; I'm delighted he wants to see you. But I don't think I should be excluded."

"You're angry because you're being left out," Nick said, scowling. "Not because of the situation, as you call it. Your Saturday afternoon riding around looking at impossibly expensive homes in clean white Connecticut has been spoiled. You don't really give a damn what Robby thinks of you."

"Nick, you are *so* wrong." Tears crept up on her. "I can't bear this any more. You've *got* to understand, you're hurting all of us, by giving in to his whims."

"Good God, Sophie, it wasn't his idea; it was mine. *I* thought we ought to be alone, not Robby."

"Oh Lord help us," breathed Sophie, "it'll *never* work."

It seemed as if some rain fell every day in April. Of course it didn't, but it felt like it to Sophie who was damp inside and out. It rained and poured and spattered and drizzled. Water barreled along the sidewalks propelled by cold and persistent winds. In two weeks Sophie lost two umbrellas, blown inside out by the wind.

As Sophie stepped into Dr. Gottlieb's office for her second appointment, her hair was dripping onto her shoulders and her toes were chilled to each tiny delicate bone. She sat down and shivered, disgusted and self-pitying. Most women needed only one man to get pregnant; it appeared that she needed at least two.

The magazine population had remained stable except for a new issue of the *Johns Hopkins Alumni Magazine* which she felt she could easily do without. The resident expectant mother sat across the room, dozing. Where did he find them all? They would come here and keep coming until the last child in the world was born. Envy and disdain took over and occupied her until she was summoned by the buxom receptionist.

Dr. Gottlieb was still blandly reassuring. After all, she asked herself in his defense, was it *his* problem? Still, the absence of passionate perplexity along the lines in his silken face troubled her. Sophie was certain, staring at his cheeks, that he kept a spare shaver in his desk drawer and shaved between patients.

Sophie forced herself to describe her failure as flatly as if she were, in fact, talking about someone else. She was determined not to show him how anxious she was. He told her to take her temperature every morning, "Immediately on waking, even before you turn over. Keep a thermometer by your bed and a piece of paper and pencil to chart it with. Once a month you will notice a drop—possibly as little as half a degree. This drop occurs as ovulation begins and indicates that you are entering a period of fertility. This is the time to have intercourse." He said it right out; she had bet herself that he would get around it somehow. Sophie gazed at him in admiration. "You will remain fertile for approximately forty-eight hours," he said significantly. "Now it's important that you take your temperature before you do anything else because if you get up or move around your temperature will rise and you will throw off the calculation. Now don't worry if your temperature registers as low as 97°; that's a perfectly normal early morning reading.

I had a woman call me just yesterday; she was hysterical because her temperature was only 96.8°. I said, 'Mrs. Brown (that's not really her name), Mrs. Brown, do you think you're dead?' She had to laugh." Sophie smiled, appalled.

Dr. Gottlieb pushed himself back on the springs of his upholstered modern. "Now I don't want to see you again—unless there's trouble of course—for at least four months. We should have a clearer picture by then about whether your difficulty suggests more than I think it does." Sophie realized prose was not his strong suit, though she had to admit he knew how to get his point across.

"You mean I don't have to have my tubes blown. You think this will work?"

"Gracious, your tubes are in fine working order; there's no reason to touch anything up there. As for what I'm now recommending, it's worked in so many cases that we hardly need discuss it."

"It seems so . . ." she hesitated.

"So calculating?" he supplied.

"Yes, exactly."

"Well, Mrs. Brean, whether you do it or not depends in part on how much you want a baby. This routine is merely an objective, visible check on a physical phenomenon; it won't make you any more or less susceptible to pregnancy."

He had got her drift but refused, apparently, to play "philosophical implications" with her. In spite of being stranded on this limb, Sophie trusted Dr. Gottlieb more than ever. What kind of man went into obstetrics, anyway?

The rain had let up during Sophie's appointment. Sophie looked across Central Park West toward the bare April branches, shiny, dripping, black, and leafless. Cars hissed and honked, jamming themselves into implausible traps. She put up her umbrella, waiting for the click as it blossomed, then put it down again, realizing she did not need it. She walked slowly, trying to muster some hope for herself, toward the subway, home, and Nick.

She repeated, later, Dr. Gottlieb's instructions to her, imitating his tutored mannerisms and the bit about the fictional Mrs. Brown.

Nick said, "It sounds reasonable to me. Somewhat calculating perhaps, but ultimately worth it—if it works. It *is* worth it, isn't it, Soph?"

"If you really want to know what I think, I think it's like holding a stopwatch before a race, on your mark, get set, go!"

"And then I jump on top of you," Nick said.

"That's hardly what I would call a moment of passion. It takes all the fun out of sex."

"Not at all," Nick said. "It's impossible to take the fun out of sex. Some of the initial spontaneity, maybe, but there are certainly ways to make up for that."

The two men, then, were in fundamental agreement. Sophie felt unaccountably defeated the next morning as she sucked on the tasteless thermometer and waited, like Hans Castorp, for something to happen. The reading was 96.8°.

Nick always and very conscientiously told Sophie about his work. She felt that he felt that by so doing he maintained an important connection with her, one that had nothing to do with sex or even friendship; it was a matter of intellectual respect. In a way, he was right to maintain this link so scrupulously.

One evening not long after Sophie started keeping temperature records (which naturally intensified her fears and hopes), Nick came home and said, "Larry Grant's in trouble." He smiled when he said this; some time previously, he had described Larry Grant as a shithouse rat—smart but sneaky.

Nick said, "I'll be right with you" and went into the bedroom. Sophie extracted an ice-cube tray from the freezer and put it on the counter. Then she got out a jar of stuffed olives, noticed that there were only three left, and wrote "olives" on the shopping-memo pad affixed to the refrigerator by a magnetized clip. She emptied the last of a large bag of corn chips into a stainless steel bowl and set out two stemmed glasses. She transferred the lot onto a tray and brought it into the living room. Nick had changed his suit jacket for a sweater. He needed to shave but hadn't; they were staying home. Sophie, still in her high heels (having preceded her husband home by five minutes), switched on the standing and table lamps and went over to kiss him; she wanted to feel the pressure of his arms across her back. Her infertility had given her, during recent weeks, many peculiarly acute moments of loneliness.

"What kind of trouble?" she asked after the kiss.

"Well, for lack of a better term, you could say it was a conflict of interest. Only three olives left; you better write it on the shopping list."

"I did," she said. "Go on."

"Grant's been doing some consulting work for one of the drug concerns. Lots of the men do it; there's nothing wrong in that. But Larry goes a little further: he's been giving them confidential stuff in return for some very attractive gifts."

"I didn't know you kept secrets. I thought you were working for humanity." Sophie watched Nick as he made them irreproachable martinis, then poured the last drops off the ice in the pitcher, and stored the leftover in the refrigerator.

"We are," he said, impatient. "Look, here's the situation. Suppose we discover, in the course of some research with viruses, that a certain type of substance or drug will attack and destroy a particular strain of virus. Naturally, this gets written up in detail in a report—a confidential report. Now, Larry Grant, who has access to all reports, takes it to the drug company he's consulting for and lets them take a confidential little peek. Then they start looking into the stuff themselves— you understand none of the other drug companies is in on it yet—and have a substantial and lucrative head start before our report is ever released to the general public. He doesn't have to tell them anything; he just sort of passes the report along with a note like 'this might be of interest to you' and they figure out the rest. Then he puts the report back into our files and no one's the wiser. In the meantime, they give Larry a nice Christmas, end-of-the-year, or Fourth-of-July bonus. What he's done is not illegal—no one's going to be able to get him into court, but it's unethical to say the least. It's in the gray land of the half-moral."

Sophie nodded, appalled. "It reminds me of the Seventh Avenue manufacturer whose business was so bad he decided to end it all by jumping out the window and as he fell past his competitor's window on the way down, he yelled back to his partner upstairs 'cut vel–l–l–l–vet.' "

"And Grant just cut his own throat. He got a little sloppy and didn't cover his tracks. We've found him out." Nick smiled.

"But how stupid of him! Didn't he realize he'd get caught sooner or later?"

"Did Goldfine think he'd get caught? A common strain runs through all these types, these smart operators. They all think they're smarter than the men they've managed, by sheer and temporary luck, to con. Once they're on top of the situation, they begin to believe they have it made for life. In a strange way they think they're untouchable. It's the only reality they can live with. It's the same with the majority of men in combat: if they really believed they were about to stop a bullet, they'd run like hell in the other direction."

"It sounds suspiciously like paranoia to me," Sophie said. "What are they going to do to Larry Grant?"

"Can him, eventually. But first, for form's sake, there's a hearing. You can't hang a man without letting him have his say. Even the Nazis were proud of their judges."

"Who hears him?"

"The trustees. It's happened a couple of times before. The man always goes straight back to the company he's been ratting to, and they reward him with a fat vice-presidency; it's part of the original unwritten agreement. He ends up making four times as much money as he ever would with us. And since money was what he was after in the first place, everybody's happy. Except that the drug company has to look for another pipeline."

"It's amazing they don't just quit their jobs and move over in the first place."

"Ah, but there you overlook the challenge of trying to get away with something, the intrinsic reward of eluding detection."

"God, I think it's incredible. It makes me feel a little ill."

"You sure you're not just pregnant?"

"Not funny. Besides I'm not."

"Why don't we just see what we can do about that?"

Sophie sighed. "I bought some watercress to go with our casserole for dinner. Come with me while I make the expensive salad."

"I can't, Sophie. I promised Graham I'd go over a proposal for him and return it by tomorrow; it's only five hundred pages long, elite type. Let me know when dinner's ready." And Nick took the manuscript out of his briefcase, sat down with it, and read, uninterrupted except to eat, until twelve-thirty, when he climbed into bed beside Sophie, already asleep and dreaming.

Two nights later the phone rang quite late, breaking into a long painful train of Sophie's thoughts, which involved several truths to which she was reluctant to commit herself. She could see that it was possible she might never be able to have a child—being the victim of one of nature's cruel inadvertencies —but she could not accept a picture of married life without children. In this respect she was a product of her own ancestral past, embracing her mother's primitive faith and sharing her fund of superstitions. It was equally bizarre to imagine that Nick would agree to adopt an orphaned or abandoned nonentity. In pushing sex to extremes of utility she had permitted it to lose some of its charm, though this was not true, apparently, for Nick. Thank God. Sophie lay rigid, fully aware of the temperature of the soup she was in and seeing, for some hideous reason, the polite and reassuring grimaces of Dr. Frank Sinatra Gottlieb. He's a beast, she decided as the phone rang. Startled, she nearly jumped out of bed.

"Is this Mrs. Brean?"

"Who *is* this?" she said, wondering which member of her family had been crushed to death. There was something in the voice she knew she ought to recognize.

"Stuart Prince. You know, the boy you see at the agency."

"Stuart," she almost shouted. Nick humped and mumbled beside her. She went to a whisper. "Stuart, what's the matter?"

"Why? Does something have to be the matter? I just wanted to talk to you."

"Do you know what time it is?"

"Sure I know. It's nighttime. What are you doing?" He paused. "Did I wake you up? Christ, I'm sorry if I woke you up."

"No, you didn't wake me, Stuart, but I can't talk to you now. If everything's honestly all right, I'll hang up." She waited.

"OK," he said, sullen. "I can take a hint. Good night again." And he hung up.

She replaced the receiver slowly, baffled, yet beginning to understand. She was sorry for Stuart; she felt so much pity that it started to ache inside her, and then she was aware that part of the pity was for Sophie herself, the childless mother. If he was the motherless child, then she was the childless mother. You *could* say that now and it was perfectly clear to her what had been happening from the first. And Nick stood outside. He was as much out of it as if he had gone to sea and were never going to come back; he preferred the life of a sailor. She wanted to cry, it ached so much; but instead she lay down again and turned out the light and tried to think of ways to solve the twin riddles of yearning and need.

Sophie knew something was wrong the minute she saw his face, for it was gray with anger and the skin seemed to have been pulled tightly toward his mouth. "That SOB," he snarled.

"Nick," Sophie said, "who? What are you talking about? What happened?"

"Remember, I told you the other day about Larry Grant and his private little information agency? Remember, I said there was going to be a hearing. Well, that bastard has implicated me. No reason except that he's always had it in for me. He's going down and he wants to take somebody with him." He sat on the couch and put his hands to his face. He looked exhausted.

"Nick," Sophie said, "I don't understand. Why should he do it? You didn't do anything wrong, did you?"

Nick looked up suddenly. Sophie could see his fingers trembling. "Oh Christ, Sophie, not you too. Of course I didn't. I haven't had anything to do with the man since he started working with us. Grant and I tend to steer clear of each other."

"Then what's it all about?"

"If you'll stop interrupting, I'll tell you," he said. "But I want a drink first." He got up and mixed himself a drink. Sophie followed him, silent and waiting. "Mind you," he said at last, "it was in a very preliminary way. He was in Graham's office, trying his best to smooth things over, pleading, of course, that he'd done only what any number of others in his position would and had done—Nick Brean for instance. Graham stopped by the lab and told me this later. He said naturally he didn't believe it but just in case Grant brought my name up again at the official hearing I should be prepared to defend myself."

"Defend yourself, but you haven't done anything!" Sophie felt the kick of the shock; it was like being hit from behind.

"Not only defend myself by denying it," Nick continued, "but be able to prove it. How the hell do you prove something negative?"

"You *can't* do it. I'm sure all you have to do is tell them. I mean *they* can't prove anything either. Isn't the burden of proof on Larry Grant?"

"Sophie, shut up a minute, will you?"

"My God, Nick, what's happening to you? Look at you. You're so jumpy anyone would think you *were* guilty." She had never seen her husband in this state.

"Please, Sophie!" He took a deep, agonized breath. "Look, Sophie, I can't think when you keep babbling at me. Just be

(117)

quiet, will you, and let me think out loud for a little while. Yes, if this were a trial the burden of proof would rest with Grant. But here it's a much subtler business. My reputation, my job, my future with the institute depend on my ability to prove beyond a doubt that I've never done anything but my own work, never told anything to anybody; that I have, in fact, been far more reticent than the most scrupulous person alive. All it took to cast doubt on me was one casual remark from Grant. I don't think I've ever felt so much like killing a man as I do this minute. That's why I'm jumpy, as you call it; I want to commit murder."

"All right," Sophie said, somewhat calmer, "but can you tell me why he did it to you; I still don't understand."

"What's he got to lose? He's always been jealous of me, especially these expense-account trips all over the country. I know for a fact that he's grumbled about that for quite a while. He's a little like a spoiled kid when it comes down to it. And, furthermore, he's deficient in a moral sense—some people are, as if they were crippled or deformed in some way. They honestly believe that what they're doing is splendid so long as they don't get caught at it. They have themselves convinced. You ought to know that, Sophie; you must deal with the same kind of thing all the time."

"With children it's different. You can't exactly tell whether they're really deficient or just undeveloped." Sophie still felt that Nick's anger and hurt were spilling all over her. It was as difficult to talk to him when he was like this as it was to take a shower with only the cold tap turned on.

"Now I've got to prepare some kind of defense for the hearing."

"What hearing?"

"I told you. My hearing."

"No, Nick, you didn't tell me. You said, 'in case.'"

"I said," Nick retorted very slowly as if he were trying to get through to an idiot, "that Graham said, 'in case.' It was his way of warning me that I would probably be investigated myself. Now do be a good little wife, will you? Go shell some peas or talk to your mother on the phone or something. I have to sort some things out."

Instead of shelling peas, Sophie played a record and listened to it, hating the music which flowed so stupidly from one idea to the next, stared out the window, and wondered why on earth his problems had assumed so great an urgency that hers were entirely obliterated.

Finally she went into the kitchen and grilled a ham steak for their dinner. She opened a can of pineapple rings and dumped them on top. Then she made a Chinese sauce from sugar, water, soy sauce, and cornstarch and poured that over the lot. It was brown, shiny, and authentic-looking. Sophie loathed ham. "Nick, dinner's ready."

Nick was talking on the phone and waved to her to be quiet. "Oh hell," she said and poured out a secret drink for herself, feeling like Ida Lupino.

Although she knew things would be easier for her if she didn't, Sophie called her mother that night to report on Nick's troubles. Her mother said loud and clear: "It's in times of trouble, darling, that the real test of a marriage is made."

Within a very short time, Nick had characteristically transformed his minor crisis into an opportunity. He found, for example, that to prove something negative was not at all the impossible task he had imagined. You assembled evidence and presented it in a logical manner; you rounded up friends and colleagues to vouch for your probity, integrity, loyalty, dedication, and other qualities which can arouse only respect and apologies; you present yourself as not merely washed, but clean to begin with. As he went along, Nick found himself enjoying the spotlight he played on himself. Its brightness was very like real warmth. He became aware of the dramatic possibilities presented by the hearing; and he wrote for the occasion a short but elegant speech on science and ethical problems in which he stated a viewpoint that had, at best, an underground popularity with most of the scientific community—namely that in proportion as technology becomes more complex, the scientist should assume a more dynamic stance in relation to problems outside his discipline. He had, in fact, discovered attitudes in himself that he had not known he possessed.

Nick read the speech to Sophie and then set about memorizing it. "I want it to seem extempore," he explained.

"But it's not; it's taken you about a week to write," Sophie said.

Nick overlooked her remark. "This little episode," he said, "has forced me to look at things in a fresh way. I've gotten new insights, you might say. It's a pretty effective talk, isn't it?"

Sophie nodded. "Very." She allowed to herself that a man *can* grow but she didn't especially like the coincidence of trouble and pragmatism. Nick was too much of a conjurer; one ought not to be able to extricate oneself so easily.

"You said Margo is coming for dinner? Great, let's open a bottle of Burgundy." He was enormously pleased with himself. "By the way," he said, uncorking a bottle to let it "breathe," "there's a movie I want to see. Maybe Margo will come along."

"I don't see how she can refuse if you've made up your mind to go," Sophie said. It was Saturday, and Sophie had spent a wasted afternoon looking for a reading lamp for the bedroom. "By the way, maybe I'll want to come along. Why don't you ask me?"

"Goodness. Sarcasm so early in life? It doesn't suit your sweet, ingenuous style," he said. "As a matter of fact I didn't ask you because I already know you want to see this movie. You said so six months ago when it first came out and we decided to wait until it hit the neighborhood." He named the picture.

Sophie admitted it, wondering how he managed to be right so much of the time. "Still," she said, suppressing her annoyance, "Margo's depressed over Ellie. She may not want to go to the movies."

"Nonsense. Movies are the best antidepressant next to goof-balls. We'll see." Nick went into the bathroom to shave.

Margo looked as if she had been hit by something large and wet. Her eyes were bloodshot and heavy-lidded, and her arms hung wearily, like a person suffering from gigantism. Her clothes (a jumper with paint splotches on the skirt, over one of Ellie's shirts) were wrinkled. The gestalt of Margo said, "I don't give a damn any more."

"Hi, Sophie," she said. "Regard the wreck of the good ship love."

"Margo," Nick said, nuzzling her shoulder as he took her coat, "you're too yummy for that joker. Come in and we'll have a restorative drink and you can tell us all about it."

"I may get weepy," she said.

"I have a large clean handkerchief," Nick said. Sophie thought he was really making an attempt, and she smiled at him. He's sweet, she thought. He's thoughtful when it counts. It did not occur to Sophie that it usually counted with people other than her.

They attempted a coherent conversation, but Margo lapsed again and again into a distracted silence. Once or twice she stopped cold in the middle of a sentence and, when urged to continue, apologized that she had forgotten what she was going to say.

"Why don't we have dinner now? Afterwards—if you'd like—there's a nifty picture up the street we might go to," Nick said to Margo.

Sophie suddenly realized that Margo had become their burden. "Fine," Sophie said, not waiting for Margo to commit herself. "Come on in the kitchen while I stir the pots."

The two women stood by the stove, Margo leaning against the wall, her head tilted back against a cupboard. She closed her eyes and breathed deeply.

"I could have warned you," Sophie said.

"Then why didn't you?" Margo's resonant voice had lost its timbre and gone flat.

"You wouldn't have believed me."

"I would."

"Maybe," Sophie said, aware that Margo might be trying to blame her, "but I doubt it."

Margo stared at her dumbly.

"I don't believe people should interfere with other people—

especially in such a flammable situation," Sophie said, reeking of piety.

Margo said evenly, "Not even when you know you can prevent something disastrous?" Then she *was* blaming Sophie.

Sophie thought, Why am *I* always made to squirm? I haven't done anything. "The thing is, Margo, supposing I had gone at length into the lamentable history of Ellie's other women, would it really have made any difference to you? Wouldn't you just have decided that this time it was going to be different, that *you* could hold onto him, the slimy thing? You shouldn't blame me for not warning you."

Margo said nothing. She reached for a cracker and ate it, then reached for a second. "I always eat too much when I'm miserable," she said. "I don't even get the satisfaction of losing a few pounds from grief. Oh hell, I'm a mess." She chewed a moment or two in silence. "Who's Diane?" she asked.

"A dancer. With a sawdust head. But then Ellie never put a premium on brains."

"Have you met her?"

"Once."

"What's she like?"

"Oh, Margo, what difference does it make? They're all the same. In another couple of months there'll be another Diane named Lulu. Look, Margo, you know what I think? I think you would never have married Ellie if he had asked you."

"Who said anything about marriage?" Margo said over her shoulder, as she walked away.

At dinner Margo confessed that a gallery on Tenth Street was willing to give her a show if she would finish three more canvasses.

"Aren't you pleased?" Sophie asked.

"Sure," Margo said. "I can now go sublimate like crazy while I'm meeting their deadline. I might even improve. You know, the beneficial effect of deep emotion on art bit." Margo accepted a second helping of pot roast.

The food seemed to restore Margo, as if she had transformed its nutritional benefits into spiritual aid, by means, perhaps, of mystical chewing. She grew almost lively and even joked about her condition. She insisted, too, on helping Sophie wash up and put every plate and pot away.

They walked up to the movie house after dinner. Nick, relieved of the pressure of the hearing, was unusually animated. Sophie, subdued now, noticed four pregnant women within three blocks. Margo walked beside Sophie but was entirely segregated with her bleeding heart. The food seemed to have worn off.

Nick paid for the three of them and made the two women wait while he bought an overpriced box of candy-coated almonds with a cellophane window against which swam the pastel-colored nuts. "Monty Clift," he said, "learned how to act when he got his face bashed in. By the way, *Time* gave this picture a great review. Whoever he is, *Time's* critic and I share a common lust for the big, the vulgar, the bloody, and the technicolored. Now if you two ladies don't like it, be sure to let me know and we'll leave."

Sophie and Margo exchanged a wry smile, a superior smile to show they recognized behind the scientist a man unable to resist the lure of the movies—almost any movie, so long as it moved.

They sat there, Margo, Sophie, then Nick, in the dark, chewing on candied nuts and staring transfixed at the Brobdingnagian images high in front of them for some time when Sophie began to be distracted by noises immediately to her left. There was a muffled gulp; a minute or so later it was followed by a breath, caught and choked on. Sophie looked over and saw with a shock of shame that Margo was dissolving in a solution of her own tears.

She poked Nick, on her right, hard in the ribs. He jumped. "Margo's crying," she said.

"That's funny," he said. "It's not a bit sad."

"It's not the movie, stupid," Sophie hissed. "It's your fine friend Ellie Shantz the lady-killer she's crying about. *I'm* going to take her home. You can come if you like." She was furious. It was as if all the trials in her marriage, the little things and the big things, had suddenly become galvanized in one great ball of fury against her husband. "I just knew we shouldn't have brought her. I knew this would happen!"

"You did not, of all the hindsight justifications," he said to her, hard and cold. They had both, it seemed, raised their voices sufficiently to receive considerable and disapproving attention from the audience.

"I'm all right," Margo sniffled. "Really I am. Sophie, please don't come with me. Really, I'd rather be alone." She was not simply protesting; she did not want sympathy. "Thanks for the pot roast, you guys. I'm sorry about this; I got carried away." A man in front of them turned around and shushed them like an angry schoolteacher. Nick muttered, "Up yours, pal," but the man did not hear him. Margo squeezed down the aisle and disappeared.

"You have no feelings. You're really a bastard," Sophie said to her husband, blaming him for all kinds of hurts, imaginary and otherwise, for her, as well as his, shortcomings.

"Listen, Sophie, you listen to me. Nobody made Margo come with us. She's a grown woman. She came of her own free will and if she broke down, that's her private business; she'll handle it the best way she knows how. Now for God's sakes, shut up and let me watch this movie."

Nick's name began to appear on full-page ads in *The New York Times* and other newspapers, either pleading for or protesting a variety of government and institutional policies. He was, for example, for fluoridation, against segregation, for extension of birth control dissemination, for greater scientific and cultural exchanges with the Soviet Union, and so on. He also accepted a place on the masthead of a magazine along with six other scientific advisory board members. Ellie told Sophie that science was definitely "in" since sputnik. Money began to reach the Breans in large chunks instead of dribs and drabs.

"What do you say we buy something big, useless, and expensive?" Nick asked Sophie as they walked home from a

restaurant along Fifth Avenue. Nick had in his wallet a check
for eight hundred dollars he had earned by giving three
lectures on RNA at Bellevue. Nick's arm was tucked against
her side. "You've put on a couple of pounds," he said, rubbing
against her hip. "Maybe we should send you to Main Chance
for a couple of weeks." Sophie said nothing. The casements of
department stores blazed; the mannikins were modeled with
such slavish accuracy they semed to be whispering to each
other behind their perfect red lips.

"Big and expensive like what?" Sophie asked. She wanted
only one thing and that she could not buy. Her obsession to
have a child had, in fact, obliterated almost every other desire;
she found the notion of something big and expensive down-
right silly.

"A painting, a car, a trip. A fur coat for you."

She laughed. "A fur coat! Are you serious, Nick? What
would Ellie say?"

"Screw what Ellie would say. What would you say?"

"I don't want one."

"You don't want one or you don't want the idea of one?
You're always cold. A fur coat would keep you warm."

"I just don't want one." She, too, thought a fur coat would
probably keep her warm.

"Well, then, how about a painting, a car?"

"We don't need a car."

"Sophie, we don't really need anything except food, clothing,
and shelter. Depending on how you choose to look at it, all the
rest is just the detritus of civilization."

That's not quite true, she said to herself. "I'll think about it,"
Sophie promised. "I tend to favor the painting—if we could
ever agree on one we both liked."

They walked in silence for several blocks, stopping in front
of windows to stare at the kind of clothes Sophie instinctively
avoided, just as she stayed away from most novels until they
had been out at least five years.

"Maybe we ought to give some of all this money away, like

to the NAACP or the Cancer society or to feed starving Korean prostitutes," she said.

"Listen, honey, I've already committed my life to cancer and CORE. As far as the NAACP is concerned, if I sent them a contribution they'd probably use it to build up their precious temperate image. What that bunch needs is for someone to light a fire under their complaisant black bottoms."

"Nick, how can you *say* that? How can you call them complaisant?"

"All right, tell me what they have accomplished in the years of their existence that wasn't Uncle Tom?"

"Worked for civil rights, brought about the Supreme Court decision on integration, provided free legal aid, and on and on."

"Have they, do you actually think they have made the slightest dent into the mind of the South, that petrification of prejudice?"

"How about integration?"

"It's a word. There's no integration in the South. One or two five-year-olds sprinkled among a thousand white kids. And that's it. They can't vote; they can't pee in a white pot; they can't eat a white sandwich. The NAACP keeps talking, and it seems you are just as ignorant as the next man on this subject. It's only our people who are getting anything accomplished." He detached his arm from her and began striding up the street, letting his indignation have free play. "You are so absorbed in your trivial problems that you cannot make the slightest effort to interest yourself in the authentic troubles of an entire race."

"That's just not true," Sophie said, angry. "You know the kind of work I do. I've spent most of my life helping other people. They have troubles, too. Maybe their troubles seem less important to you, but let me tell you, in many ways these troubles are even more crippling than being born black. And don't forget this: I help anyone who comes to me—all sizes, shapes, colors, and smells." She felt the weight of his accusation as she would the sudden recognition of an enormous personal failure—as in a catastrophic decision or a bad marriage.

"Sure you help them," he said. "It's your job. Would you do it for nothing?"

"I can't answer that question—it's too hypothetical. I've been trained for this. In our society people get paid for their training and their skills."

"No. What about doing it for nothing, sacrificing your time, your career, your life maybe, for something?"

"For a principle? I don't know. It's too hypothetical," she said, repeating herself. They had stopped walking and were just standing on a corner. She had the feeling that all they were standing on was shifting ground.

"That's nonsense," he told her.

"And I suppose that's why you want to buy an expensive car. Why not a Bentley while we're at it?"

"There you go again. All or nothing. I'm not suggesting we give away everything we own and go about in rags begging for a few crumbs. Nor founding a spiritual community like Tolstoy and other mystics. What I *am* trying to suggest is that I doubt that you are capable of the kind of vision and emotional range that would make sacrifice a practical possibility."

"Are you, then?" she asked. She felt abandoned.

"I think so," he said soberly. "Yes, I think I am."

"But how can anyone be sure?" They were walking again. They passed a display filled with the brilliance of an artificial sun and underneath it two tipsy striped beach umbrellas and a pair of plastic ladies in skimpy bathing suits of impeccable design and bright color.

Nick said, "I know myself, that's about it. If threatened, I'll fight. If one of my beliefs is threatened, I will fight for it."

"You sound like that melodrama we saw the other night, Nick." Sophie could hardly believe what she was hearing; no one she knew talked like this. She doubted, in fact, that people actually lived like that. She believed instead that what they did when literally threatened preceded any rationale they might later hold for their extreme acts. "You've changed," she said, half hoping he would not be listening.

"Not as much as you wish," he said mysteriously. If there existed within him a fire (and she looked at his eyes, as icy and determined as a recruiting-poster soldier), it would be the kind you can turn out by removing a plug from the wall—glowing handsomely but spurious. "The world has changed," he went on. "The climate's altered; ordinary men—not just soldiers—are now obliged to act in ways that were closed to them before."

"Are you referring to the South again?"

"In part."

"We can't all be brave in the same way," she murmured but he was not interested. She was, by now, quite certain that Nick was going to commit himself to a posture she could never imitate and that he had done it without realizing that his messianic ardor might be selfish as well as charitable. For a man of insight, Nick was peculiarly dense about his self-inflicted role, as a parent is who, in the grip of compulsive spasms of vanity, inspires his children to bring home only A's.

Sophie saw many children and adolescents in the course of her work. None, however, appealed to her in the special and unprofessional way that Stuart had. For this she was relieved; it was reassuring not to fall into the same trap again. Three or four times Dr. Strauss offered her spontaneous and public praise during staff conferences; this she accepted with gratitude but also with a sense of ironic reservation. In one case she had restored to life a large clumsy child of four named Gabe. Gabe, his parents told her with guilty directness, was hopelessly retarded; he could not, in fact, speak. After five visits to Sophie's office, where he manipulated her toys as if in a trance, he had said to her, "Why won't they let me open the door?" It was his first sentence, ever. Sophie then concentrated on discovering which door he was talking about and why they insisted on keeping it closed and so on, excavating her way back to where Gabe had first found the tool of speech and decided to bury it. Sophie sent him down the hall to Mrs. Magid, who, in the course of tabulating his test results, found that Gabe was just as bright as everyone else and in fact had some highly original fantasies going on inside his head, fantasies that might finally turn into something useful. In the end, Sophie managed to fit Gabe back into the family jigsaw; his parents looked at him as if they had never seen him before. The mother sent Sophie a present, a box of lavender cocktail napkins.

"You did a splendid job with that child," Dr. Strauss said. "His parents were about to sacrifice their other child's education to send him to a special school."

"Thank you," she said, eyes downcast. She had liked Gabe— the child had a mind of his own and a charming way of standing, as if he were about to take a dive from the highest board.

Then there was Dorothy, a fourteen-year-old whose eyes were always red and watery and who for weeks denied that she ever cried. Dorothy had had intercourse with nineteen different boys. One day, shortly before the girl was dragged into Sophie's office, her mother had found Dorothy's diaphragm at the bottom of a box of tissues and had fainted. What Sophie uncovered, in the course of getting Dorothy to unburden herself, was that although Dorothy was a neophyte prostitute—with rates, hours, and restrictions—she actually knew very little about sex and cared less. She did not know from which orifice babies emerged into the world and confessed that she had done what she had because her clients— mainly boys no older then seventeen—had paid her in cash with which she bought what she referred to as "decent clothes." For his own curious reasons her father had refused to buy her any clothes at all. It took Sophie almost a year to straighten the girl out; her psyche had got as complex and twisted as an adult intestine. In addition, Dorothy's addiction to Sophie had became particularly adhesive; Sophie had been forced into the role of good mother and poor deprived Dorothy hung on for dear life. Dorothy had cried continually during the last few months of treatment; her consumption of handkerchiefs was phenomenal. Dorothy had called Sophie at home several times, and once or twice Nick had answered and pretended to be a Russian butler, which didn't make things any easier for either Dorothy or Sophie.

Sophie considered her work and found it difficult to resist the temptation of believing Dr. Strauss; she possessed an undeniable knack for untying the knots that children seemed bent on tying themselves into without the slightest knowledge of how to get out.

May, June. Sophie spotted hundreds of pregnant women; they seemed to be multiplying like laboratory mice. Nick kept up a steady stream of contributions to scientific journals; his name appeared here and there in stories about the coming, always coming, breakthrough to the secret of cellular life. A shiny national picture magazine wanted to do a story about him. He was called at work.

"May I speak to Dr. Nicholas Brean?"

"This is Dr. Brean." Nick tipped back in his chair and watched two pigeons pecking at the concrete ledge outside his window. Jamming the phone between neck and shoulder, he snapped a paper clip at one of them via a rubber-band slingshot. It struck one on the thigh and the birds flew off squawking and fluttering in panic. Nick held the phone in his hand again. "What can I do for you?"

"This is William Clutch, sir, of *Cool Magazine*. I'd like to come by some time when it's convenient for you and discuss the possibility of our doing a story about you and your work over there."

Nick tipped his chair upright. "Sure, of course," he said. "No, wait. I think I'd like to talk this over with the director, Dr. Graham."

"I've already cleared this with Dr. Graham," the man said. He sounded pleased with himself.

"He said it was all right?"

"Yes, sir."

"Well, in that case I think I'd better clear it with my wife." He laughed.

"Your wife?"

"Yes, my wife, Mrs. Brean. I never let anyone take my picture or record my secrets without obtaining my wife's permission." From the silence on the other end, Nick was sure Mr. Clutch did not know whether Nick was joking or serious. "Why don't you call back tomorrow morning after I've had a chance to talk with Mrs. Brean?"

"I can assure you, Dr. Brean, that we wouldn't publish anything without your final approval."

"Naturally, of course," Nick said, "that goes without saying. Thanks for calling." He hung up and smiled. He was not sure himself whether he was keeping the man on the hook or was genuinely reluctant.

That night Nick reached home before his wife. This happened so infrequently that he was uneasy about it and impatient with her for not turning on the lights first. He looked in the refrigerator and found nothing in it that could conceivably be transformed into an edible dinner for a grown man. On this evidence he decided that Sophie must be shopping for dinner; her planning was really impossible. Nick made himself a drink and stood by the window looking for Sophie in the street. His picture, quite possibly, would be on the cover; he would be dressed in a clean white coat, unbuttoned to exhibit his striped shirt, and a vest, buttoned to exhibit his integrity. He would hold his reading glasses lightly in his fingers and be looking directly into the eye of the camera: the searcher in the saddle. He took a satisfying sip that burned its way past his gullet and warmed his heart.

Presently Nick heard Sophie's heels tapping on the corridor outside. He opened the front door.

"Hi," she said. "Thanks, I couldn't find my key. What luck you were here. What are you doing home so early?"

"It's not early," he said, taking a bundle from her. "You're late."

"I had to stop off at the market for some food. I miscalculated again."

"I know," he said. "What'd you get?"

"Veal—it was on sale. I'll be right with you." She went into the bathroom and stayed and stayed. Nick unloaded the bags and put the food away. He made her a drink and himself a second. Still she did not reappear.

"What in heck are you doing in there?" He stood outside the bathroom door and shouted at it.

"I took a shower," she yelled. "Did I forget to get your permission?"

He decided she was in a bad mood. "I made you a gin and tonic," he said.

"Thanks."

"I have something to tell you," Nick shouted.

"What?"

"Oh, never mind. When are you going to get out of there?"

"When I'm finished," she said.

"Oh hell," Nick said. He pulled some work out of his attaché case and sat down with it, totally absorbed. He did not even hear Sophie when she emerged at last.

"Did I hear you say you had something to tell me?"

"It'll keep," he said. "I'm right in the middle of something and I don't want to interrupt myself."

"Good heavens, Nick."

"I'll tell you later," Nick said again. "Now, don't you think you'd better get on with dinner? Veal should be well done."

"It's scallopini," she said, disgusted. He was paying her back for taking so long in the shower. He's nothing but a big baby, she thought, deliberately banging pots and pans until he yelled at her. "Be quiet, for Christ sake. It sounds like a goddamn kindergarten in there!"

Well, she decided, in the tedium of everyday life our true personality does stick up its ugly little head.

Nick said almost nothing until coffee. They had dined like two strangers who happen to be sharing a table in a cafeteria, treating one another with both exaggerated politeness and undercover suspicion.

"I don't know why I shouldn't tell you now," he said.

"Oh? Suppose I don't care to hear."

"Come here, you big baby; let's go sit down together and stop this nonsense. I want to hold your pretty soft hands and feel your pretty soft thighs. You're beautiful, Sophie."

"Why are you so mean?" she said, refusing, although she was aching to give in. "The impossible part about your meanness is that you're mean when you really don't want to be. You have no control over your meanness."

"Just stop talking like a psychologist. If I was mean to you, I apologize. Sincerely. Now come over here—forget the dishes— come over here."

"Oh, Nick, I'm sorry. I don't feel well. I got my period today; it's so depressing."

"Not again?" He smiled.

"How can you smile?" she wailed. "Why can't I get pregnant?"

"Now listen: you'll never get pregnant until you let up a little and stop agonizing. You've simply got to relax and let life have a crack at you."

"I can't." She began to cry.

"Don't cry."

"Why?"

"I don't know." He got up and paced about the room while Sophie cried. At last she said, "I'm all cried out."

"That's a mercy," he said. "I was just about to take a nice long walk. Do you think you could stop feeling sorry for yourself long enough to listen to something about me?"

Sophie nodded, sniffing. She shifted her legs to the couch and stretched out with two pillows behind her head. "Shoot."

Nick's left profile, the one she could see now, was regular and strong, like a marble Augustus. Even after all this time, the sight of it made her catch her breath with desire. The right profile was the one where something was slightly out of whack, which gave him a somewhat nasty look, like an actor playing Al Capone.

"*Cool Magazine* wants to do a story about me, about our work in the lab. I suppose they think we have the answer to the great questions. I put them off; what do you think?" He had not in fact, meant to do it this way; he was asking her advice now to his own surprise.

Sophie threw it back to him. "What do *you* think about it?"

"Naturally, I'm flattered. But the idea sticks in my throat."

"Are we snobs?" she said, aware of what he was trying to say, thinking the same thing herself but uneasy about it.

"Maybe," he said. He wondered what the few people whose opinions really mattered to him would say when they saw him buttoned up and down while waiting to get their hair trimmed or their teeth filled. What he imagined made him twitch with shame. Like "When are you going on the 'Ed Sullivan show'?" or worse, even, than that. Doors might swing silently shut.

"If we're snobs," he said, consoling himself but not her, "we're the only acceptable variety." Suddenly things shifted comfortably into place for him, and he wanted his wife. For once they had agreed; it was almost a miracle. "Darling, I'm truly sorry about your condition." He came over to where she lay and kneeled, dropping his head to her breast.

"In more ways than one?" she asked, rubbing his ear as if it were soft and furry.

"In more ways than one," he murmured.

It was almost August again. Sophie found that summer vacation no longer held promises of delight, for August meant J. Robert and J. Robert meant putting herself to a prolonged test. J. Robert, one might say, was Sophie's unpropitious Stuart Prince. She could do with Stuart (admitting only to herself a powerful role in shaping him) what she could not even attempt with Robby. The boy was, after all, her stepson—which made her, in turn, the wicked stepmother. He could not now or ever be a moist lump of clay, like Stuart. Even Ellie would agree that as for personality Robby was a lemon, a hard, dry wrinkled lemon with perhaps a little mold creeping along the skin; and if she could not blame herself for this, or Nick (who had lost him long ago), she could still find his presence a positive torment. You were supposed to relax during your vacation, not get all worked up over some small child.

Thinking about Robby made Sophie jump to Stuart. She was pleased with how his last hour had gone; in fact it had all the dramatic tension of a scene in which baffled emotions struggled to get out but were finally restrained from exploding. He had greeted her with an air of infant bravado. No child writing down his first readable alphabet could have been more pleased than Stuart was with this complicated and long-awaited finale. During the hour they talked about his graduation; they discussed his physical symptoms, most of which had disappeared; they encountered his mother along the way and dealt with her in a way Sophie found brilliantly objective. Then it was time to go. Stuart lingered, spending some minutes gathering his belongings to leave. Sophie stood patiently by the door, looking at him and seeing him three inches taller than when he had first arrived, noticing the broad, flat mass of his back and shoulders, the Middle-European triangle of his head. The boy was put together like an athlete, a composition that was rarely a liability; few men will turn their back on such obvious strength—and probably few women.

He fumbled inside his book bag and came up with a large sheet of heavy stock paper.

"This is for you," he said, pushing it toward Sophie.

Surprised, she took it from him. It was a charcoal drawing. She thought she could see a bridge in it. "It's beautiful, Stuart. Thank you." The paper felt warm, almost moist in her fingers.

"It's not beautiful. It *is* strong." The feminine word obviously disgusted him. "I thought you could hang it there," he said, motioning to the only appropriate spot on the wall. "That is, if you like it enough."

"I *do* like it enough, Stuart. I'm terribly pleased to have it. When did you do it?"

"A couple of weeks ago, I guess." He held out his hand. "I better go now; the next one must be waiting."

Sophie felt the earnest pull of his hesitation through his hand. "Good-bye, Stuart," she said, realizing it was the first time she and he had touched. "And good luck," she added, attaching a neat, clipped tail to the backside of his treatment. She hated to say it; it was the kind of phrase he would find no meaning in. He discovered her eyes and, for a moment, their hands still joined, she saw them plead for more words, words like "I love you," "I need you," "Don't go yet," or even "Kiss me good-bye." She would not say them and their hands slid apart like a well-oiled coupling.

Sophie cleared her throat and steered him through the door. "Remember, Stuart, you can come back to see me any time you feel like talking."

He looked doubtful. "Yeah, sure. Well good-bye, Mrs. Brean." And he flew away.

Sophie shut the door and sighed heavily. She sat at her desk and propped the drawing in front of her. It was somewhat stiff, perhaps, but it was controlled; he knew exactly what he was doing. The bridge was recognizable. A bridge between him and her? between him and life? between generations? between the sexes? Any one would be nice; all of them and he'd have smooth sailing.

6

It was not unusual for the parent of a patient to want to interfere during a treatment; in fact it happened so often that the agency had advised its staff to anticipate all varieties of anger, hidden and open, threatening and cringing. It *was*, however, unusual for parents—who after all had been seen right along—to try to make trouble after the treatment was over and the patient turned loose. But Stuart was different; his personality left traces. He was not like Robin, for instance, whom people forget as soon as she left the room (and no amount of treatment was going to change that). Stuart continued to radiate heat after he left.

The trouble began, as so much trouble does, with the ringing of a telephone.

"Sophie," Nick called, "it's for you." He raised his eyebrows, indicating he did not recognize the caller, handed her the receiver, and resumed packing.

"Hello?"

"Mrs. Brean. This is Joseph Prince. I'd like to have a talk with you. It's about Stuart."

"Is anything wrong with Stuart?" Unexpectedly, her heart began thumping.

"I'll say! First of all, he's left his mother's home and he's living in sin with that girl what's her name, that shiksa. He hasn't even got a job."

Sophie was relieved. "I'll be glad to make an appointment to discuss this with you, Mr. Prince. If you'll just call me at my office tomorrow morning, I'll make a date to see you and Mrs. Prince, though it will have to wait, I'm afraid, until the first week in September. I'm about to go off on my vacation."

She heard him put his hand over his receiver and shout, "She's going away!" Then he took his hand off. "It's important. I want to know what you did to my son and I want to talk to you about undoing it. My wife is in such an emotional state I had to stay home from work, miss a night's pay, just to stay with her and keep her from hurting herself." This was not mere talk; Sophie detected an overtone of threat in Mr. Prince's voice.

"Mr. Prince," she said, and was aware that Nick had stopped moving about the room and was standing listening to her side of the conversation, "I'm aware that this is important to you but I don't think this is the best time or way to talk about it. If you like I'll come into the office early tomorrow morning and see you then." She grimaced to Nick whose face remained noncommittal.

Mr. Prince said, "I have to ask Pearl."

Sophie heard him tell Mrs. Prince that they would have to be there at eight in the morning. "We'll be there, Mrs. Brean," he said. "You sure made a hell of a mess out of our son. Better he should have dropped out of school than live the way he does now, a beatnik. I might as well tell you now, Mrs.

Prince and I are pretty sore about this. But we want to hear your side of the story first."

"Thank you," Sophie said, without the slightest trace of what she actually felt. "I'll see you at eight, then, in my office."

"I had a feeling this might happen," she said to Nick.

"What's it all about?"

"Remember the boy I told you about, Stuart, the one we kept from dropping out of school? Well, he's finally made the break and left his mother's bed and board and assumed responsibility for his own debts. His parents have decided to blame me for his rebellion, which they just can't stomach. Oh yes, he's also, in Papa's words, 'living in sin with a shiksa.'"

"Like us," Nick said.

"Hardly."

"Other side of the same coin," he said.

"Now I've got to see these two people and explain every-thing—which they'll never understand anyway because they don't want to hear any of it."

"What do they want to hear?" He seemed faintly amused and Sophie found this irritating. After all, he worked only with dead things, in tubes and smeared over slides, and she worked with human beings, people with smashed spirits and bruised egos. Where did he get off being entertained?

"They want me to assuage their unbearable Jewish guilt," she said severely.

"And?"

"And I'm not going to do it."

The Brean alarm clock went off at six-thirty the following morning. Shivering, though it was not cold, Sophie brewed her small pot of coffee, ate a slice of whole wheat toast spread with processed cheese, stuck a peach in her purse, and woke her husband by leaning over him and whispering into his ear. He smelled of warm, human flesh accustomed to itself, with no foreign odors intruding. With her cheek near his warm creased neck, she was a victim of the same persuasive sexual radiance that had startled and intrigued her from the moment she had first seen him. But Nick was a sexual bully; he used it where other men might use kindness or generosity. She passed up the impulse to pinch his neck as hard as she could.

"Get up," she said. "It's time to get up." She kissed him lightly. The pillowcase had creased his cheek. He looked very young.

"Where the hell are you off to, so early? It must be all of seven o'clock."

"To see Mr. and Mrs. Prince, remember?"

"Oh yes, the wrathful parents of the wicked boy."

"He's not a bad boy. They're wicked parents."

"Isn't that the way you always read it?"

"No, of course it isn't. And you know it." The idea of starting to fight so early in the morning nauseated her.

"Aren't you going to have breakfast with me?"

"I've had mine," she said evenly. "I've got to leave now, Nick, or I'll be late."

Nick tried to pull her down onto the bed beside him.

"Nick, please!"

"What's the matter, honey pot, do I have bad breath?"

"Nick, don't." She wrenched away. "I've got to be uptown in half an hour. I can't keep them waiting; it just isn't right, after they agreed to be in my office so early. I'll see you tonight."

"You are far too seductive to sit behind a desk in an office." He started to peel himself out of bed. He was entirely naked.

"Why do you say that?" she accused him, still unwilling to leave, to let the echo of his last words ring in her head like a television commercial. She detested his knack for giving every compliment a reverse twist. "Why do you always belittle my work and my job?" she demanded.

"Sophie, this all sounds far too disagreeable to continue before my cup of tea. I'll be glad to investigate your accusations further if you want to stick around for a while." Sophie looked at his gorgeous body and despised it.

"It isn't a question," she said, pulling on her gloves, "of choosing whether I stick around or not. I *can't* stay. That's exactly what I'm talking about. You act as if my work had no real meaning, like a volunteer sorting clothes in a thrift shop or something; as if whether I go or not in the morning depends on my mood or whatever else I may have planned for the day that I might enjoy more. That's what I mean by belittling—don't you see?"

His coolness infuriated her. "And what about me?" he said, pulling on his trousers, his back toward her. He found a clean shirt, ripped out the laundry cardboard, and threw it on the bed along with the paper strip. "What about children—if you ever have any? Don't we enter into the precious career picture at all?"

"That's something else again. You knew I wanted to go on working when you married me. What's all this fuss now? You act as if you had just discovered a terrible secret in my past that changed your picture of me. I'm the same Sophie you married, the same selfish Sophie."

Nick shrugged and his tone changed abruptly, without transition, pausing only momentarily between the second and third movements. "Aren't you going to kiss me good-bye?" he pleaded, advancing on her like the Sheik.

"No," she said, and walked out through the front door, closing it too hard.

Riding uptown on the subway, Sophie found she could not shake her fury at Nick. After all this time, why should she be forced to explain herself in such simplistic terms? Why did he choose such an unfortunate moment to start questioning what he ought to have accepted from the very beginning? Part of it was that Sophie had a sneaking suspicion that basically Nick did not give a damn, that he really did not care whether she worked or not; he simply wanted to make waves in their marriage.

By the time Joseph Prince strode into her office, with Mrs. Prince not far behind, Sophie was still so angry she almost called him Nick.

"So," she said, after indicating chairs for them, "you think Stuart's made a dreadful mistake?" She glowered at Mr. Prince and watched with satisfaction as Mrs. Prince withdrew a crumpled handkerchief from her purse and began dabbing at her eyes with it.

"Mistake!" Sarcasm dilated his words. "*You* can call it that. *I* call it a disaster. He started out only lazy; now he's in real trouble. His chances are ruined, finished. There's nothing left for him; he might as well be paralyzed, living inside an iron lung." Mr. Prince, *mezzo forte,* waved his hands about as he spoke. Mrs. Prince's eyes became clogged up and seemed about to spill over.

"Can you be a little more specific, Mr. Prince? What has Stuart done to ruin his chances? I take it you mean his chances for earning what you think of as a decent living?" Sophie concentrated on this man; she still saw, like a double exposure, the supercilious face of her husband as he had abused her an hour earlier.

"Yes, I mean a decent living, a life that means something. You know what he is now, since he came here? He's a bum. He hasn't got a real job; he only goes to a couple of art classes a week. And then there's this shiksa, this Amy what's her name; they live in one filthy room on Avenue B. They're probably both dope fiends, too, I don't know. What kind of a life is that? What did you say to him to make him do this?" The force of Joseph Prince's anger nearly lifted him to his feet, like a seat full of buckshot.

"You've seen his apartment?" Sophie asked, determined to ask the questions herself.

"You mean his room. Sure I seen it."

"Did Stuart invite you?"

Mrs. Prince began to blubber, her eyes red. "I wouldn't set foot in the place," she wept. "He" (and she indicated her husband by a tilt of the head) "went."

"For supper," Mr. Prince went on. "The girl cooked. Italian sausages and spaghetti."

"It sounds," Sophie said, "as if Stuart is trying to be friends."

"Friends, maybe, with that girl. Why should I have to be friends with my own son?" he said, illogic joining his anger.

"Look at the way he's living! Everything about the way he lives means he's thumbing his nose at his mother and father. He's a beatnik and he's happy being a beatnik. He says 'look at me, old man, I'm a nothing, and I'm not ever going to be an anything.' He asked me down there so he could gloat." The man paused to let his words sink in. "The girl plays the guitar." This last appeared to be the final outrage.

"But you're a musician yourself," Sophie said softly, the image of Nick mercifully fading.

"That's different," he said and did not bother to explain how.

It was quite clear to Sophie that whatever Stuart did, it would not be acceptable to his parents so long as he remained outside the realm of their own experience.

"Now what we want to know," Mr. Prince said, "is what are you going to do about this situation?"

"Do? I don't understand."

"Do, to get my son back," Mrs. Prince said. Sophie could hardly believe her ears.

"You must understand," she said, her fury at Nick finally swallowed by the rationale of her own strength, "I am not going to interfere in Stuart's life. He came to me of his own will and—if you'll remember—with your blessing; he came here in some conscious attempt to create order and meaning from his life, which didn't seem to matter very much to him at the time. When he started seeing me he was about eleven years old emotionally. When he stopped he was just about ready to be an adult. I *will* take some of the credit for that but you must realize that most of this growth originated from Stuart. One of the adjustments he had to make concerned the two of you. Maybe the adjustment he's made will turn out to be temporary, but it seems to be a satisfactory one, a good one. Whether or not he marries Amy isn't really important at this moment, but the fact that he can have an apparently gratifying relationship with a woman *is*. And I think you ought to know that I think this would have been quite impossible for him if

(143)

he hadn't come here and tried to help himself. From what you say, Mr. Prince, it sounds as if he were trying to learn to paint. Considering his background and the obstacles, his accomplishments appear rather larger than even I expected." Sophie sat back.

Her audience seemed shattered. This was not what they had come to hear. Mrs. Prince's eyes had grown dry and hard like blue clay balls. The man and woman looked at each other as if they had just heard that Stuart was not really their son, but an adopted child.

"I never heard such disgusting talk in my life. Mrs. Brean, you're an immoral woman," Mrs. Prince said, pulling herself together for the encounter. She had, in fact, shut her ears after the first few sentences. "I don't want to talk to her any more," Mrs. Prince said to her husband. "I think we should go see the director and tell him what we just heard."

Sophie felt a little sick but quite undefeated. She had a point to make and she had made it, having been given an opportunity often denied her. Generally the wounded ones simply slunk away; these two, for their own reasons, had to face her and be told. "It's perfectly all right with me if you feel you want to talk about Stuart with Dr. Strauss. But I think I ought to tell you that he'll probably ask me to be present when you see him—that's the way it's usually done." She looked at Mrs. Prince with what she hoped would seem utter candor and turned the knife a little. "It's our policy," she said.

"This is terrible," Mrs. Prince said.

"It's like a conspiracy," her husband added. "Just like in Russia. You brainwashed him!"

"Please, Mr. and Mrs. Prince, please listen to me; try to listen." Sophie heard her own voice rise with concern for herself. "All I did was help Stuart climb out of a hole he had somehow fallen into. He wasn't pushed; he just fell. Some of us do; it's the way we're born, the way we stand up to the forces around us, something. Anyway, what I mainly did was listen to him. Actually I told him very little. I listened to him and I got him to listen to himself. Whatever I did tell him I merely suggested and then, most often, it was in the form of a question. I think you should understand there was no magic, no hypnosis, no subliminal suggestion in Stuart's treatment. If I *wanted* to I couldn't brainwash anyone; it requires a special technique I've little knowledge of and no training in." This was not her idiom at all, but the Princes did not know this and it seemed to throw them somewhat off balance. Mr. Prince was flustered by the speech, by its logic.

"I still think," he said lamely, "that you did something to Stuart to change him and make him live like he does. You know how the rent's getting paid? He delivers lunches and *she* works in some kind of jewelry store in Greenwich Village that's open practically all night."

Everything Mr. Prince told her about Stuart was just right; things were working out for him the way Sophie hoped they would. As Mr. Prince grew more outraged, Sophie grew happier. Finally she could not suppress a smile.

"Joseph, I'm leaving." Mrs. Prince stood, spilling her handkerchief on the floor.

"Stay," her husband said, "or go if you want. I'm not finished yet." Pearl Prince wavered, considering the consequences of both actions. At last she stood tentatively touching the doorknob, listening to her husband deliver the last words.

"Mrs. Brean," Joseph Prince said, "I don't know what kind of woman you are but you have made a disaster out of a fine boy. We are not going to let this matter drop; you can be sure of that." Mr. Prince seemed to be using someone else's words with his voice, like a ventriloquist. The effect was startling but ludicrous. Sophie coughed.

She said, "I'm awfully sorry that we can't come to some kind of agreement or understanding, Mr. Prince, truly I am. I wish you were able to see Stuart's remarkable development the way I do. It's a pity we have to disagree about him this way."

This speech had the effect of propelling them both out of Sophie's office. The intense satisfaction that settled around Sophie like a warm blast of recirculated air was not altogether healthy for it contained particles of revenge and germs of self-righteousness.

Sophie and Nick left the city for their vacation at the beach on a Friday, after work. The night before they left, Thursday, Margo called to say good-bye. She exhibited what seemed to Sophie a suspiciously giddy frame of mind, giggling about how she was managing to juggle four men who had never met each other. "It's just like a Restoration comedy," she said. "They hide from each other under the bed. By the way, how's Ellie?"

"The same. Except that he's more at loose ends than ever; he's finally finished the novel."

"That's nice," Margo said. "Has anyone bought it?"

"His agent's been reading it for three weeks. It's called *Itching*. You're supposed to ask itching what?"

"OK, itching what?"

"No, you're supposed to ask the author. And he says itching piles. But it isn't about itching at all. Unless of course you read it as America's neural itch. Anyway, his agent hasn't said anything yet. Ellie put in a scene in which some radioactive isotopes get left in a cathouse by mistake, because he thinks he'll have a better chance of selling the book to the movies with that in it. Actually it's a very funny scene."

No laughter issued from Margo. She asked, "Does he have a girl?" The question came out as a squeak.

"Sure he has a girl. Did you ever see Ellie without a girl? He needs girls like other people need a bath."

"Diane?"

"I don't think so. Dee-ann got summoned home to Lake Forest by Papa when he discovered she was sleeping with a non-Aryan and so he found her a nice Wasp investment broker with an airplane of his very own instead. She decided that dancing was making her legs too muscular and her chest too flat anyway. She also discovered that Ellie had no intention of marrying and so it all worked out neatly. She sent Ellie an invitation to the wedding. He was going to go, for a lark, but

Nick dissuaded him on the grounds that he'd be bored stiff at the reception. Do you know something odd: Ellie told us she slept with him for over a month before she found out he was Jewish and then she told him he was the first Jewish male she had ever touched. Ellie found this hysterical. Nick and I didn't think it was quite so funny. Anyway, I believe the present incumbent's name is Moira. Ellie says Irish girls smell like clover and cow dung."

"Lovely," Margo said. "Well, you two have a fine time at the beach. Me, I'm going to stick around here and paint and screw. Maybe I'll come on out and stay with you for a couple of days when I've worked up a good enough sweat, but I'll call or write first just to make sure you're not entertaining Mr. Shantz."

"Please come, Margo. We have plenty of room. And I need some protection from J. Robert, my adorable stepson."

"I'll try," Margo promised.

J. Robert was bigger. He was more substantial. He was nastier and more difficult than ever to reach. He had acquired a kind of laminated style, like a smooth British schoolboy—and was just as subterranean. Sophie could imagine him giving his seat to an old lady in a bus and then making an obscene gesture behind her back.

As soon as Robby saw her, Sophie could tell he knew she was on to him. What surprised—and wounded—her was that Nick could not see anything wrong with him.

"He's a darn good-looking kid, isn't he?" Nick said to Sophie. They sat together on a large towel, watching Robby comb the beach. Sophie nodded. They saw different things. To Sophie, Robby's precocious height and build was upsetting, like a dream figure who assumes, in a nightmare, the surrealistic proportions of anxiety.

"Strong," Nick said. "It's almost too bad he wasn't born with the brains of a professional football player." The scientist could afford to envy the athlete, Sophie figured. It was all part of his special perversity.

Sophie laughed. "As if money mattered to you."

"Money does matter to me. I wish I had more of it."

She assumed, from the set of his mouth, that he meant it but that it was a latter-day thought; what, she wondered, would he say if she asked him what he would do with more? She herself could not imagine living another way; a new coat each year, maybe, or a steak every Thursday, or a trip. She began to think of places to go.

"I'm not going to do any work at all for one week," Nick said, slipping backward until he was lying quite flat against the towel. Sophie noticed that the hairs on his chest had gone gray, tiny gray clusters of wire, like the inside of a computer. The muscles of his chest and shoulders were solid and knotty, like his mythical football player's biceps. He cared. He ate carefully and stepped on his doctor's scales each morning, dropping his bathrobe to the floor behind him and fixing the sliding weight with cautious accuracy.

"I'm going to grow tomatoes out back," Sophie announced.

"Splendid," Nick said, "but don't expect me to help; I loathe rutting around in the dirt."

"No," she said quietly, watching with detached curiosity while Robby dragged an old scrap of canvas filled with something, up the sand toward them. "I don't expect you to help." Sophie felt a twinge in her abdomen and recognized it as *mittelschmerz*. She sighed.

J. Robert came up to them and breathed adenoidally on her shoulders. "Hi, Robby," she said. "What'd you find?"

"Just a lot of junk," he said, not talking. If he had found something valuable, she wondered, would he tell anyone?

"I'll stash it under the house. Then I'm going in and get some milk. OK?"

"Sure, Robby. You don't have to ask me. Why don't you have some fruit and crackers, too. I left some apricots on top of the refrigerator."

"No, just milk." He walked away, depositing a tiny mound of sand behind every heel print throughout the house. There was a shallow pan of water by the sliding door to dip sandy feet in. Robby didn't ignore it: he never even saw it.

Altogether, in the day and a half since he had been with Nick and Sophie, Robby had said very little but enough for Sophie to observe a new habit. Each time he spoke he took in a large gulp of air, releasing it along with the words in small puffs and a final leftover puff, as if he were restraining a terrific blast of anger.

"Did you ever notice," Sophie said, "that when we're inside the house Robby's out and when we're out Robby's in? And the same thing with the beach. We're swimming, he's wandering around on the beach; we come out of the water and he goes in."

From behind his closed face, Nick said, "As a matter of fact I haven't. I think you're misrepresenting Robby's independence. The kid just wants to be off by himself. I imagine it's a relief to get away from his stepfather—and from all adults for a little while. Don't forget, this is *his* vacation, too. By the way, what time is it? I promised to take him kite-flying before lunch."

Sophie said, "That's funny. I don't seem to have my watch on. I could swear I put it on this morning."

"Why on earth do you wear a watch down here anyway? Whose schedule are you trying to meet?"

"Yours." Sophie made a face. "I'll be right back," she said.

Sophie had an uneasy feeling about her watch. She climbed up the dune toward the house as if she were about to interview Ilse Koch and ask her why she'd done it.

"Have you seen my wristwatch, Robby?" The boy stood by the refrigerator, looking down into a glass of milk the way alcoholics stare into their liquor, ponderously grateful, except that Robby's eyes were always intelligent, always afloat.

"I think I saw it in the bathroom," he said, giving her a look that said nothing.

Sophie went into the bathroom and found her watch on the shelf above the basin. Relief and disappointment melted together and formed a sigh. A flush of shame spread over her face, warming her ears and causing a tiny tremble in the corner of her mouth. Robby wasn't a thief after all; he just put on a convincing thief act. He got her every time; there hadn't been a single skirmish she had won.

Sophie thanked her stepson as if nothing had taken place, as indeed it hadn't. "By the way I think Nick wanted to fly a kite or something before lunch. You'd better go down and tell him it's after eleven. Take the kite with you; it's on the chest in our bedroom."

Robby set his glass down on the edge of the sink without rinsing it. "OK," he said. "You coming?"

"No, I have a few chores to do up here. I'll see you later."

He left and Sophie did not even try to guess whether he was relieved not to have her along or merely felt nothing. His reactions were hidden under something whose composition she could only guess at. Besides, when Nick and Robby were together, the merger of *that* man and *that* boy made her shudder; it was as if she were the enemy. There was no doubt that some of this was jealousy and no doubt that the rest was real enough. She looked down at herself: striped top, short shorts, bare feet, her legs just a little heavy and crinkled above the knee, her hair, as she ran her hand over it, sprinkled with sand and stiff with salt water. The sand swept up from the beach and in from the dunes and was everywhere; it even crept into bed with them at night. She was Sophie here but who was Sophie? Out of her mental uniform, the one she wore all year long, disabusing the abused, her confidence drained and crumbled into sand and was swallowed by the Atlantic Ocean along with all the other salty detritus. She did not know if Nick noticed the change in her but that did not seem as crucial as the fact that when she was down—as now—Nick seemed committed, in an almost lethal way, to making things tough for her, to testing her, to exploiting her inadequacies.

Sophie walked out onto the cantilevered deck, with her big toe drew designs in the sand, and then wrote *merde* in it. She giggled like Robby and went inside and made a peanut-butter sandwich for herself, eating it in lonely guttony.

Nick came back from a trip to the post office three days later and handed her an envelope.

"Seems they want to keep tabs on you," he said, indicating the agency's letterhead.

Sophie opened the letter, looking for the signature first. To her, letters were like stories in *The New Yorker;* she could never read either without first exposing the author. In this case it was Dr. Strauss. It was a letter redolent with goodwill and brimming with unpleasant news. It reported on a "mildly paranoid" telephone call from Joseph Prince. "The man seems determined to create some kind of trouble for you and, by extension, for the entire staff. It would be extremely helpful under the circumstances if you would make available to me your complete files on the Prince boy and also if you will give me at your convenience, of course, a simple written statement of the boy's original and subsequent status. In other words, prognosis, diagnosis, and treatment provided. I realize, Sophie, that this is going to be a nuisance for you, especially since you are on vacation and one should not have to think about such matters on holiday, but considering the urgency of Mr. Prince's accusations, if not threats (something about bringing suit, for which, rest assured, he has absolutely no legal grounds), I think that this calm course of action will be most efficient in ridding ourselves of this bad apple once and for all." Still reading, Sophie dropped into a chair. She was perspiring freely. "I considered," the letter went on, "postponing this news until you returned from your vacation but after talking to Burt Kidder, our attorney, I decided that it should not have to wait. The sooner we reply the better our chances that this matter will not grow out of its purely nuisance proportions." Dr. Strauss sent Sophie, in conclusion, "Most affectionate regards."

Sophie was shattered. She was afraid, suddenly, and felt as

if someone had pushed her violently. "Nick," she whispered, "come here and read this."

He read it quickly. "Looks as if this charming client of yours has dunked you into some fairly hot water."

"No," she protested, "you misunderstand. I'm not in trouble. The man is clearly out of his head. Even Dr. Strauss says so. He calls him paranoid."

"I can read, Sophie. But it's quite clear that Dr. Strauss is concerned about the outcome of this; you can read it between every single line."

"But that's absurd," Sophie cried. "I helped this boy. This is one of the few that really would have sunk without my help. He was absolutely lost when he first came in; he didn't know which end was up." Sophie felt tears accumulating in her throat. "Mr. Prince is just angry because he gave Stuart nothing to envy, nothing to love. It bothers him now. It should have bothered him seventeen or eighteen years ago."

"Don't worry, Sophie; I'm sure this isn't going to get any worse than it is right now. It's the surprise you're reacting to now. Give it a couple of days and all this will seem like a joke." Nick's unexpected reassurance caught Sophie off guard, and she responded to it like a child who has located her father after being lost for an hour in Macy's basement. "You know, darling," Nick said, wrapping her up in his arms like a precious gift, "I believe you're beginning to be aware that even absolute good is relative. Someone nailed up Jesus; someone else popped off Lincoln; now Sophie's neatest triumph has been turned upside down, so you can see all the nastiness underneath."

"Am I a whited sepulcher?" she asked.

He laughed. "Of course not. I just wish you could accept the fact that nothing ever turns out quite the way you expect it to. I'll say it again: even absolute good is relative."

"How can it be? Even the words are a contradiction."

"You really aren't ready to understand, are you?" he said. He was, for Nick, surprisingly gentle. "You look a little pale. How about a glass of beer or something to restore the color?"

She nodded. "OK. Then I better get busy on my statement for Dr. Strauss."

"No," Nick said. "Wait a few days. Think about it first; wait until your judgment comes back. Then I'll help you with it if you'd like."

"Oh, Nick, will you? Thank you." She was embarrassed by his offer, though she did not understand why. "You don't really think this monster can cause any real trouble, do you?"

"He hasn't got a chance. But getting rid of him may not be as easy as Dr. Strauss hopes it is."

Sophie began to circle the room in agitation. "Why did this have to happen?" she wailed. "I was so pleased: even after the Princes came to complain I thought everything was all right." Sophie could feel herself slip into a puddle of self-pity.

"There's absolutely no reason not to be pleased. In fact you might almost measure your success with this kid by his parents' anger. Now, stop feeling sorry for yourself—you did a perfectly adequate job but not everyone's going to love you for it."

Sophie wondered why Nick always sounded so moral. He said the most moral things she had ever heard. Half of what he said sounded like a sermon on how to be a better person. She didn't especially want to be a better person. She only wanted love in several palpable forms.

"What's up?" J. Robert came in, dripping water on the floor like a leaky faucet.

"Would you like a towel?" Sophie asked him.

"No." The boy scratched his arm ferociously. "Frigging mosquitoes," he said. "I met a kid on the beach. He wants me to come back to his place for lunch."

"Who is it?" Nick said.

"I don't know. His name's Peter."

"He must be the Carter's kid. Sure you can go. But be back in time for dinner, please."

Later, as they ate their lunch together on the deck, Sophie said, "Is that the couple with the Franz Kline in the bathroom? The man keeps a harem of padded girl friends?"

"And the wife is always half stoned? Yup. They're the ones." Nick was amused.

"You want Robby to spend the day there? They'll probably pour gin in his milk instead of chocolate syrup."

"He won't like the taste," Nick told her and drained a glass of beer. "Besides," he added, rubbing her flesh below the margin of her very short shorts. "Isn't it nice to be alone?"

"We're always alone," she said. "And *my* besides is I'm not sure I like Robby's being at the Carters' all day."

"Listen, honey," Nick told her, taking her hand, her arm, and zeroing in on the rest of her, "Robby's not going to be morally contaminated by one afternoon with those people. It's good for a child to see the way the other half lives. He should be exposed to the seamy side of life. You and I, we're just conventional types. Anyway, he needs a friend down here and Peter will do for that very nicely."

"In other words," she said, smiling at him, "you're feeling horny."

"It always takes two," he said. "You know, even with your hair that way, you're incredibly attractive; you're so attractive you make me twitch all over."

"OK," she said, submitting willingly. "Only this letter, this business with the crazy Princes may ruin it for me."

"I doubt it." He rubbed the inside of her thigh. She stood up and her knees softened; she fell against him. Nick picked her up like a baby and carried her into the bedroom as if he were the most powerful man in the world, which, for the moment, he was.

Together, they worked on the statement Dr. Strauss asked for. Sophie wrote the first draft and then Nick improved it. Her version was longer, more detailed, but she discovered Nick could do crafty things with a blue pencil. The whole thing ended up less than a page long and was circumstantial and direct; it sounded as if it had been written by a disinterested outsider. Nick warned her against defensiveness and hysteria. "At this point reason must appear the ultimate weapon, even if in later rounds we may have to fight dirty."

They sent it off. "Now forget about it," he ordered. "You're on vacation."

"Sure," she said.

They played some tennis and went to two cocktail parties in the sand, but Sophie was preoccupied and did not have a very good time. She kept watching the mail for reassurance.

Instead, she got a card from Margo saying she planned to come out for a few days the following week.

"We're not expecting Ellie, are we?"

"Not that I'm aware of. But you know how Ellie is. He might show up here at midnight in a scuba outfit with ten dancing girls on gold leashes. Is there any special reason why Ellie and Margo shouldn't see each other? I mean it isn't exactly as if he were Bertie and she was Queen Elizabeth."

"Margo would just rather not see him, that's all."

"As I said, he's not coming as far as I know but one never expects him; he just appears, like Peter Quint."

"I'll write her that the coast is clear and we'll take our chances with the ghost."

Sophie sat down and wrote Margo: "All clear, even the sky."

"Mail it for me, will you, Nick? You have to make a trip to town anyway, don't you?"

"Today or tomorrow," he said from his favorite chair.

"Today?" she persisted. "Besides, we're out of vermouth."

"That settles it—today." He bounced up and went to put on a pair of chinos. "I think I'll take Robby," he called from the bedroom. "Robby!" Nick's voice found every corner of the house. "Where *is* that kid?"

"I think he's out back, weeding my tomato patch. I'm paying him twenty cents an hour. Robby!"

There was no answer. Sophie looked out of the kitchen window. The tomato vines were deserted. "He's not there," she told her husband.

"Well, tough luck. When he turns up, tell him I tried to find him and I'll take him next trip. Anything else you want?" he asked, sounding like a perfectly normal husband.

"Yes, but I'm embarrassed to tell you."

"Some kind of female apparatus?"

"No."

"Come on, what is it?"

"A copy of *McCalls*."

"He laughed. "You're kidding."

She shook her head. "You told me to relax, didn't you? I have a secret appetite for ladies' magazines—the way some grown men read Ian Fleming."

He looked at her as if she were a small child asking for a bag of marshmallows.

"OK, Soph, a copy of ladies' pap and a bottle of vermouth. I'll be back soon. Don't forget to apologize to Robby for me. I promised to take him the next time I went. He's probably a mile down the beach. I think I'll get a haircut too as long as I'm there."

He left. Sophie lay down in his chair and closed her eyes, immediately seeing the distorted face of Joseph Prince. She felt the morning sun hit her legs and arms like a hot, silent slap. Her eyelids burned. She felt the perspiration begin to accumulate under her arms and then trickle down her sides. She would stay there until she couldn't bear it any longer and then quickly change into her bathing suit and run down for a swim.

Sophie lay motionless for nearly half an hour at which time she heard a noise inside the house. She turned her head and saw Robby standing in the center of the room, obviously unaware of being watched. He was behaving oddly, very oddly, as if he were in a ritual trance or acting under a posthypnotic suggestion. She shuddered, utterly fascinated, as he slowly revolved in the center of the room, like the "it" in a game of blindman's buff. After perhaps ten revolutions he stopped, opened his eyes, and began walking slowly toward the closet where raincoats, parkas, and odd sweaters were jammed together like Korean orphans. Sophie raised herself quietly to see better. Methodically, Robby went through

(156)

every pocket and collected the change. She heard him say "shit" once, indicating that he had not found as much as he had hoped. He transferred the loot to his own pockets and moved on, still in the same trancelike walk. He tried all the drawers in the kitchen area, fund two metal bottle recappers, and pocketed them. With dismay, Sophie heard herself breathing hoarsely, as if *she* were the thief. Robby, a look of impartial purpose on his perfect little face, walked back to the middle of the room once more, turned completely around twice, and, to Sophie's horror, started off toward her bedroom, where she could not follow him. She considered abandoning her passive role and taking off after him, but something restrained her and she lay there breathing like a racer and waiting for Robby to come back. After two or three minutes, J. Robert emerged, started visibly at the sound of a car on the distant road, and, hearing it pass, continued to look for things to steal. In the meantime, Sophie concentrated on trying to recall what she had left in her room that would be worth taking: a guard ring left on the bureau, an inexpensive and pretty pair of onyx earrings, a traveling clock in a genuine pigskin case that her mother had given her when she started off on her honeymoon (he wouldn't dare, too large and too obvious), and a charcoal sketch on the wall, (if he wanted to go to the trouble of breaking the glass and rolling the thing up and hiding it in his pants). She was aware then that Robby was opening the shallow chest containing the house's few valuables, an odd collection: a pair of silver candlesticks, an amethyst paperweight, and a first edition of *The Torrents of Spring* they were always meaning but forgetting to bring back to the city, away from the moisture; also an inappropriate embroidered linen tablecloth and an emergency bottle of ten-year-old Scotch. Robby bent over and inspected the lot, with apparent disgust and disappointment. He took the paperweight and held the stone to his eyes, watching a lavender world and smiling oddly at what he saw. Sophie decided it was time to strike.

"What are you doing with that?" she demanded, charging

into the open like the suddenly recognized source of a humiliating dream. She felt as unsure of herself as if Robby had been holding a loaded gun.

"Where's Dad?" he demanded back. His self-possession was remarkable.

"He's gone to town. I asked you what you were doing with that?"

"He promised to take me," the boy said. "I'm looking at it." She realized that he was probably trying to figure out just how much she had seen.

"I see. And what about the money you were looking at and the bottle tops and the things you took from my bedroom?" She was perfectly aware you don't ask a child questions that leave him a hole to wriggle through but she found herself compelled—because of his incredible coolness, his cockiness—to play with him.

"What money?" he asked, stalling.

"The money you took from those coat pockets. Would you care to tell me how much it came to?"

The boy paused, clearly attempting a decision between confession and denial, weighing the consequences of this difficult choice to the best of his considerable ability. "One dollar and twelve cents," he said, as confident as Willie Sutton that he would find a way out.

"Are you fully aware, Robby, that taking money from your father's pockets is the same thing as stealing? *Is* stealing?"

"No," he said. "I was going to put it back."

"Robby!"

"I said I was going to put it back."

Sophie's impulse to slap his face was so strong her knees trembled. "What about the stuff from the bedroom?" She realized this was a risky question but still a risk worth taking.

"What stuff? I didn't take anything from there. Hey, what is this, the third degree? When are you going to bring out the rubber hose?"

She ignored his question. "You went into the bedroom right after you took the bottle caps. Now what did you find? I want you to empty your pockets here, right now in front of me." In all her dealings with children, she had never been so angry. It disturbed her to realize how little control she had with him.

"No, I don't want to and you can't make me."

"Unless you do it right now, right this minute, I will tell Nick." Immediately she detested the price of her bargain. She could not take it back. I'm an idiot, she thought. He's not afraid of me anyway; he's afraid of Nick.

The boy's face showed him to be half unbelieving but immensely relieved. "You won't tell him?"

"Not if you put back every single thing you took and never steal anything else again. You must promise me that."

Again he paused, considering, with the logic of a practiced criminal, the merits of the various ways open to him. His detachment shocked Sophie even though she was at the same time aware that he never did respond fully, like other children.

"OK," he said at last. "Here's your ring. It's junk anyway." He held out her guard ring in the flat of his palm. She scooped it out of his hand, scratching his flesh with her long fingernails as she did so. He gave her a look of such malevolence that she was certain he was quite capable of acts more brutal than theft and lies. "Is that all?" she asked, desperate for the tension to slacken but not knowing what to do about it.

"Yes, that's all."

"Give me the rest."

"There isn't any rest."

"If you don't give me the other things you've taken, I'll go into your room and search it like a policeman and you won't like that, I assure you." Her educated guess paid off.

"There's a book," he said. With this confession his face went to pieces. "I'll get it," he mumbled and went into the tiny back room where he slept. He returned carrying the book, which he handed to Sophie without a word.

It was a book about divorce. A glib, how-to-live-with-your-problem book. "Where did you get this?"

"At Peter's house."

"You took it from the Carter's? Do they know?" Pity began to eat into her fury like a small worm.

"We can tell them I borrowed it."

"Why did you take this?" Sophie spoke around a small lump that had formed in the back of her throat.

"Because I wanted to read it, naturally."

"About divorce?"

"Yes. About divorce."

"You've never talked about it," she said, guessing again.

"Why should I?"

"Oh, Robby," she sighed, hoping he'd left himself open at last.

"You gonna take it back for me and tell them I borrowed it?" He had started to pull himself together. She could see the gates to his emotions moving slowly toward one another, about to clang shut forever.

"I'll make another deal with you," she said. "I'll take the book back and give the Carters a perfectly reasonable excuse for our having it if you'll sit down with me and talk about what you've read and how you feel about it and maybe some other things that are on your mind." She held her breath.

"I don't want to talk about it."

"I realize you don't. That's the whole point. Sometimes, though, you can find out a lot more by talking with a grown-up than you can from a book. Sometimes talking about them makes the troubles disappear."

"Well, I don't want to talk about them. And you can't make me."

She sighed, wondering if, had she been a stranger, he would have consented. "All right, Robby, it's your decision. You'll have to return this book yourself." She tried to hand it back to him.

He would not accept it. "But what'll I say?" he whined. He squirmed inside his clothes as if he were covered by a swarm of ants.

"That's for you to figure out. I offered to do it for you. You can still change your mind. Now, I'm going to change into my suit and go down for a swim. Why don't you stay here and think about it for a while? And remember, if you take so much as a box of matches without asking first, I will not only tell your father but I'll make certain that you never come out here to the beach with us again."

As she walked down to the ocean, Sophie once more scolded herself for promising not to tell Nick. She stepped out of her sandals and faced the waves, which rose five feet and more above themselves in a melodramatic orgy of self-destruction; eventually a sloppy but adequate solution suggested itself to her; she had promised not to tell his father but she had not promised not to tell his mother. Maybe she would write that peculiar woman whom she had never met and dump the problem in her immense lap. The slipshod quality of this solution disgusted Sophie, and her anger at Robby, and Nick's continual siding with him, turned inward. She dove into the Atlantic and swam parallel to the shore with long, energetic strokes, kicking furiously until her ankles and calves ached. She had the strongest impression that she was handling Robby's problems in a way that did her very little credit, that was even cowardly. But she could not now undo anything for she had promised the boy, and if she broke the promise he would never trust anyone else again.

"How come you were so helpful with that statement I sent Dr. Strauss?" Sophie asked her husband some time later.

"What's the matter?" he said, bland as ready-made eggnog. "Life not exciting enough for you out here? You want to engage in fisticuffs?" He thought he was teasing her.

"No, seriously, I'm interested. Generally you stay miles away from my work and anything that has to do with it."

"Aren't husbands supposed to be useful in times of trouble? And don't forget, your experience with the Princes is not so wildly different from mine with that cretin Grant at my lab."

"And you wanted me to profit by your experience?"

"If you insist on putting it that way. There's no point in losing your head because some poor bastard, baffled by his own frustrations, turns them against you. Why should you or I have to be victims?"

"Being a victim when it's your turn is just part of life, isn't it, Nick? Sometimes we're on top; sometimes they are."

"That's all too mystical for me," Nick said. "Listen, Soph, please don't make anything out of my helping you. If you hadn't sought it, I mightn't have given it. I don't really see what you're bitching about."

Nick's features, meanwhile, had arranged themselves into sharp lines and angles, as if he had suddenly lost ten pounds. Sophie herself had no clear idea why she had started this pointless inquiry; it seemed, even to her, deliberately perverse. "I'm not bitching, as you call it! I merely want to know why, after never even asking me about what I do all day—how it's going and so on—you offered to, well, I could say, rescue me. Not that I'm not grateful, of course, for the final product. It was much better than the one I wrote."

"Perhaps," he said, controlling himself admirably, "you'd better ask yourself why you can't seem to accept my assistance without acting as if you were being publicly humiliated."

He sounded so sane she couldn't bear it. "Oh hell, I'm going out back." She got down on her knees in the sand and took up the weeding fork, noticing that Robby had earned less than five cents. Teardrops arranged themselves and then rolled down her cheeks, falling onto the sand with a tiny ping, like seed pearls from a necklace whose thread has snapped. Still Sophie blamed the mutual, black tensions on her infertility.

Margo arrived. Sophie was so glad to see her old friend that her own relief surprised her.

"No Ellie?" Margo said, putting down her straw handbag and sniffing, as if she expected to smell him out.

"No Ellie," Sophie said. "Just like I promised. What's in that thing, half a wildebeest?"

"No, my nightgown, my bathing suit, and a bottle of wine. Christ, but it's like the insides of a cat in heat in New York.

Why do I stay when I don't have to? I must be some kind of masochist."

"Aren't we all? Would you like to swim right away? There's plenty of time before dinner. We're not on much of a schedule out here anyway."

"Sure, I'd adore a swim; that's what I came out here for. Where's Nicholas?" Margo, pasty white and spectacular in a lemon-colored cotton dress that pulled ridges across her bosom and stuck moistly to her back, her feet in thonged sandals, and her hair caught up in an abundant pony-tail, inspected the house with nervous pleasure. "Hey, how come it took me three years to come out here? It's a neat setup."

"It does for almost a month. Then you begin to feel as if you were eating sand with everything. Nick's off somewhere with his beamish boy, J. Robert. They've been gone since after breakfast. Snorkling for gold or something."

"You didn't tell me Nick's son was here."

"Oh yes I did. The night before we left, when you called. Did you ever pause to think: four's company, three's a crowd?"

"I take it you and your stepson are hearing different drummers?"

"Me and my stepson hear different everything. We live together in a state of armed truce. But we've got a secret we're sharing. I'll tell you about it later. I feel like the GPU."

Margo raised her eyebrows. "Where do I sleep?"

"Here, you say the magic words and this couch pulls open and it's a bed. Nick's invented a bed that converts into a couch after the company leaves. I hope you don't mind."

"Not unless your husband sleepwalks."

"Or J. Robert turns into a vampire."

"Do I detect the tiniest traces of hatred?"

"Margo, you just can't imagine. Robby's one of those fantastically bright kids with X-ray minds who are incapable of feeling any single normal emotion. I'm certain he spends his spare time thinking up and perfecting any number of antisocial acts, and Nick thinks he's the cat's pajamas. Besides, as

I told you, I'm keeping an ugly secret for him and that sort of burden rarely makes a relationship flourish."

"It sounds like it was just about time for Margo to show up. Is it all right to undress here?" Sophie nodded. Margo stripped and eyed herself in an oval mirror hanging on the wall. "Talk about hourglass figures. I was born a hundred years too late."

"Nick doesn't think so, if that makes you feel any better."

"Just a little. Let's go swim, for Christ's sake; I've been looking forward to this for a week."

Nick and Margo got along reasonably well; since they were essentially incurious about one another, the friendship was easy but hardly intimate. Sophie suspected that Nick saw Margo as he had once described another girl: meat on the hoof. Nice meat but still merely flesh. It rather hurt Sophie that he had to be reminded Margo was a painter.

At the same time Sophie suspected that Margo considered Nick to be somewhat thorny—not one to rub against by accident or on purpose. She approached Nick with caution and kept her mouth shut.

It was odd then—and here in a particularly striking way— about taste, taste in people as well as in things and attitudes. Sophie could like Margo and be married to Nick and they in turn could mean as much to one another as two strangers sharing a seat on a bus. If Sophie suddenly disappeared, Nick and Margo would no doubt never exchange another word. There was no valid reason on earth why one of them should feel warm toward the other if they were not so inclined; still, at moments, Sophie wished that Nick could enjoy Margo in a way that wasn't so outspokenly sexual. What if Margo had been plain? Would Nick have ignored her or been rude?

"You're smashing in that bathing costume," Nick said to Margo. He stood on their strip of beach, his snorkling gear piled neatly on a rock, watching the two women stumble down the steep cliff of sand. Robby was still under water, his white breathing tube poking through the surface of the water, a miniature periscope.

"Hello, Nicholas," Margo said bravely. She marched toward him and stuck out her hand.

"I thought the New York style demanded a kiss on either cheek," he said, refusing her hand and pulling her off balance so that she was obliged to be kissed.

Sophie watched them without jealousy; it was all an act. And yet, a momentary twinge went through her: Margo found Nick's kiss unpleasant.

Nick said, "Too bad Ellie Shantz can't see you in that outfit." Sophie looked in his face for signs of malicious mischief.

"Why?" Margo asked.

"*Everyone* should see you like this. It makes you look like a Titian Venus. Sophie, you should get one like it; you hide far too much of your anatomy. Margo, have you met my son? Robby!"

"He can't possibly hear you, Nick. Margo wants to swim. She can introduce herself in the water."

"I'm anxious to see that suit wet," Nick said.

Later, while Sophie put together ingredients for their dinner, Margo told her, "I wish Nick hadn't said that about Ellie."

"I know. I apologize for him. Sometimes I think he says things like that just so he can make waves. I'm sure he didn't mean to upset you. He likes you. I don't think he really understands about you and Ellie." Sophie held several leaves of Boston lettuce under the faucet until her fingers turned numb with cold. She hadn't had a chance to mention it to him, but she wanted Nick to know that he had ruffled Margo. This was the same kind of game he played with Sophie's mother; some could take it more easily than others, but basically, they were games that gave absolutely no one but him pleasure.

"He didn't upset me, dear; he just reminded me of how furious I am at Ellie. I'm so angry that sometimes I feel like murdering him. I really do, so he won't go around doing the same thing to other poor ladies. Actually, I find this kind of sensation more exhilarating than being bored or lonely."

"What about all those other men you keep alluding to? Don't they help take your mind off Ellie?"

"Sure they do—in bed. It's the 3:00 A.M. horrors I'm talking about. And also breakfast. Did you ever eat breakfast for two mornings in a row with a man who belches after every bite? And scratches?"

"I guess if you loved him—whoever he is—it wouldn't matter."

"I guess so," Margo said.

Robby walked up and looked at their halibut, dotted with butter as if it were raw sheep's eyes. "What's that glop?" he said to Sophie.

"That's dinner," Sophie said. "Fish."

"Fish is for cats."

"What are you?" she asked.

Robby looked at her icily. "Hey, Dad, do I have to eat fish?"

Nick looked up from his collection of shells. "Is there anything else for Robby, Sophie?" Margo pretended not to hear what was going on.

"He can have some hash if he wants," Sophie said evenly.

Margo said, "Cafeteria? I'll have the Salisbury steak."

"Just when Robby's here," Sophie whispered back. She was so annoyed that she cut her hand on the lid of the hash can and bled, holding her hand under running water and cursing softly. Meanwhile the sky, perfectly behaved up to now, had begun to gather itself into an angry mass of dark clouds. In the distance, on the horizon, a line of lightning ripped through the dusk and thunder rolled up the beach like an ancient wagon.

"Rain," Margo said mournfully. "Got here just when I did. Margo's inevitable luck."

"That's the way the cookie crumbles," Robby said to her, his brilliant eyes shining with malice.

Margo stayed four days, two of which were filled with rain. They sat inside and read, played Monopoly and a cautious

(166)

form of poker. Margo and Nick won at cards. Robby argued with his father.

"I want to play. I know how."

"I'm sure you do, Robby," Nick said. "But I don't want you gambling for real money."

"If I can't play for real money, I won't play at all."

"Suit yourself."

"We don't have to play for real money, Nick," Sophie suggested.

"It's no game unless the chips mean something," Nick told her.

"You're a bastard," Robby said to his father.

"Go to your room!" Nick said, his face going crimson.

Margo sat stonestill, staring into her lap, her own face reddening slightly. Robby obeyed Nick, scraping his feet along the sandy floor as he went. "Did you hear what he called me?" Nick said.

"Nick," Sophie said, agonized that Margo was forced to be a witness, "maybe if you gave him a few more boundaries. . . ."

"Sophie, if you don't mind, please don't tell me how to raise my own child. I'm not one of your clients."

"Oh Christ," Sophie said. "I give up!"

Margo said, "Why don't you two shut up and let me deal?"

Wanting a baby with such intensity that its absence was an obsession, it could not at the time strike Sophie as it did Margo—with noxious force—that Nick might not make the ideal father for her child.

The next morning they awoke to a downpour, a thick curtain of water that pounded on the roof like a thousand hammers or like dwarves trying to get in. Robby, at his uncommunicative best, escaped to his room with, Sophie thought, a book. "Either it's got dirty pictures in it or he's going to rip out some of the pages," she said to Margo, knowing Margo would not confuse malevolence with truth and realize Sophie did not mean it. Margo just smiled.

"Did you have enough breakfast?" Sophie asked the guest. There was no point in talking about the weather. It was the kind of obstinate rain that falls in the tropics for months and months.

"Plenty, thanks," Margo said and sighed.

From across the room Nick said, "I think I'll get a little work done this morning."

"Oh, Nick, you promised!"

"I know I did," Nick told her, unlocking his portfolio and spreading a sheaf of papers in front of him on the teak coffee table. "But what the hell else is there to do in this rain? Work or sleep." Sophie was aware that he had deliberately left something out.

"Why don't you sleep then?"

"Because I just got up and I'm not tired."

"What about your new Ian Fleming?" As she spoke Sophie watched Margo moon over to the sliding glass wall and lean her forehead against the pane, depositing a potato-shaped smudge of oil against it.

"I finished it last night. It's not as good as *Goldfinger*—too much sadism, not enough screwing. Hey, Sophie, lay off, will you? I'm just going to type a couple of memos. Then I'll do what you want. Maybe a round of Monopoly. How about it, Margo? How do you feel about Marvin Gardens?"

Margo was ignoring what went on behind her. Nick shrugged and went into the bedroom to get something he needed for his work.

Sophie chose not to try to enter Margo's retreat; the girl obviously wanted to be alone. A casual housekeeper at best, Sophie was seized with an unfamiliar urge to clean the kitchen. She scrubbed the face of the range, scoured the sink, removed all the spices from the cabinet, and washed its floor. The typewriter was clacking away behind her. Typewriter keys and running water, they combined to create the kind of domestic scene that pleased her. There existed, for a little while, a definite harmony, even if it was in the wrong house. When she finished cleaning she made their bed, replaced all the used towels with fresh ones, and then stood and looked with satisfaction at the result of her labor. "I cleaned up," she said to her husband.

"That's a novelty," he said. "Where's Margo?"

"I don't know," she answered, realizing that she hadn't seen her for at least half an hour. "Margo!" she called.

"Stop shouting," Nick said, for no reason except to give an order.

"Where do you think she could be?" Sophie said. "She doesn't have a raincoat with her; she couldn't have gone out in this rain. Where could she be?"

"Why do you always panic the second things turn uncertain?"

"Why do you always find fault with me?" she challenged.

"You're getting to be as touchy as your mother. Come on, I'll help you look for her." Nick got up, making it perfectly clear, in the exaggerated way he took his time about it, that he would much rather stay where he was. "Your friend," he said, handing Sophie her slicker and sou'wester and getting into his own, "is probably trying to see what it's like to be wet all over at the same time."

Sophie said nothing as they left the house. The rain was uncomfortably cool. It chilled Sophie's bare feet. She shivered inside the oily coat. They circled the house. "No Margo," Nick announced. "Maybe she's down at the beach."

They started across the top of the dune, over sand that was packed down hard. Sophie's face was as wet as if she had been swimming under water. She watched a large drop at the end of Nick's long straight nose form, waver, and fall off to be replaced by another. He rubbed the back of his hand over his face. "The gods are angry," he muttered.

"There she is!" Sophie said, pointing.

Below them sat Margo, by the edge of the waves, like a Winslow Homer child, her arms embracing her legs, her chin on her knees. From the distance the pose was as grotesquely isolated as it was poignant. Sophie resisted the temptation to call to Margo. "Nick," she said, "she's soaked to the skin."

"A little water never hurt anyone," he said.

They approached Margo. Her hair was flattened by the water; it seemed pasted to her head and cheeks like a thin black scarf. Her striped cotton shirt and shorts were soaked and dripping. She sat quite still, her eyes apparently piercing the rain looking for a horizon which no one could see.

"Margo," Sophie said, softly, "how long have you been here?"

"I don't really know," Margo said, raising her misty face.

"Is anything the matter?" It was an idiotic question. Nick seemed embarrassed and impatient.

"Oh, I don't know," Margo answered, from what sounded like a great distance.

"Come on back to the house," Sophie said. "I'll give you some dry things to put on. You're absolutely soaked." Margo's nipples seemed about to pierce her shirt. Nick looked at them openly and Margo did not care. "Thanks," she said. "I'll be up in a few minutes. I want to stay here awhile."

"Come on, Sophie," Nick said.

"But, Margo, you'll get a chill. It's cold."

"I don't really care," Margo said.

Sophie turned to Nick, who repeated his suggestion that they go back. "Margo wants to be alone," he said. "She'll be all right. Come on, Sophie."

They climbed back up to the house without speaking. "What do you suppose she's thinking about?" Sophie said.

"My guess is nothing. We did what we could. If she wants to get pneumonia, it's none of our business now. Gad, it's wet enough for a crocodile."

"I don't like the way Margo's acting," Sophie said. "There's something terribly disturbing in the way she's locking everybody out, and no matter what she's thinking about, there must come a point when it's just terribly unpleasant being rained on that way."

"For once, I can't argue with you," Nick said, teasing her. "Now, where the hell is Robby?"

7

In spite of the measures she had taken, Sophie continued to produce nothing. In fantasy she became less of a woman, half a woman, though consciously she would have admitted that this was foolish. She wasted time in front of the mirror, looking at her image through half-closed eyes, straining to catch sight of a sign or a quality that would betray an underlying reason for her barrenness, something in her face, perhaps, as definitive as a brand on the backside of a steer.

Like a child who has done something unforgivable and is ashamed, Sophie found it difficult to face her mother. Actually, Mrs. Golderman was anything but a help. Her mother implied that it had something to do with "a mixture of bloods."

"Mother, what on earth are you talking about?"

"You know what I mean."

"You mean because Nick's not Jewish and I am? I can't believe you're still stewing over that. Besides, that business about blood is plain nonsense. Ask Daddy."

Sophie and her mother sat across from one another at a shiny wooden table in Schrafft's, waiting for tea.

"You sure you want tea, Mama? It's a tea bag."

"It'll have to do," Mrs. Golderman said, smoothing her long white gloves where they lay in her lap. "Where did you say Nick was?"

"Washington, no Maryland really, the naval hospital. But he's staying in Washington. He'll be back Monday."

"Do they always have these conferences on weekends?"

"Yes. They can count on a lot of people who don't want to leave work during the week. They don't mind so much about leaving their families." Sophie smiled to let her mother know that she did not really feel neglected.

"Who gets the tea sandwiches?" The black and white waitress held a plate of sandwiches over the table, accusing the ladies.

Mrs. Golderman inspected the sandwiches. "A dollar thirty for five cents' worth of food," she whispered to Sophie.

"Ah, but Mama, they're all different colors and shapes. They're pretty."

Mrs. Golderman laughed and then zeroed back in on Sophie's problems. "Now tell me again, what did the doctor say? I wish you'd let your father talk to him."

"Mama, there's no point in Daddy's talking to Dr. Gottlieb. It would only irritate Nick and besides, he wouldn't tell Daddy anything he hasn't told me. Don't forget, Nick's a doctor too and he's satisfied."

"And what *has* Dr. Gottlieb told you? That's what I'm trying to find out and it seems very hard."

"He doesn't know," Sophie sipped at her tea. It tasted like asphalt.

"Oh."

(172)

"Mama, listen. First of all, there's absolutely nothing wrong with me. Second, Nick has a child already—by his first wife—so presumably he's capable of having another. Whatever is keeping me from getting pregnant is a medical mystery. Any one or a combination of factors could be responsible. And he can't do anything about any of them."

"Factors such as?" Florence Golderman bit into a circle of black bread smeared with something white. "Plain cream cheese," she said.

"Such as my emotional state."

"Nonsense," Florence said, dismissing the idea. "If you're a healthy girl and live with your husband, the next thing that happens is a baby."

"And I suppose you don't know any other healthy married women who don't have children?"

Florence's was a theme without appreciable variation; it was beginning to have the merciful effect of numbing Sophie to nuances. At the same time, Sophie's sense of being fed up doubled the tedium of treading the same useless ground. "A few, perhaps," Florence admitted. "But in those cases I always thought there was something wrong to start with in the marriage, at home. For example, my cousin Janice. Janice's husband Stanley made love to one of the high school girls in the stockroom. I don't mean he actually made love to her in there; she just worked there, after school. But Janice cried all the time when she found out what Stanley was doing—and this was, oh, only a couple of years after their beautiful wedding—making love to this little sleep-easy from his father's company behind Janice's back."

It was so like Florence to say "making love" like that. Sophie had to smile. "And the sleep-easy, did she get pregnant?"

"I never found out. I didn't want to. All I know is that *Janice* never did."

"And probably a lucky thing, too," Sophie said.

"Maybe, maybe. But what I'm trying to get across, if you'll only listen to me a minute and stop changing the subject, is that it is natural for a married woman to bear a child—many children, unless something is wrong."

"Mama, would it surprise you to know that one couple out of twelve has difficulty producing children?"

"Sounds high to me. I don't trust that kind of statistic anyway."

"What kind of statistic *do* you trust?"

"I just have a hard time believing that one," Florence said.

"Mama, please, we're really just going around in circles. You act as if I'm not having a baby on purpose. I *want* a baby; Nick wants a baby. *Dr. Gottlieb* would be delighted if I had a baby. I could talk about it, analyze it until we were both blue in the face, and it still would not alter the facts."

"Well, as you say, of course, talking about it won't change things but it might make the circumstances a little easier to understand. Sophie, you look a little peaked. Are you sure you're not sick or coming down with something?" She pronounced it *peek-id*.

"I'm sure, Mama; I'm not sick. And I'm not pale either. I just got back from a month at the beach."

"I'm not talking about that fancy tan you acquired on the Island; I see underneath, your cheeks, they're awfully pale."

"You ought to know me by now, Mama; I've never been what you'd call rosy. I have a good idea; let's stop discussing Sophie and her troubles."

"What are you planning to do tonight? Why don't you come over for dinner? The Barrons are coming, after dinner, for bridge. It may be a little boring for you, just to watch, but that's better than sitting alone in an apartment all by yourself on a Saturday night."

"No thanks, Mama. I think I'll just read a book and drink a glass of wine and go to bed."

Her mother gazed at Sophie and oozed pity, as if her child were a quadruple amputee. "You poor baby," she said. The tea sandwiches had long since disappeared down Mrs. Golderman's alimentary canal and were now being churned and ground into new tissue for her ripe round elbows, her honey-dew breasts, and her bottle-brown hair.

Sophie had to laugh. "You're good for me, Mama. You make me realize how lucky I really am. After all, I could have been married to Cousin Stanley."

"Sophie, I just have to tell you something: I think you're making a mistake turning your marriage and your life into a joke. You can avoid *anything* by ridiculing it."

As they left the restaurant, Florence said, "You could at least have ordered some cinnamon toast to go with your tea. You'll waste away to nothing."

Joseph Prince waited for his boy to drown in the mainstream of life. When it was apparent that Stuart was still afloat, Joseph went to see his cousin Archie Asch, a lawyer, about starting a suit against either Sophie, the agency, or both. Archie's clientele was composed chiefly of small businessmen who needed someone to incorporate them, help them file their income-tax returns, and instruct them in avoiding trifling legal difficulties. His courtroom delivery, never one of his strong points, was rusty. In addition, he was not at all certain that he could work up a case for Joe Prince.

"I suppose I could look into the precedents in malpractice," Archie told Joe. "Is this Mrs. Brean an M.D.?"

Mr. Prince looked at Archie's law-school diploma and was distracted by the Latin. "I don't know," he said. "I don't think so."

Archie was older than Joe; they had played handball and stickball in the old days in East Harlem. "If you really want to go into this," Archie said, biting the tip off a cigar and spitting it into a wastebasket placed for that purpose alongside his knee, "I'll look into the possibilities." When Archie was ten years old, he had fallen down holding a bottle of cream soda. The glass sliced through a tendon in his palm, curling his fingers so that his hand resembled a chimpanzee's. His nickname was Chimp.

Joe, because of the rigid shape of his mind, was poor at inferences, but even he could tell that Archie was reluctant. "Why shouldn't I go into this? This woman has destroyed my son. I want her to pay for it."

Archie scratched at his liver-spotted scalp with the curled-up hand, unselfconscious. "Expense, for one thing," he said, inspecting the nails. "The dollar. Any lawsuit is expensive, even if you win. Also, Joe, look at it this way. What'll you get out of it? More tzuris. Vengeance is, legally speaking, a poor motive. Besides, it won't make any difference to your boy, to Stuart; it won't change *him*. It may give you a feeling of revenge but I assure you, nothing more. I've seen too many of these cases not to know that the plaintiff is never really satisfied. And then, there's no guarantee you could win such a case. Frankly, I've never heard of one quite like it—though I could be mistaken. There's always unpleasantness connected with a lawsuit; things you never thought of can be brought to light and embarrass you one way or another. Do me a favor, will you, Joe? Go home and think it over. If you decide, after you've given it a little time to percolate, that you *do* want to go ahead, I'll probably refer you to another firm, a firm that specializes in court work of this kind."

"You couldn't handle it for me, Chimp?" Joseph Prince looked as stunned as if he had just found a monkey sitting on his violin.

"Now, Joe, be sensible for once. I can't handle this kind of case. I haven't argued in court for twenty years." The chimp's hand clawed through a pile of papers on his desk. "You know what these are? Sara Steinberg wants to enlarge her corset shop; she's trying to buy the place next door and I'm handling the transaction for her. *That's* what I'm good at, Joe, not getting up in front of a judge or jury like, who's that fat guy, Perry Mason?"

The scene became grotesque to Joseph Prince. He could not get his son back by punishing Mrs. Brean. The truth—which hit him abruptly—was that he had never given much thought to his son. Stuart's mother had seemed to want to bring him up by herself, and he had let her mainly because it was so much easier that way.

"You're one hell of a big help, Chimp!" he said, bolting from Archie's office and crashing into a secretary in the corridor.

Archie was startled. "Son of a bitch," he said. "Joe must be flipping. Malpractice against a harmless lady head doctor. Next thing, he'll probably want to start a suit for alienation of affections. You see, Miss Regan," he said to the woman who had come in after the collision, "you see what happens to a man when he discovers he's been doing the wrong thing more than half his life—a man like that, he wants to blame everybody else for his aches and pains, for his own mistakes. Even when we were kids together, this guy was a sore loser. He used to go off and sulk when I beat him at checkers or handball. But he could play the violin—like Mischa Elman. I wonder where all that talent went to."

"I'm sure I don't know," Miss Regan said. "Do you have some dictation for me, Mr. Asch?"

The only serious threat to Sophie Brean lay in the mind of Joseph Prince; but Sophie did not know that, and her distress, if anything, worsened. It seemed to her morally implausible that the good she had done Stuart could be subverted by one angry man.

"Don't you think," she asked Nick, not once, but often, "that what I did for Stuart is somehow less valuable because of this business with his father?"

"Absolutely not," Nick said. "I don't see how you can come to a conclusion like that, how you still can expect things to go all one way or the other."

"I don't expect things to go all one way, but it seems to me that I ought to have reached the father as well as the son."

"Love doesn't always spread itself like germs spread disease," Nick said. "Be satisfied with what you *have* accomplished; it's enough. What do you care about a nutty old coot like Prince? He'll never have his way; don't agonize so much."

"I should have reached him," she said, repeating herself.

"Are you trying to play God?" Nick said, finally.

"I give up," Sophie said.

Sophie began, then, to notice questions in the eyes of Dr. Gottlieb. She attributed them to a fresh crop of doubts in the man.

"I have examined you from every angle"—his little joke—"and I fail to find any pathological basis for your not becoming pregnant."

Sophie looked around the doctor's office and released a small, poisonous sigh. With each visit the place seemed more and more a chamber of horrors. It was furnished with deliberate taste, which, definitely not her own, she figured must belong to the doctor's wife. The walls were mossy green against which hung three pale watercolor views of Manhattan, no doubt to reassure him that he had made it and to orient patients who might become temporarily erratic. The floor was hidden beneath a vast black rug of a soft, hard-wearing fibrous composition. His desk was a highly polished table, also black, with a set of shallow drawers at one end and two brass legs at the other. There were several lamps resembling brass driftwood topped by enormous shades with their cellophane bandages still intact. Dr. Gottlieb's chair matched the patient's in a larger, more richly padded version, both distinctly contemporary and far from sleazy. Sophie figured four hundred for his, two fifty for hers. The curtains were never drawn because, Sophie reasoned, he liked things kept as cheerful as possible. She could tell from the wadded-up turquoise geometric pattern on the linen that the curtains had been selected with care, caution, and an ample checking account.

She thought she would love this hideous room if in it she found hope.

"Well," she said, "where do we go from here?"

Frank Gottlieb found dealing with uncertainty the most grueling part of his work—worse than a double breach delivery. A terminal pelvic cancer was a solid fact; so was a month-old fetus. But what could one do with an insoluble and persistent infertility? Generally he fell back on rather elegant verbal footwork whose effect lasted just as long as it took the patient to reach home and start thinking it over. He rubbed his palms together, pleased at the restorative effective of a new hand cream he had been using for several days.

"Mrs. Brean, Sophie, if I may, there simply isn't anywhere to go at this point. I don't frankly feel you've given yourself sufficient time under the most relaxed circumstances—though I realize, of course, that from where you sit it seems like too much time. I could prescribe radical treatment, but I hesitate because of the potential dangers involved in fooling around with the body's normal hormonal balance. My advice remains the same: try to forget how hard you're trying. Relax. Babies are not miracles; they are a predictable, everyday event. You are a normal woman; your husband appears to be a normal male. This little trouble may simply reflect the difficulty in establishing a coincidence of fertile periods. But you must not think of yourself as permanently sterile—such a negative attitude can do as much harm as contraception. My last point has been proved time and time again by women who adopt after years of trying and then get pregnant for the first time."

"Are you trying to tell me it's psychogenic?"

"Sophie, I just can't be sure, in your case, which are the dominant factors. You are, you must be aware, rather high-strung. Have you always been high-strung?"

Sophie had to laugh. She laughed. "I never considered myself high-strung," she said. "I'll have to think about it."

"He called babies an event," Sophie told Nick later.

"At least he could get his case endings right," Nick said. He was packing again, this time for Chicago. Although Sophie had grown somewhat accustomed to Nick's frequent expeditions, she always slept fitfully when he was away. Then she read until her eyes watered or she listened to the radio for hours, straight through the center of the night: men discussing un-identified flying objects, ESP, and other marginal topics. Sometimes they put her to sleep, and she would wake in the morning with the radio still on.

"Don't forget the dental floss this time," Sophie said. "He also said I was high-strung," she added. "Do you think he's right?"

"Not that I've noticed, particularly," was Nick's answer. "A little bit sensitive, perhaps, but not high-strung."

"It makes me sound like a race horse," she said, remarkably relieved.

"Hey, Sophie, what are you going to this bird for, medical treatment or psychoanalysis? By the way, as long as we're on this subject again, you might as well know that I feel you could start thinking about seeing a man who specializes in sterility."

"But I'm not sterile. He said so!"

"Why are you so upset? I should think you'd welcome a chance to investigate this in a more scientific way. This man you're seeing is obviously at sea. But, of course it's your decision. By the way, where the hell *is* the dental floss? I can't find it."

"You'll just have to buy some," Sophie told him. "We're fresh out. I think Dr. Gottlieb is doing fine." Sophie found herself defending him in spite of the fact she could just as easily have agreed with Nick.

"Sophie, good heavens, you like this man because he tells you you're not sterile. Does what other people say really matter that much to you? They're just words. The fact is we've tried for well over a year now to get you pregnant without the slightest indication of success. What difference does it make what you name your condition?"

"Apparently it makes a great difference," she said, and tears built up again.

"And she's not even a bona fide head shrinker," Nick said at one of Ellie's parties. Sophie shrank at the word "shrinker." She managed a smile though she felt like tearing out her husband's hair. Ellie sent her a swift look of loyalty but it did not help much; after all she was Nick's wife and he had been the one to say it.

At this party were several writers whose names Sophie recognized. Ellie had told her often that writers were generally poor company—with the exception of the great talkers—because they were jealous and shifty and drank too much. Sophie wondered why Ellie had bothered to invite them.

The ice ran out. Ellie had bought a giant ice cream container full of ice cubes but still it was not enough. Bottles of blended whiskey and gin stood in tiny pools of liquid in various stages of emptiness on the counter of Ellie's pullman kitchen alongside splits of mixers—emerald green ginger ale bottles, pebbly white soda and tonic. A pair of shaggy men with tab collars and striped shirts stood with their hips smack against the bar, arguing about Alfred Hitchcock, and blocking access to the drinks. Ellie floated from one female to another. It appeared he had asked four or five extra women to dress the place up. Sophie found them implausibly beautiful. She wondered where he found these creatures with their tiny perfect lips, shimmering shoulder-length hair, large saucer eyes, meager hips and tummies, and surprisingly healthy breasts. Most of them, she discovered after eavesdropping for a while, talked like imbeciles. Sophie liked this discrepancy; it was poetically apt. She watched, fascinated, as Ellie fondled each in turn; they all looked at him as if he were Darryl Zanuck.

"Tell me about the head-shrinking racket," someone said to Sophie.

"You heard him," she said. "He said I'm not a psychiatrist." She looked at the speaker's face. It belonged to one of the names she recognized: rugged, going to flab. Fascinating but unspeakably narcissistic.

"OK, then what are you?"

"A psychologist. A counselor. I work with children, mostly, and adolescents. They come to me when their parents can't stand them any more. I'm supposed to make them sunny." If he asked her if she could read his mind she was going to leave the party.

"How come you let your husband treat you that way in front of all these people? I know his type; I bet he's tried to get you to quit working and stay home and take care of the kiddies."

"There *are* no kiddies," Sophie said.

"He tried to make you look stupid; you know that don't you? Why do you let him do that?"

"Hey," she said, "aren't you getting just a little bit too personal? I don't" (she lied) "even know your name."

With mock formality he introduced himself to Sophie, presenting his hand for her to shake. He squeezed too hard. He mentioned his novel. She said she hadn't read it. "Now that I've introduced myself," he said, "let's get personal again."

"I'd rather we didn't," she said. He was wearing a fuzzy red sports jacket. Sophie wanted to touch it.

"What does your husband do in the daytime?" he asked.

"He's a research scientist."

"He looks like a painter." The man was staring quite openly at Nick, who did not appear to notice. "It's his long hair, I guess."

"I didn't know writers went in for stereotypes," Sophie said.

He laughed unpleasantly. "Stereotypes are our bread and butter. Every character in every single novel and every short story is a stereotype. The measure of a writer's craft is in how he can dress them up to look different, disguise them. Underneath you got the identical five or six archetypal slobs that everyone else is writing about." He began to list them. "You got the trembly virginal type—male or female—you got the wise old geezer, you got the troublemaker with ants in his pants, you got . . ."

She cut him off. She guessed he was either seeing how much she would swallow or else he was a complete fool. "Stop," she said, "you'll ruin the plot."

Again he laughed, this time more warmly. "What are you drinking—you need a refill."

"Whiskey and water. I think Ellie's run out of ice."

(182)

"He usually does. He's a cheap bastard. But nice. He's got a lovable spirit, Ellie, a fine liquid Jewish soul. I love Jews."

"How nice for you," she said.

"I'm putting a Jew in my next book. They're easier than jigs."

"A stereotype?" she said.

"Whadda ya mean?" he said. He was wounded. "What kind of writer do you think I am? The trouble with Jews in most novels is they come out either boobs like Hyman Kaplan or mythically doomed like Anne Frank. They're caricatures. My Jew's gonna be shifty just like everyone else."

"You mean you think there might be something in between?"

He gave her a withering smile. "You're trying to make with the joke work, I read you," he said.

"I thought you were going to get me a drink."

"OK, honey," he said. He walked across the room to the bar, stumbling twice.

Sophie said to Ellie, "Is he real?"

"Considering what that cat had to overcome in the way of a background, I'd say he's going to make it. He writes kind of wild stuff, his own stuff, not like anybody else. But he's got to work on his censor; he doesn't know what to leave out yet. Don't pay any attention to what he says; he's stoned. Also, he hates women. He says they give him gas pains."

Sophie laughed. "You don't know how many times a year I hear that: 'he hates women.' Doesn't anybody appreciate us any more?"

"What do you think?" Ellie said, fondling her.

In response to Sophie's letter to J. Robert's mother, a letter in which she suggested that the boy needed a little "outside help" and specifically mentioned "an incident" when Robby went through his father's pockets and took some money from them, later denying that he'd done so, Sophie received a semihysterical letter in which she was accused of harboring malicious resentment against J. Robert, against his mother, and of "being too smart for your own good." Then the woman, too, was beyond reach. So Robby seemed headed straight for a life of petty crime, not necessarily stealing but helping himself to things and people that did not belong to him and which he had no reason to expect.

For a long time the urge to confess to Nick grew in Sophie, but her sense of loyalty to Robby remained obscurely strong. It was like being caught between devotion to the law and an anarchist brother with plans to blow up *The New York Times*.

She tried to convince herself that Robby was not really a thief, that he had merely been experimenting with her to see how much she would go along with. She listened to the echo of Ellie's voice assuring her that her suspicions about Robby were projected from her own intense dislike of the boy. None of this worked in the least. She was as certain as ever that her husband's child was a sport, a human mistake.

"Nick, what was Sydney like when you were married to her?"

"A whiner. She complained about everything and if there wasn't anything to complain about, she made something up. She also had a raging case of hypochondria. She imagined a cancer in every mole, TB in every cough, and when Robby was an infant she'd ask you to walk through live steam before you could get near him."

"How grim. What did you do?"

"I tried to joke her out of it, but you don't know what people like Sydney will do to protect their fantasies. She'd start crying and accuse me of being cold, you know, the you-don't-under-stand-me-and-what's-more-you-don't-care bit. Which eventually turned into you-don't-love-me."

"And you didn't," Sophie said.

"Not after six years of that sort of thing. No man should have to live with Cassandra."

"Do you suppose she's changed at all?"

"How the hell should I know? I have no reason to think so. To me, she was always a little nuts, and a lot of other people thought so too. I was extremely patient with her, considering

(184)

the provocation. Besides, I was concerned about Robby and what would happen if she were left in charge of bringing him up."

"Why did you let her then?"

"Haven't I ever told you about Lois?" Nick stretched. He sat on the couch and threw his arms back as if preparing himself for an embrace. He seemed expansive, pleased to contemplate his own history. The apartment was illuminated by half-light, revealing the shabbiness of New York interiors immediately before dusk, before the lights are turned on. Sophie noticed a ragged tear on the arm of their couch, as if some small animal with sharp teeth had been gnawing at it. The furniture was no longer new. A desperate feeling of emptiness emerged from somewhere inside her and swung around, hitting her like a left to the heart. She sighed deeply. "No," she murmured. "I don't remember Lois."

"Lois was the lever Sydney used to pry away most of my money. It was just what she needed, to adjust the divorce settlement her way. Lois was my lab assistant."

"And you had an affair with Lois."

"I screwed her a few times."

"She fell in love with you."

"I believe *I'm* telling the story."

"You are."

"Well, we shouldn't be too hard on Lois. She's partly responsible for bringing on the inevitable. In a way you should be grateful to her—you and I were available at the same time. Incidentally, Lois had a miserable complexion."

"And so," Sophie said, "they were married and lived happily ever after."

"When will dinner be ready?" Nick said. "This recital makes you uneasy. I'm sorry, I shouldn't have started it." There was something wrong with his apology although she could not have said what.

"That's all right," she said. "Neither of us came to the marriage exactly spotless. Not me, not you." She wanted to rub it in. "Dinner will be ready soon. Before we eat, though, there's

(185)

something I've got to tell you. It's a secret I can't keep any longer, even though I promised I would." She stopped and took a deep breath. "It's about Robby. That's why I asked you about his mother."

"What about Robby?" Nick sat forward.

"He's got a little behavior problem. He takes things."

Nick threw it back at her like a computer rejecting the wrong instruction: "You must be kidding," he said.

"No, Nick, I'm not kidding. I'm absolutely not kidding."

"Sophie, can you tell me just where these incredible ideas of yours originate?" She saw immediately that the incredible was also the unacceptable. Sophie knew all about the blind spots in perfectionist parents, but she had not been prepared for it in Nick.

"From Robby himself." Cautious and accurate, as if she were walking barefoot near broken glass, Sophie told Nick everything that had happened. He listened, not moving, not saying a word until she was finished.

"You must be exaggerating," he said at last.

"How can I be exaggerating? I'm reporting, not interpreting." It appeared that this was to develop into another contest. Her stomach contracted.

"All kids go through their parents' coat pockets. You may be shocked, you poor girl, but even your perfect husband did it. I can vividly remember finding a quarter in my father's overcoat and exactly what I bought with it. It was a balsa-wood plane with a rubber-band engine. The dog ate it before I had a chance to fly it."

"Why do you suppose you still remember it so vividly? Because it was an isolated incident and you knew you shouldn't have done it. You probably even fed it to the dog yourself. Listen, Robby didn't just happen to find one quarter —he went through the house systematically, taking anything that appealed to him. He would have taken more if there'd been more to steal. He's a thief—he's sick, Nick, he needs help."

"Now you listen, Sophie," Nick said, rising and pacing back and forth across the aging carpet, "I appreciate your concern over Robby. I myself can see things that indicate he may grow into a troubled and questioning adult, but I refuse to listen, do you understand—once and for all, *I will not listen* to you sitting there on your Olympian throne diagnosing Robby as if he were one of your neurotic kids at the agency. Save that kind of thing for your clients!"

"Nick, listen," she pleaded. Sophie could find no words. She stopped altogether.

"I will *not* listen if it's about Robby," he told her. "I'm going out for a walk. I have to get out of here."

"But dinner. . . ."

"I'll get a bite somewhere," he said. "Good night."

He left without slamming the door, which made it worse. The unsteady truth about her husband began at last to seep into Sophie's consciousness like tiny particles of memory during a moment of insight.

Sophie carried this beginning truth around uncomfortably, like several overweight pounds—wanting to be rid of them but finding there were not enough to make her revolutionize her life.

Margo's opening fell on an evening when Nick was busy, and Sophie went alone. The gallery, when she arrived, was packed with Margo's friends and admirers. It was a cocktail party; they stood with their backs to the whitewashed walls and gabbled urgently. Several people, who did not know any better, crept around the perimeter of the room, inspecting the pictures. But the canvases were so large that they could be taken in only a fraction at a time, and the whole performance was rather like the blind men and the elephant.

California white wine was being poured from gallon jugs into paper cups by the exuberant gallery owner who handed a drink to everyone who came by.

Margo spotted Sophie as soon as she entered. "Where's Nick?" she said. Margo wore a black linen sheath, the kind of dress Nick generally approved of because it was just a little too tight.

"He's at a meeting. He said to tell you he'd be here some time next week. It's very impressive, Margo," Sophie said.

"Want one? This one here is only $850. Sy says 'think money.' That's why he buys that expensive wine."

"I don't have a wall big enough for any of these," Sophie said, "though I suppose I could hang it on the outside of the building. Wait till we acquire our weekend cottage in Florence. Then I'll hang one in every room." Margo brought her a cup of wine.

"You look a little pale around the eyes," Sophie said.

"Romantic trouble," Margo said and went off to greet a man with a white Harpo Marx wig and a florid face.

"Who's that show-off?" Sophie asked Ellie Shantz who snuggled up behind her.

Ellie told her the name. "Ginkgo's an art critic."

"He's the image of Harpo," Sophie said.

"He's not nearly as funny," Ellie told her.

"Where's our boy Enders?"

"Oh Nick—he's plotting a protest in Yonkers. What do you think of the show?"

"I like that black and gray one over there, the one with the three fat fingers in it. Margo's starting to paint like a man."

"And that's better, naturally, than painting like a woman?"

"Naturally. I'll be back in a flash, doll, I want to congratulate the father."

Ellie shoved through the crowd. Sophie watched his squat heavy back, the curling hair that was beginning to gray, his wrinkled flannels, and the jacket that sat crookedly and was much too large, as if he had bought it at a thrift shop and didn't know his own size. Sophie realized that Ellie was a man whose own appearance mattered less to him than the identity of a stray dog. She had, in fact, never met anyone who cared so little and still seemed so solidly held together by psychic glue. The encounter between Ellie and Margo was as swift as an accidental collision. Ellie was back at Sophie's side in less than two minutes.

"That was brief," she said, not liking what she saw on Ellie's face.

"The kid's got spirit," he said grimly.

"What did she say?"

"She said 'up yours.' Just like those fingers in the painting. I'll lay odds she meant for me. Come on, doll, let's blow this joint and get a real drink somewhere."

"OK, only I've got to say good-bye to Margo first."

"I'll wait for you outside," Ellie said. He left.

"That's not like you," Sophie scolded Margo. Margo's dress seemed tighter; her hips bulged under the linen like rising pastry. Threads of hair strayed from her French knot and clung to her cheeks, which shimmered with warmth and excitement.

"Kiddo," she said, "you don't know the half of it."

"Well, I'd like to be filled in sometime if you want to talk about it."

"It's a drag," Margo said. "Look, Sophie, take him out of here, will you? He's spoiling my party."

"He's gone already," Sophie said. "I'm sorry about this. I'll be back with Nick soon; I can't see anything with this mob here anyway." Unexpectedly—for both of them—she leaned forward and hugged Margo. Margo was solid, substantial, like a large bundle of clean laundry.

Ellie steered Sophie into a bar near the gallery. He ordered Scotch and water and sat contemplating his dirty fingernails until the drinks arrived. Sophie said, "I can't stay long; I'm meeting Nick uptown for dinner. We're celebrating our anniversary with lasagna."

"This isn't your anniversary," Ellie said, puzzled.

"It's one of them." She sighed.

"I see," he said. "That's cute."

"How come no date tonight?" Sophie asked.

"What do you call yourself? *You're* my date. Besides, I've got to work tonight. Earning a little money on the side. I've been transmogrified into the ghost of a dipsomaniac movie queen. No names, please." He took a drink. "You know what, doll? You look the way I feel."

"It's this baby business. The longer it goes on, the more I want one. Even *I* know I'm getting to be repulsive about it. The other night I found myself telling a complete stranger at a party all about my private obstetrical problems. If anyone did that to me I'd just get up and walk away."

"And like what does the doctor say? I mean can't he pump you full of female hormones or something?"

"He says he doesn't want to fool around with hormones. I guess he's doing the best he can. If you really want to know, Nick thinks he hasn't any more idea why I can't conceive than I do myself."

"You need maybe a whole new monkey?"

"What does that mean?"

"Well, there's this man who can't seem to get it up any more so he goes to a doctor with his problem and the doctor fixes him up like new with a complete set of monkey glands. Pretty soon the wife is having the same kind of trouble, she's getting frigid. So she goes to the same doctor and says, 'Can't you fix me up with some monkey glands like you did to my husband?' So the doc examines her and when it's all over he says, 'Lady, you don't need a new set of glands—you need a whole new monkey.'"

Sophie laughed until she almost cried.

"Hey," Ellie said, "it's not *that* funny."

"Oh yes it is, Ellie."

"Well, maybe it is. Did you ever consider the possibility that the trouble might be in Nick?"

"It can't be," Sophie said, blowing her nose. "Nick already has a child—if we can assume Robby is human."

"Well, maybe it's the combination."

She looked up at him, startled. "What are you talking about? You sound just like my old lady. You can't mean that literally?"

"I mean maybe your genes are incompatible or something. After all, he's a foreign body and you're the host."

"A neat theory but hardly scientific."

"I am, you beautiful doll, almost persuaded to make a pass at you," Ellie said. His eyes insisted. They told her something that was terribly close to love. "Maybe you and I could give you what you want." His hands twisted and wove themselves together under the table.

"Ellie?"

"What, doll?"

"You'd lose Nick." She paused and something she did not recognize herself as possessing yearned in quite an original way. "And so would I," she added. She could not bring herself to imagine what it would be like, Ellie and she having intercourse.

"I said 'almost,' remember?" He tried to smile. "Even amoral Ellie occasionally considers the risks."

"As soon as there is life there is danger," Sophie murmured.

"Emerson," Ellie said. "A nice clean old man."

"He went dotty in his old age," she said. The risk floated away, like garbage heaved overboard, but it left her giddy.

"How did you know that?" Ellie said.

"I don't know. Sometimes I read books. At night, when I can't sleep. I'll read yours when it's published."

"Next year," he said. "I can't decide whether to dedicate it to my old man or to you."

"Ellie! *Really?*"

8

Sophie always thought of what happened next as terribly out of key; it was as if a signature from *Forever Amber* had found its way into the text of *Anna Karenina*. It would have been grisly out of context, and it was still more grisly because it was totally unpredictable in the circumstances. You learned to expect things from the people you knew; you could be fairly certain, for example, that in such and such a circumstance, one man will manage and another go to pieces, this child will cry after a fall and that one will be stoic, this woman will spread your secret and that one will keep it. But when a person defies his own personality, transcends the limits of his own possibilities, this in itself creates obstacles and even inside the most ancient friendship there may be moments of genuine horror and revulsion, moments when the wish to disassociate yourself may overwhelm the tutored reactions of civilization.

It was about two weeks after Margo's show opened. The show was successful on two counts: two museums bought the two largest canvases and three millionaires bought another three. Only five paintings remained unsold after the first ten days, mainly because of their gigantic size. And then Harpo called Margo's work "visionary and vitriolic" in print. On the strength of this triumph, Margo went up to Ellie's apartment at two in the morning with a small but excessively sharpened penknife in her pocket.

Margo found Ellie lying on his unmade bed, snoring and grunting in his sleep, his shoes off and his socks on. He was wearing a shirt and trousers. His string tie curled over his chest like a wide black snake dozing in the dark. He barely stirred as Margo entered the apartment with a key she had never returned, did not even wake as she stood in the doorway of his tiny bedroom. The window was shut tight and Margo's nose twitched at the odors that had accumulated for weeks: sweat, beer, bad breath, used linens, and damp towels accounting for most of it. She stood by his bed, trembling as if the room were in fact freezing, and stared at the man she considered the principal torment in her life. At the same time, she remained remote from the scene and watched herself watching him, feeling courage and anger surge and ebb as regularly as his breath.

"Ellie," she whispered.

He grunted in his sleep again, like the pig he was. His right hand came up and scratched his left armpit. Margo watched, enchanted, enjoying the last few impulses of his life; at the same time, they were so trivial that she found them slightly disgusting. Giving him no credit for physical courage, she imagined him crying for mercy like a German soldier.

"You louse," she whispered. Involuntarily her body arched in hate and prurience.

Margo tired of the one-sided quality of the confrontation.

Experimenting, she stepped out of her shoes and quietly lowered herself onto the bed beside Ellie. He stirred, and his near arm, so accustomed to a female in the bed, responded like saliva and found her hip, caressing it faintly. Margo shuddered.

She reached down her flank and found her pocket and the knife in it. The knife was solid and pebbly under her fingers. The balance of the thing was perfect. She had some trouble with the blade; her fingernails kept slipping. Finally, she freed the blade though she tore a nail doing it. She moved closer to Ellie and arranged her body so that her head was exactly on a line with his. His breath smelled of beer and garlic. He never brushed his teeth, merely scrubbed at them with a towel whenever he remembered to take a shower. His breath had once been aphrodisiac for Margo.

She shifted slightly, brought her mouth close to his ear, and bit the lobe, hard, as if she were biting into a tough steak.

"Hey!" he cried. At the same moment, Margo bounced up and was standing again.

"You stinking bastard," she answered, dropping to her knees. "You don't deserve to live." And as if she were about to kill an eight-inch roach with a shoe, she raised her arm with the knife point down in her hand, high up over her rich brown curling hair, and drove it into his groin.

His scream seemed wildly appropriate. High and sustained, it revealed as much self-pity as actual pain. He screamed hard and long, while Margo rose slowly to her feet and trembled as if someone were trying to loosen her teeth. Ellie reached out and grabbed her wrist, nearly breaking it, his strength emanating from a full reservoir of self-preservation.

"You crazy bitch," he shouted at her, "you're killing me!" He managed to raise himself high enough to clout her on her mouth, so successfully, in fact, that she fell backward and landed on the floor with a tooth in her lap and a mouthful of blood, which she spat out along with a portion of her dinner. Then she began to laugh and cry, choking on her own hysterics.

"If you don't get an ambulance for me this second," Ellie said to her, his voice already weakening, "I will kill you with this." He had the knife in his hand now and Margo believed him.

Margo crawled to the telephone and dialed *O*.

Barely in control, she said, "We need an ambulance quick. A man's bleeding to death. Hurry, please."

"What is your address please?" the voice said.

Margo almost gave her own address. "And hurry, please," she added.

"We will have an ambulance there as soon as we can." The voice told her to be a good and patient child.

"Oh Christ," she said, "what am I going to do?"

Ellie had collapsed. He was lying alone, the way Margo had originally discovered him. His breath sounded as if he had just run the mile against a difficult field. His eyes opened and shut convulsively, and when they were open they asked a stream of wild questions; Margo did not have the courage to look at them.

"Why did you kill me?" he gasped as he began to slip. She was sitting on the bed now, nearly touching her victim, an invasion of tears swarming down over her cheeks. "You have blood on your chin," he said as he passed out.

Margo forced herself to look at the place. Ellie's pants were wet and dark; a stain, almost black, was widening slowly and with neat symmetry. The sheet beneath him was red and sticky.

Margo turned her eyes away. She said a few words of a Hebrew prayer she had not heard since her father buried her grandfather in a Queens cemetery ten years before.

The ambulance arrived in twelve minutes, although Margo could have sworn it was twelve hours. Two men appeared and lifted Ellie carefully, like an atomic warhead, onto a low stretcher on wheels. One of them whistled. "Right in the nuts," he said. "Lady, did you do this?"

Margo nodded numbly.

"Why the hell didn't somebody get a cop up here? Lady, you

better come along with us to the hospital. We ain't the police, for Christ's sake," he said to the other man.

"I guess I should have told her," Margo said.

"Listen," the other man said, "let's not stand here while this guy bleeds to death. Come on, they'll figure out what to do with her later."

Margo rode beside Ellie in the ambulance, which shrieked through the sleeping streets, landing at Roosevelt Hospital. She was not aware of anything that was happening but existed inside a grayish blur. She fainted onto the tiles in the emergency entrance and was put to bed for the night. A police guard slept outside her room in a wooden armchair.

Ellie spent ninety minutes in the operating room where a Pakistani surgeon cut, patched, and sewed him back together again. When he woke up at ten-thirty in the morning, he made such a fuss about the pain that a nurse eventually injected a shot of morphine into the main artery of his arm. "Just one of these, buster," she told him. "We got enough junkies here to worry about."

"He's not going to press charges," Margo said limply. Her face looked as if it had been dismantled and then clumsily reassembled.

Sophie wondered if Margo were capable of doing the same thing again. "Thank goodness," she said. "Nick says you could have got five years." Vaguely but pervasively Sophie felt betrayed by Margo's violence; she could not understand. She wanted to ask Margo very badly if she had meant to kill Ellie. The question lingered in her mouth like the aftertaste of something strong and bitter.

Margo said, "I can't sleep. I'm like Lady Macbeth. The doctor gave me some pills but they make me want to burp. Besides, they're constipating. God only knows what's in them, but whatever it is, it's poison for me. While I'm lying here not sleeping, I keep seeing all that blood oozing out of his crotch and hearing him scream. My dear, have I told you about Ellie's lungs? He screamed just like an animal being gelded or something. It wasn't until he started shrieking, as a matter of fact, that I came out of my trance. But by that time, of course, it was too late." She fell back and closed her eyes.

"Don't think about it, then. Try to forget the details; picking at the scab isn't going to make it feel any better."

"Think about it, see it, hear it," Margo answered. "All the old clichés about reliving a moment of horror are true. But I see it in triple-technicolor-stereo. And all alone. I don't even have a hand to hold."

"Your superego seems to be very active these days," Sophie said.

"Active, but hardly the fast-acting variety," Margo said.

Margo lay across her daybed, wretched, exhausted, as much a victim as her victim. Seeing her so haggard, Sophie betrayed her own resolve to be poised and paced back and forth in Margo's huge loft, zigzagging about, avoiding odd bits and chunks of wood, scattered canvases, a stone jar large enough for Ali Baba filled with used paint tubes and old brushes. The place smelled of dry rot and turpentine. It could not have been anyone's home but Margo's, and yet she had never consciously made it into anything; it simply expressed her personality in concrete terms the way no decorator could for any client and no wife could for any husband. Sophie looked at her friend and noticed that the skin over her throat had loosened and was crisscrossed with tiny, irregular lines.

"I wish I understood it all," Sophie admitted.

"Well," Margo said, "you brought me a loaf of chalah and some strawberries. If you can't do anything for my spirit at least you've come to the aid of my poor wracked body."

"Why isn't Ellie pressing charges?" Sophie asked.

Margo said, "You sound as if you can't wait to get me behind bars."

"Oh no," Sophie said, horrified. "My God, Margo." She began, inexplicably, to cry. "I love you both."

"Hey, cut it out, it was just a joke. Good heavens, girl, don't carry on so; you'll have us both in tears."

"I'm sorry," Sophie said, "it just happened." She stared at Margo and again wanted to ask her if she had meant to kill Ellie.

Margo lit a cigarette and closed her eyes. Limp against a bank of brilliantly colored pillows, she was a dead plant in a spring garden.

"Would you like me to make you a sandwich or warm some soup or serve you a bowl of strawberries? You look as if you hadn't eaten in a week."

"No thanks," Margo said. "I'm on the nine-day miracle diet. You don't have to do anything but commit an act of violence on the first day and just sit back and watch the pounds roll off without any additional effort. I recommend it for all those plagued by overweight and lack of willpower."

"Come on, Margo, have a nice sticky peanut-butter sandwich."

"You sound like my old lady, Sophie. Honestly, kid, I've tried to eat but I can't swallow yet."

"But what are you going to do?"

"I'll pull out of it sooner or later. Or maybe I won't. Who knows?"

"Would you like some help?"

"You mean," Margo said, opening her eyes at last, "what is so deliciously known as 'outside help'?"

Sophie nodded and sat in Margo's Victorian loveseat, feeling she was losing contact and not knowing how to hold on.

"No thanks again. If I once got started with a shrink, I might never finish. I mean like doesn't that kind of help keep you helpless for years and years?"

"Not necessarily," Sophie said. "I guess this isn't exactly the best time to talk about it."

"Be my guest," Margo said, and acted as if she were sleeping. They sat in silence, Sophie wondering how much ground she could cover safely. "You never said why Ellie wasn't pressing charges," she said at last.

Margo remained silent. It was impossible to tell whether she had heard the question. Sophie sighed and got up to leave. She saw that the telephone receiver was off its cradle. Margo said, "People keep calling. Even *Time*. I had no idea Ellie was so chic, really. On the strength of our little episode he'll probably sell that crazy novel to the movies for a million dollars."

Sophie crossed the loft. Its low, die-stamped ceiling was suddenly oppressive; it seemed about to lower and squash her like a cockroach. She went back over to Margo, who was now lighting another cigarette, and leaned over and hugged her. She no longer felt hard like clean laundry but like a bundle of rags. Margo said, "Cheer up, kid, things have nowhere to go but up."

Sophie said softly, "I'll come again tomorrow or the next day. Or will you come uptown?"

"I'm too beat," Margo said. "Maybe in a week or two. In the meantime I'm going to sit here by myself and contemplate my crime."

"Why do *you* think Ellie isn't going to press charges?" Sophie asked Nick later.

"Maybe he can't be bothered. Maybe he finds the whole incident too humiliating. Can you picture him describing to a jury—or even just a judge—the details of an attack on his genitals?"

"She tried to kill him," Sophie said.

"I don't see how you can be so certain, Sophie. If a person wants to kill a man, he aims for a vital organ, not his sexual organs. I think it was just malice, revenge if you want to get fancy, self-pity, perhaps, but hardly intent to kill."

"Maybe she was going to stab him there first and then finish him off in a more orthodox way. Besides, you *can* kill a person there. He could have bled to death."

"I don't think that's what Margo had in mind," Nick said. "She's not the type. She *is* the type who might want to cut off a man's balls."

"Every woman wants to castrate every man. Isn't that what you really think?"

"No, Sophie, not at all. Not *every* woman."

"I guess I'm fairly upset by this business. I can't seem to accept it."

"What? That your volatile girl friend is capable of slashing at a man when he's asleep? Listen, Sophie, most people have murder inside them, trying to get out. Some of us control it better than others. But all of us are unpredictable when sufficiently provoked. It's merely a matter of our threshold of provocation."

"You're such an expert on human behavior—you always know just a little bit more about people than I do."

"You *must* be upset or you wouldn't talk this way," Nick said, resisting the battle. "How about a movie? There's a good revival around the corner."

"You're a movie junkie. Anything unpleasant happens—'let's go to the movies.' I'm *sick* of the movies!"

Nick was grim. "You're behaving like a small child. You better can it, Sophie, or I'm not going to stay around to listen."

"Why don't you go to the movies?" she said.

"I think that's a splendid idea," he said; and without waiting for dinner, he left the apartment, where Sophie spent an hour pacing, tearing at her fingernails until her fingers bled, cursing her husband silently. He seemed, suddenly, a crueler and more dangerous threat than Ellie ever had been to Margo.

Sophie could not shake a sense of indignity she had over Margo's act, an indignity that had nothing whatever moralistic about it. There were ways and ways to punctuate a separation; Margo had chosen the way that was at once the most dramatic, the most outrageous, and the most meaningless. (Stuart, on the other hand, had slipped away neatly and without fuss.) Margo had dreamed up many of the wrongs done to her by Ellie, simply imagined them. She and Ellie had had nothing to do with one another for a long time, but Margo had been unable to conclude the affair without violence. After she attacked Ellie, Margo thought herself free—and in a way she was. But it was not a freedom she could enjoy, for she was the captive of a rigid and hostile imagination whose form Sophie had not even suspected. Sophie could not shake the sense of trouble that began with Margo's assault on Ellie.

Harmony seemed more and more just another fantasy. Sophie would commit herself to one way, only to be uncertain of it a moment later. Nick's subtle needling, for example, caused her to abandon Dr. Gottlieb. The man she turned to was Kenneth Campbell, a doctor who specialized in infertility and who was, in most respects, his predecessor's opposite.

His diploma had been granted by Harvard and his manner, too, carried the Harvard seal; he was impeccably thorough and wonderfully cool. His movements were like a tiny bird's, darting and sure. He had been, at one time, a colleague of Nick's, and somehow that made Nick seem an eavesdropper on their conversations and an observer at the examinations.

Dr. Campbell's office was in a hospital, an institution whose very name reflected the utmost in Christian care and antisepsis. The space occupied by his office was as utilitarian as Dr. Gottlieb's was wasteful; if it spoke to her at all it spoke in a whisper. The moment she stepped inside the waiting room she knew, like a convert to Catholicism, that she had come to the right place, and she sighed with relief as she sat down. Here was unmistakable optimism, down to the scrubbed face of the college girl sitting at his reception desk, where the light from a small window bounced off the gold circlet on her cashmere breast and flung itself about the room.

"Well, Mrs. Brean," Dr. Campbell began, "I understand from my nurse that you've been having some difficulty in conceiving. I'll do the best I can to reverse this condition. Remarkably few women, by the way, are permanently sterile, you understand; and we have many different avenues available in approaching the problem. The main thing is to be exhaustive and not give up. So." He stood. His long white coat was identical to Nick's. Unbuttoned, it revealed an immaculately tailored bluish-gray suit and a diagonally striped tie that Sophie guessed represented membership in a final club. Sophie also noticed a gold seal ring on the little finger of his right hand; she wondered if he would remove it to examine her.

The word had been spoken and Sophie prepared herself for the tenth or twelfth time—she had lost count. By now the examination was as routine as chopping onions for a meatloaf. She was no longer embarrassed by its intricacies. If the bearded lady could tolerate the prurient gape of the crowd, why Sophie Brean could stand with similar equanimity the humbling quality of a pelvic examination—even one by a man as impassive as Kenneth Campbell. He was, as it turned out, so expert in his work that the whole thing was over in less than five minutes. Dressed once more, she sat in his office looking at his face for signs, but she saw nothing but the blandness and assurance of confidences immaculately kept.

The man looked as if he never needed to shave, although the backs of his hands were black with hair. "Mrs. Brean," he said, "you've had an endometrial biopsy?"

Sophie was not sure whether this was a question or a statement. In any case, the word *biopsy* frightened her. He waited while she tried to think and then repeated the question.

"I don't think so," she said.

"A microscopic examination of the endometrial—uterine—tissue is one way," he explained, lightly caressing his gold-tipped crimson Sheaffer pen, "that we can tell if ovulation has occurred."

"How?" she asked, realizing that the mechanics did not in any way matter to her.

"The menstrual cycle is an extremely intricate—and provocative—process," he said, willing, apparently, to cast her in the role of student. "Basically, the ovary produces two hormones, estrogen and progesterone. Under the influence of hormonal activity, the endometrium changes its physical characteristics during the month-long cycle. By removing a piece of tissue no larger than five milimeters and examining it microscopically for the presence of one of these hormones—progesterone—we can ascertain whether a patient is ovulating. In other words," he continued, now carried along by the clarity of

(202)

his recital, "if progesterone is present during the latter half of the cycle, we can assume—with all probability—that you have ovulated. And if you have ovulated, you can conceive. If, on the other hand, as I suspect, you are deficient or even lacking in progesterone, we can prescribe hormonal therapy." Dr. Campbell smiled his cooling smile and asked her to come back in ten days, the most propitious time for the biopsy.

Sophie wanted to ask if the procedure would be painful, but decided against it and opted for stoical ignorance over vulnerable curiosity.

"This little operation should bother you very little; generally it is painless—in case you're worried about that aspect of it. I do this sort of thing here several times every week."

Sophie disliked him heartily for reading her mind. And, in spite of the reassurance, she invented an anxiety whose elements she could not differentiate: was it the "little operation" itself which caused her apprehension or what it would tell her?

Just before she left his office, Dr. Campbell told Sophie, "If my suspicions are borne out, you should be expecting an heir within the year. If I'm wrong, I'll vote Kennedy."

Sophie thought he must be joking. "You will in any case, won't you?"

He looked up at her, surprise written all over his obedient features. "Heavens no," he said. "Campbells who vote democrat are drummed out of the clan."

Ten days later, bright as a kitchen-gadget salesman in the basement of the five-and-ten, Dr. Campbell greeted his patient. His nurse, an incongruous element—for she wore emphatic makeup and violet lipstick, and Sophie would have guessed that the doctor would have thrown his hands up in genuine horror—was ready by the autoclave stirring instruments around with the delighted vigor of a witch brewing something nasty. As Sophie emerged from the dressing alcove, the nurse helped her hop back onto the examining table, guided her feet into the icy stirrups, and brought her down to the edge of the table. Characteristically helpless, Sophie tried to repeat lines from a miscellany of poems but was unable to concentrate on anything but what was happening to her. She tried, for a moment, to imagine whom her baby—if she ever had one—would resemble but got nowhere; it had as little character as a doll in the toy store, frilly and so grotesque in the face as to be faceless.

The nurse powdered Dr. Campbell's hands, which he then slid into a pair of ochre rubber gloves. Watching this, Sophie felt the contents of her stomach slosh around like thick shampoo in a half-empty bottle. She closed her eyes. The instruments rattled discretely and expressively; each had a separate tone of its own, the whole a chorus of intent probing. Dr. Campbell scraped his stainless steel stool in for a close look.

"Now, Mrs. Brean," he announced, raising his tanned forehead, "I am going to insert this curet"—he held up what appeared to be a steel crochet hook, very long and gleaming naughtily—"through your cervix and into the endometrial cavity and remove a bit of tissue with it. Please try to relax; the more relaxed you are, the less discomfort you'll feel. It will only take a moment or two. Now, inhale deeply please."

As Sophie did as she was ordered, perspiration exploded all over her face; she had a moustache of it, and a beard. The probe went in through an opening she knew for a fact was as small as the buttonhole on a christening gown. The pain that reached her brain was not sharp or burning but large and hollow, an atomic explosion of pain, devouring her and sending radiations and ripples of pain even into her fingers. The pain cast a spell of doom on her; nothing good could possibly come of this. How perverse of him to tell her it would be painless but, then, how would *he* know? (The torments of her life with Nick might be imaginary, too.)

"Lie still, please, Mrs. Brean," the doctor commanded her. "I'm almost through."

"Oh," she said foolishly. She felt the nurse's hand on her shoulder; it lay there lightly, only diffidently reassuring. She saw the bone of the girl's young jaw, and from this peculiar angle it seemed to take a wonderful, invulnerable journey up

(204)

the side of her pancaked face, disappearing into her orderly hair like a straight path into the jungle. Her eyes were stupid, Sophie realized; they pointed somewhere irrelevant, such as back to last night's kisses or forward to the shape of her wedding veil.

"What's your name?" Sophie said.

"Vera," the girl said, bringing her silly eyes to focus on Sophie.

"Alas," Dr. Campbell said, from the depths, his forehead now broken out in little Anglo-Saxon droplets of sweat, "Vera is forsaking us. She's going to marry her young man." The quality of his grief was only in the words; his voice remained as impersonal as an electronic announcement.

Sophie could not talk; the effort of withstanding this precise medical assault had exhausted her.

"Aha," Dr. Campbell announced. He held up the hook for her inspection. Then he picked up a pair of curved tweezers and removed something from it which he then transferred to a jar containing a solution held in one of Vera's manicured hands. "All through. That wasn't so bad, was it?"

"Well," she said weakly, "I wouldn't want to go through it every day."

He ignored her complaint, banishing her forever into the company of "tense females"—a judgment he had silently passed on at least half his patients. In spite of their commonness, they were more difficult to treat because their problems never looked the same twice.

"We should have our answer within the week," he said. "No need to come into my other office when you're dressed. Just go on home, if you can, and lie down for a bit. You may experience slight bleeding or staining—it's normal after a biopsy—nothing to be concerned about."

Sophie was flustered. "I can't go home now, Dr. Campbell, I have to go back to my office; I have several children to see this afternoon. That's all right, isn't it? I mean you didn't mention anything about having to lie down when I made this appointment."

"Certainly, it's all right," Kenneth Campbell said, restraining impatience. "I simply meant that if you were feeling somewhat shaky, you might benefit from a nap. Actually, you're in perfectly fine shape and could play nine holes of golf if you felt like it." He stripped the gloves from his hands; they snapped like rubber bands. He stood in the doorway ready for his next tense female. It confused Sophie that Dr. Campbell adapted so easily. Either she should nap or she shouldn't.

"I'll compromise," she said. "I'll take a taxi back to work instead of the subway."

"Splendid," he said, nodding. "You'll be hearing from us as soon as the results of the test come in. Then we will proceed with whatever is necessary to get you that baby." The doctor had an infallible way of putting the proper words into the wrong slots. At this moment, Sophie lost her scorn and began to be amused.

During the afternoon Sophie felt twitches and echoes of pain. She thought she was bleeding, excused herself, and found nothing at all. The three children she saw that day suspected nothing, so successful was she at camouflaging her preoccupations, so involved were they in trying to escape from imaginary bullies.

Exactly a week after the biopsy, Dr. Campbell's receptionist called Sophie at work. "The doctor," she said, "would like you to come in and see him next week."

Sophie's heart thumped wildly, then lodged in her throat like a sour ball swallowed whole. "Do you know what he found?" she asked.

"I'm afraid I can't give you the information you want. If you'd like, I'll have Dr. Campbell call you when he comes into the office tomorrow afternoon. He's in the *clinic*, now," she added as if to make Sophie ashamed of her demands.

"No thanks," Sophie said. "I'll wait till I see him."

She repeated the news—or lack of any—to Nick that night. The running report on the state of her hidden organs had taken on a ludicrous aspect that Sophie was only just beginning to appreciate. It was as if she had pledged herself to make a written note of each new gray hair or count the sneezes of a child with a cold or keep track of every murderous or indelicate thought.

Nick listened to her, only half listening, the evening paper which he held in his hands obscuring the entire right side of his face.

"I think we may be getting somewhere," she ventured. "I'm going back to see Dr. Campbell next Wednesday."

"Probably wants to dose you up to the ears with hormones," Nick said.

"Well, maybe."

"Not maybe. Certainly. Why else do you suppose he took the trouble to examine your endometrial tissue?"

"He didn't know beforehand. That's why he did the biopsy." Sophie tasted the familiar acid of a quarrel in her mouth and wanted to spit.

"It was his job to make certain. You can't prescribe at random." Nick mulled over the necessity for double checking, assuring himself that his own laboratory work was exemplary, and then continued. "Hormones," he said. "Tricky business."

Oh God, she thought, here we go again. "Nick," she began, "it was you, remember, who advised me to consult Dr. Campbell. This time it was *not* my father *or* my mother *or* my Aunt Fanny *or* the lady next door. It was *you*. Dr. Campbell is *your* selection."

"What in hell are you getting all worked up about? Did I say or suggest anything that would cast the slightest doubt on Ken Campbell's credentials or competence? I did not. I merely stated the truth, I might even say the obvious: hormones are a tricky business. Sophie, you're getting much too sensitive. You're so jumpy that if I sneezed in the middle of the night and we had a gun, you might very easily shoot me first and then bother to find out I wasn't a thief after you'd killed me. Thank God we don't own a gun."

Sophie did not trust herself with a response so she held her tongue. In fact, she very nearly bit a hole in it.

Dr. Campbell honored Nick's armchair prediction: he dosed

Sophie with progesterone, a hormone he described to her as "tricky, but amazingly effective in cases like yours—these deficiencies. It's a pity, really, that a slight anomaly like yours wasn't detected earlier."

He's dying to knock Dr. Gottlieb, Sophie interpreted, but he's damned if he'll violate the code. "Do you think," she asked him, capturing his eyes with a bold turn of her head, "that Dr. Gottlieb, the man I was seeing before I came to you, should have done this biopsy and prescribed hormones for me right away?" She saw the shock of ethical outrage cross Kenneth Campbell's features and then fly off, to be followed by the faint gleam of annoyance. "How can I say positively?" he said, fingering her folder. "I'm a specialist in infertility problems; Dr. Gottlieb isn't."

"Then perhaps he ought to have referred me to one," she suggested, wanting him to commit himself as much for his own sake as for hers.

Dr. Campbell once more avoided the hook with dexterity. "I imagine Dr. Gottlieb felt there was no reason—given the limited circumstances—to believe you could not get pregnant without treatment. Even your temperature chart was misleading. It *did* indicate, as I recall, that you *were* ovulating. Why not simply be satisfied with what's been accomplished here and go on from that point? If we stick with this hormonal therapy, I have every reason to believe you will become pregnant within a few months. That's really the important thing, isn't it?"

Sophie realized the man was both devious and far from brave. "You actually mean," she persisted, "that Dr. Gottlieb should have tried this therapy two years ago when I was two years younger?" She wanted him to acknowledge the waste.

He could not have been more deaf to her if he had shut off the battery of a hearing aid. He would not have talked if tortured: the brotherhood was too thick with the clots of loyalty. He dismissed the subject of Dr. Gottlieb's delinquency as finally as he dismissed her: "Mrs. Brean, I have patients waiting for me; I'll be glad to continue exploring this rather complex topic some other time—though I seriously doubt its ultimate fruitfulness. You know, in medicine it's frequently helpful to attack a problem as if it had no history whatsoever. But I can't afford the time right now; it's not fair to my other patients." He had risen as his last sentence fell and obviously expected Sophie to imitate him. She did so, full of reluctance and ingratitude, in spite of the fact that here, held in this man's incredibly steady fingers, was the prescription, the gift she had longed for for almost three years.

I am, she decided, as wretched as he is.

"Of course I was right," Nick said later. "Frank Gottlieb is a horse's ass."

"Dr. Campbell wouldn't admit that Dr. Gottlieb fleeced me out of two years of genuine motherhood. We'll have to move if we have a baby," she added.

"Wait until you're pregnant and then we can talk about moving," Nick said. "Maybe we could rent a couple of floors in a brownstone in the Village."

"You mean it?" she said, surprised.

"Why not? We can afford it," Nick told her. Sophie had only a vague idea of what the Breans were worth as a couple, though she was aware her salary counted for less than a third of what they were making. Nick's numerous consulting jobs, his lectures, his articles all brought them sums that, as far as Sophie could tell, they did not spend much of—except to buy some reliable stock issues. And Nick was characteristically clever at that, too. "But getting back to Dr. Campbell," he said, "you should know by now, we all have our little personality defects. Ken's may be reticence."

"Have you ever heard one doctor discredit another doctor in front of an ordinary citizen?" Sophie asked.

"Yes: me."

"You're a different case," she said. And she could have elaborated in a hundred ways.

"You're right, honey, and that's one reason I stopped seeing patients. I got tired of having to filter so much information."

"What's another?"

"Somebody—I forget who—told me I was a genius and was wasting my time diagnosing hemorrhoids." He was teasing her. For a moment—made more poignant by its abrupt clarity— Sophie saw still sputtering the spark of her lover, her fiancé, her new husband. But it went dead as Nick began to speculate on the ultimate lengths to which his genius (which she recognized in the same way she recognized he had certain inflexible habits) might take him.

"Why don't you run for mayor?" she said at last.

"You can't bear it, can you, to admit that I might be able to function more efficiently than most men? What in heaven's name did you expect when you married me?"

"What did *you* expect?"

"I expected nothing but you."

"It sounds so adorable," she said, aroused, her cheeks burning. "I don't really think you expected only me. Why, tell me for once, if you have any honesty, honestly, why *did* you marry me?"

And for once Nick was honest, although he could not know it himself and thought only that he sounded plausible and sentimental, two accents he imagined to be sweet to the female ear. "I needed you," he said.

Sophie was confused because she recognized how closely he had brushed the truth and she did not know whether he was aware of it or not. His face was handsome—he was growing older with magnificent physical control as if he had simply willed himself the sideburns of a movie star, the direct blueness of a tinted contact lens, the straight jaw of a judge—his manner dispassionate. One of his most sickening habits was to tell people he never lost his temper, which was all too true; he sailed through scenes that might have led to violence without ruffling anything more than a lock of his silvering hair.

"You needed me," she scoffed. "But what for? What for?"

"Sophie," he said, "whenever you get into one of your let's-psychoanalyze-Nicholas moods, you're beyond my reach or the reach of any logic. I might just as well be talking to a deaf-mute."

"Sometimes I *feel* like a deaf-mute, Nick; I feel as if I'd lost the use of my senses." Under ordinary circumstances Sophie would have given in to tears, but now there were none to fall back on; she was dry, even her hands were powdery dry. She sat at the dinner table—where the majority of their disagreements seemed to take place (as if nourished by the food they both consumed) and looked away from her husband, in dry grief.

"Come on, Sophie," he said, almost gay, "let's not argue any more. The doctor gave you good news. Think about *that*."

"I am," she said grimly. "It's just about all there is."

Sophie said, "But Nick, you hate buses."

"In this case that's entirely irrelevant." Nick shone with virtue. Sophie thought he actually looked younger. His walk was springy, like a runner's, and he had lost several pounds. He had bought an expensive but inconspicuous sports jacket for the occasion. "Sophie dear, this bus ride is to be one of the most important journeys of my life. Why don't you change your mind and come along?"

"I can't leave my children for this," she said. "I've thought about it a lot. It's very upsetting to them for me to interrupt their treatment." She was so certain Nick thought her a coward that she had begun to wonder herself if she were. She tried to imagine riding into the South, a country so hostile, it was even more dangerous than the unknown, sunburned faces lining the road like featherless vultures, killing with looks, hating with an impersonal passion that would make ordinary fear seem niggling in comparison.

"What exactly are you going to do when you get there?"

"We're going to do something called sit-in. You just walk into a restaurant—well not quite a restaurant, probably one of those wretched greasy spoons in the five-and-ten—and sit alongside the colored men and women who came in with you."

"And you order a ham on rye?"

"You order a ham on rye or even just a cup of coffee."

"And naturally they refuse to serve you."

"That's the whole idea," Nick said. "We know damn well the frightened little red-neck behind the counter isn't going to serve no niggers and no nigger-lovers."

"And your presence is a protest against the system?"

"Yup. It's a form of passive resistance, like Indians lying down on the railroad tracks. It worked there. This has all been very carefully thought out."

"You're a brave man," she said. And she believed it despite a deep suspicion about the impulses which led him to courage. There was no doubt about it; the man had physical courage and it confused Sophie, who had, until now, thought of this kind of courage as something either puerile or irrelevant. Were you a better man if you were brave as well as honest; or could you, lacking a supply of physical intrepidity, be equally "good," deserving, fulfilled? Nick's need for approval was as persistent and demanding as the conflicts in a troublesome child; where did his bravery originate?

Nick accepted her compliment and continued. "And then, if you don't get beaten up immediately or kicked in the balls by one of the spectators—and they gather round, apparently, like flies on a custard, to watch the incredible spectacle of black and white sitting side by side without either one of them dropping dead or getting a case of the clap—then you get carted off to the pokey where they shove you around a little bit, charge you with disturbing the peace, and put you behind segregated bars. The colored ones are likely to get a good old-fashioned going over, maybe with a broken pipe, maybe simply with a pair of toughened fists."

"Oh, Nick, do they really do that?"

"You bet your life they do. Some of the men who have come back have had their scalps split open. It's amazing how little you seem to know—or care—about this." He was openly contemptuous.

"It's not true that I don't care," she said. "I care terribly. But you can't change me. I'll go on doing what I can do best, which is helping people who need me. I do that with all the sympathy and skill I have. If I feel that I'm not the one to get beaten up you can accuse me, if you like, of being a coward—which may or may not be true—but you can't accuse me of not caring. I'm convinced the only way to purge people of the kind of hatred that seems to flourish down there is to get them when they're young enough to understand their own crippling fears, the kind that develop later into brutality and violence. The sort of hate you're going down there to face is sick. I treat sick people. We're both trying to accomplish the same thing in different ways."

"That sounds suspiciously like a speech to me," Nick said. "I distrust speeches from you in moments like this—they're apt to disguise an unpleasant truth."

"Nick, you really *are* a dog. You can make a very high-sounding call to moral arms but if I try and state my position I'm accused of lying."

"I didn't say you were lying. Dear God, listen to her."

"We're fighting again," she said through clenched teeth. They were lying in bed, not touching. Sophie felt tears dribbling down into her ears. She turned over onto her stomach and moaned softly.

"I trust that someday you'll wake up and understand that the world does not revolve around Sophie Brean, but quite the opposite," he said, getting out of bed. He put on his robe and went into the living room where he read until three in the morning, the dead of night.

9

ONE OF ELLIE's friends gave a party for him when his novel was published. Iris Jonquil lived on Central Park South in five puce rooms with two white poodles and one black maid.

"Look at those lobster sandwiches," Ellie said, greedily.

Iris (recently divorced from Mr. Jonquil) was wearing slim eggshell satin pants, a cerise blouse, also satin, and gold, high-heeled sandals.

"Nice knockers," Nick said to Ellie, indicating Mrs. Jonquil's. Sophie thought her hostess might have overheard the remark from the way her mouth, upturned in a smile, froze tight. Sophie noticed, at the same time, that Iris' breasts were singularly prominent.

Contained in every lobster canape was half of the tail meat of one lobster. They lay in a circular platter; an entire sturgeon filled another plate. There were silver bowls studded with cold boiled shrimp, hot hors d'oeuvres called pig-in-a-blanket, chopped chicken liver in soft round hills, and salted cashew nuts in palm-sized silver leaves. The bar was stocked with the usual drinks plus a Greek apéritif Mrs. Jonquil had discovered when she went to Crete to get over the shock of her separation. "What does Mr. J. do?" Sophie asked Ellie.

"Digital and analogue computers, doll," he said. "Don't you know, computers are the coming thing?"

"I think your book is simply fascinating, Mr. Shantz. I stayed up all night reading it." A snug postadolescent girl in black slid up against Ellie and gazed at him as if he were Hemingway and Norman Mailer rolled into one. "Will you autograph a copy for me?"

"If you'll buy one, honey, I'll be just delighted to sign it for you. What's your name?"

"Michele," she said. "I've already bought your book. I've got it right here." And indeed she had it right there, thrusting it at Ellie like the evidence of a crime.

"Not here, you fool," he told her severely. "Come into the bedroom with me. I never sign anything except in a room with a bed in it. It's bad luck otherwise."

"She thinks he's Marlon Brando," Sophie said to Nick. "What's he going to do in there?"

"Autograph *Itching* naturally," Nick said, helping himself to a sandwich held by a young man dressed up as a waiter. He bit into it and scraps of mayonnaised lobster fell from between the slices of bread, slid down his silk tie, bounced off his knee, and landed on his glossy moccasins. "Damn," he said, looking at the expensive damage. "She ought to know better than to serve whatchamacallits this big."

"I think they're cute," Sophie said, in order to disagree.

"They're vulgar," Nick said.

"It's vulgar to nit-pick," Sophie said and walked away from her husband. She was accustomed to getting her own drink and finding her own way about. She would approach the bar (in this case it was the dining-room table covered with a white cloth and presided over by two men in white monkey jackets and black bow ties, stoic and bored) and say "a gin and tonic" with a self-consciousness that had been brutalized into acerbity. Her solo trips around rooms and through apartments full of people or half empty—rooms that were either strange or familiar, the life histories of their occupants invisibly present like dust in the furniture—often gave Sophie the illusion that she really was alone.

"I made a date with that broad," Ellie said to Sophie. "She wants to interview me for her magazine. I set it up for tomorrow night at my pad."

"A mutual interview, I take it," Sophie said, watching Nick stalk a vividly wasted woman standing by herself and looking as if she needed a drink. Ellie said, "That's Iris' sister, Violet."

"Ellie," Sophie said shrugging, "what's the matter with you?"

Ellie sagged. "You want to hear? You really want to hear?"

Sophie nodded. "If you want to tell me."

He led her to a small study lined with unread books, some bound in red leather, others with dust jackets intact. An enormous plump color television set dominated the room like Queen Victoria at Windsor.

"I've never seen one of those things on," Sophie said.

"It's the same slop, doll; only you can taste it easier in color." Ellie lowered himself into a man-sized leather chair whose skin matched the bound books. "Iris calls this her den. She likes to do it in here; it seems to give an ultra high-frequency charge."

"Yes?" Sophie could wait.

"Yes and no," Ellie said with a flash of self-dramatization. "You might want to hear what's happened to Ellias Shantz. Well, it's a simple case of cause and effect."

Sophie took a wild guess: "Margo?"

Ellie nodded, glumly, like a child admitting to misbehavior. "She hurt you?"

"It's this way," he began, wearier than Oblomov. "The doc assured me there's no functional impairment and that the wound's completely healed. But he's not inside me and I am. I've lost the old bezazz. Sometimes, get this, I can't make it at all. Can you appreciate the beauty of it—Ellie Shantz can't get it up any more? This is, you understand, a tough thing to complain about to one of those clean old M.D.'s but I did it. You know what he said, he said it was just a matter of time before my system absorbed the trauma and it became another footnote in my body's history. He thinks he's got to be literary with me. But, as I said, he's not inside me. It ain't getting any better, that's all I know."

"Oh, Ellie."

He tried to smile but looked, instead, as if he were about to cry. "Cut down in the prime of its life," he said. Sophie suspected he was a little drunk.

"Give yourself a chance, Ellie; it has to improve if there's no functional damage."

"Maybe so, doll," he said. He closed his eyes.

"Does Margo know?"

"Are you kidding? Do you think I'd give her the satisfaction of crowing over her victory? She put Ellie out of commission but I'm damned if she's gonna know about it. The fact that Margo lost her marbles that night doesn't excuse her. I'll let you in on another gamey secret. The reason I didn't press charges against that crazy female is that I didn't want to go into the details in front of some prurient judge or a bug-eyed jury. Let them get that sort of thing from the tabloids over breakfast. If she'd stabbed me anywhere else, you can count on it: I would have had her behind bars until she was way past the menopause. Your pal Margo is a sex maniac."

Sophie cringed from the force of his anger but she could not blame Ellie for wallowing in it. "Ellie," she said, "ever since it happened I've been trying to decide something: did she really try to kill you or was she just trying to hurt you?"

"If you'd seen her eyes that night you would have seen murder in them. That's why I insist she was crazy. But I'm not sure she had the guts to go through with it. The fact is I'm still alive."

"You're thinking the whole thing has a kind of ghastly poetic justice, aren't you?"

"Well, doll, aren't you?"

"I'm afraid I don't, Ellie," she said, as serious as he was contemptuous. And Sophie realized, all at once, that whether his impotence were real or imaginary mattered very little. The man was now as out of work as General MacArthur on his way home from Korea.

Whenever Sophie listened to Nick on the subject of the civil-rights movement, she was amazed at how the right words could sound so off-key, as if the trumpet were bent out of shape. She rarely accompanied him to the meetings because seeing his wife as spectator seemed to enrage him—though no one but Sophie was aware of it.

He came home one night and said to her, as she was propped in bed with her pillow and his, reading and wondering if the pinches of pain in her breasts meant she was pregnant or just the opposite, "Tonight we had a demonstration of how to avoid having our gonads crushed by a boot." He got down on the floor; Sophie had to lean over the side of the bed to watch as he assumed a foetal position. "On the other hand," he went on, his voice muffled by his arms, "once you've committed yourself to this pose it's difficult to protect the back of your head where your brains are." Sophie guessed that Nick was trying to scare her; she remained unmoved by his performance.

"Why don't you tell me something reassuring," she said. He lay curled up like a baby in a crib.

"Such as what?" He got up off the floor and brushed his pants by slapping at them sharply. "We're leaving a week from tomorrow. You want to celebrate on Saturday?"

The threat of danger reached her at last like a cooking odor snaking its way through a large house; it made Nick seem attractive in the old way. For a moment, seeing his prodigiously handsome face, she forgot the persistent pain involved in trying to live with him on some rational, human basis. "If you're sure you want to," she said. "But wouldn't it make more sense to celebrate when you get back?"

"You're afraid I won't come back, aren't you, Sophie?"

"Everybody has fantasies they play with, both good ones and bad," she said. "But I'm not actually afraid you won't come back. After all, this isn't a war. You're not going out to join the International Brigade."

"Your choice of analogy is not as inept as you wish it were," he said solemnly. There was the unmistakable odor, in the man, of pure escalating excitement. Sophie sighed.

They were together in the apartment—she in bed, he standing by a window—they now shared much as two cell-mates share their home. His habits were as familiar to her as her own. Her medicine bottles stood next to his on the bathroom cabinet shelf. Every time she washed it out, lining the contents along the side of the sink and on the windowsill, she was appalled at how the collection had grown, especially his share of it—pills for tension, for restraining his appetite, pills to ease his semiannual muscular spasms, suppositories for recurrent piles, leftover antibiotics from an attack of streptococcus, something cobalt blue and mysterious she had never asked about, and more. He required, it appeared, a great many pills to keep him in working order the way old automobiles need constant attention, gas, and lubrication.

"Are you going to take any pills along with you?" she asked.

"What do you mean?" he said.

"Oh nothing. Do you realize, Nick, that we've been living in some intimacy for nearly five years and we aren't even related?"

Nick was caught off guard. First he smiled, and then he began to laugh. He laughed harder and harder and ended by embracing his wife on the bed where she lay. It was chiefly these sexual conversations, combined with Sophie's obsession to bear children, or even just one child, that kept Sophie's eyes, metaphorically speaking, half shut to the whole truth.

When it was time for Nick to go, Sophie went with him to the bus terminal. The place was basking under blue neon lights—"Do-nut Shoppe," "Gifts," "Rest Rooms"—lining the interior of the buildings like incandescent arteries. In fact, the whole crowd seemed bluish, even the Negroes. Sophie found that it was difficult to move; those waiting to board buses filled the entire waiting room and spilled over onto the concrete platforms outside. They shuffled and changed places with each other, impatience mingling with slight and anxious laughter. Sophie noticed that most of the men and women were younger than she and Nick. Their enthusiasm touched her. She clung, for a moment, to Nick's arm and then, feeling him pull away, released her hold; he was free. He went to talk with a round-faced man she guessed (from the authority of his clothes and manner) to be one of the leaders. In Nick's face she saw signs of intense and well controlled excitement. His lips thinned in tightness; his eyes moved constantly; his legs were springy, like a runner's before the dash. She envied him this excitement and wondered if perhaps it was partly for the claim on this sensation that he had committed himself. Sophie watched and watched, standing uneasily by a bank of twenty-five cent lockers. Nick led his friend over to meet her.

"Sophie, this is Jim Kaye. He and I are going to sit together on the way down." It seemed to Sophie he was making a big thing out of sitting next to a colored man—but then, it was probably just her basic distrust that led her to overinterpret everything Nick said. She stuck out her hand and said, "I'm sorry not to be going with you, Mr. Kaye," and was surprised because she had not intended to make such an admission.

"So am I, Mrs. Brean," Jim Kaye said. "Perhaps on the next trip?"

Nick stopped her from answering: "Jim teaches biology," he said as if he were announcing that Miss America could read.

"Where do you teach, Mr. Kaye?" Sophie asked.

"At a junior high school in Queens," he said. "Nick here is going to give me something special I can pass on to my own students. Your husband is a very fine man, Mrs. Brean." He smiled at Nick and at her, including them both in his gratitude, which was as real and as valid as his ambivalence toward anyone with a white skin. "We're all immensely proud to have him with us." The man with the honest round face and desperate eyes looked from Nick to Sophie and back again, saying much and making no noise at all.

Sophie said at last, "He's proud to be going with you, Mr. Kaye." He told Sophie to call him Jim; everybody called him Jim. Sophie felt loathesome and helpless for knowing Nick so well.

No one, she decided, ought to penetrate the hero's armor; that he has put it on at all is enough. She said, "I hope this isn't going to be too rough on you."

"Rough," Jim repeated as if she had said a word in a language he could not understand. "Oh no, Sophie, this isn't going to be rough; we've been waiting to make this trip for over a hundred years. The only thing I'm worried about is keeping the kids from using their fists. If they start a rumble down there we're worse off than we would be dead. They'll hang us up by the heels."

Nick changed weight, shifting from one foot to the other three times while Jim talked—Sophie was counting. "I've got to buy a few things," he said. "I'll be right back."

A young man, it seemed to Sophie he could not have been more than seventeen, rushed up to Jim Kaye and urgently pulled him away somewhere, leaving Sophie alone once more. Though she was not one of them, she experienced a sense of empathy with the bus riders that amazed her by its force. The girls particularly, with their air of innocent and cool bravery, worn as palpably as the first application of grown-up makeup, stirred Sophie as she was not often stirred. They reminded her of children evacuated from London during the blitz; their courage was as artless as Nick's was sophisticated. I must be getting soft, she thought. I am exaggerating the dangers. Her raw silk suit seemed a complaisant mistake.

"I ought to be in blue jeans," she said to Nick who came up then carrying a copy of *U.S. News & World Report* and several candy bars of different gooey varieties.

"Nonsense, you won't find a single girl here in pants. I believe they were instructed not to appear in slacks but to look as ladylike as possible. Obviously, the order was difficult for some of them to carry out."

"I meant it symbolically, Nick," Sophie said. "When are you actually going to leave?" The tension had started to pinch her and she felt as if she too were about to board one of the huge buses charted by the organization, lined up now in their slots outside, waiting and growling.

"In about five minutes," he said, looking up at the wall clock. "Now," he wondered out loud, "do I have everything?" She knew he had fifty dollars in his wallet.

"Are you sure you need all that?" she asked.

"Relatively," he said.

"I don't quite understand why you're taking it in the first place. This isn't exactly a shopping expedition," she said.

"I'm not planning to spend it," he said. "It's for an emergency. You never can tell when fifty bucks will come in handy."

Something about his attitude struck Sophie as odd. She was certain they were told not to bring money with them (it would simply be confiscated and never returned), and she doubted if anyone knew about Nick's violation. But she trusted her husband; the wise owl had an unerring instinct in this kind of situation, where the possibilities as well as the certainties could be played with like two matching dice.

The kiss that they exchanged just before Nick climbed into the bus was elegant with meaning and had the power to send Sophie home more convinced than ever that her husband would willingly enslave almost anyone who offered himself for the job.

The accounts of what happened to this wave of sitters-in varied, naturally, according to where they were published. In several Northern papers, Nick was shown being led away from the scene by a cigar-chewing policeman who apparently made no attempt to hide either his contempt or the enormous bulge of stomach which hung suspended over his garrison belt, as large and solid as a stuffed turkey. The expression on Nick's face caught by the camera and frozen for eternity to admire was unmistakably beatific and a source of particular pride to the organization. Sophie, seeing it for the first time, correctly guessed that the picture would be used for propaganda purposes; its blackness was so black, its whiteness so manifest. And, in fact, six months later the photograph of Nick and his captor appeared on the cover of a fund-raising leaflet mailed out by the hundreds of thousands.

"That cop looks as if he were accustomed to cleaning up after elephants in the zoo," she said to Nick later.

"He's a deputy sheriff," Nick said. "He takes pride in his work. He felt it a privilege to tell me that the South will never accept integration. He was as certain of that as his wife is that God is looking over her shoulder when she scours her toilet bowl."

"How can they be so wrong and so certain at the same time?" Sophie mused, knowing the answer. "It's discouraging," she said. "I've seen children whose only good qualities have been irretrievably lost by the age of eight. What can I expect?"

"We can only keep doing what we've *been* doing," Nick said in a rare moment of generous and simple clarity. Sophie considered the task and felt inadequate.

If Nick's trip did not accomplish anything concrete, it did make its point. Similar trips followed it and eventually the point became too sharp for even mayors and governors to ignore. Nick had ridden with the first wave; this in itself exhilarated him and increased his stature; the circles made by his pebble of influence grew larger. Sophie often found him insufferable at home.

Unlike some secrets shared, Ellie's brought him closer to Sophie than ever before. On her side she continued to see in him an ideal companion; they played few games together. Once in a while, when Ellie had business—always mysterious —uptown, they met in a chrome and plastic delicatessen off Sixth Avenue, owned by a cousin of Ellie's father. They always got one of the three booths. The food was only fair. Sophie sat opposite Ellie, watching with fascination as he ate, and said, "Nick thinks he's the new leader of the black race. He's got a genuine T. E. Lawrence complex about all this which, while there's no disputing its effectiveness, makes him unbearable. I wouldn't think of teasing him about it."

"Listen, doll, you've got to understand. This whatever you want to call it—movement, revolution, whatever—is the most reassuring thing that's happened in this country since F.D.R. hired starving artists. I mean, you can't feel halfway about this, Soph; there's some people even going to get knocked off for their belief in this thing. You know, it's like we just woke up. You can't blame old Nick for throwing himself into it."

"Oh, Ellie, don't. I know all about how important it is. I'm with it. There's mustard on your chin. I'm not talking about involvement or commitment. I'm talking about what it's doing to Nick Brean. He's messianic. He won't even hang up his towels any more. The whole apartment is strewn with damp towels. No, I'm kidding; I pick them up."

"That's what a wife is for," Ellie told her. He speared several slices of pastrami that had escaped from between slices of dark rye and shoved them into his mouth. "Delicious," he murmured. "I've started turning to food now that sex has lost its kick. I've put on five pounds in the last month." He looked miserable.

"But you're happy about the book, aren't you?"

"The book," he repeated, as if he had forgotten it existed. "*Commentary* loved it; *Midstream* compared me to Joyce; *Partisan Review* called it the funniest satire since The Three Stooges. As of last Friday it's sold eight thousand copies, most of them, for some mysterious reason, in Philadelphia."

Sophie did not know whether eight thousand was good or bad. "How does your publisher feel about it?" she asked.

"Ecchh," he said, "who knows? But next week, ask me about Hollywood. I understand Sonny Tufts is considering the part of the cat with the itch."

Sophie laughed. Then she remembered the money. She had determined not to share this one secret but somehow, encoun-

tering Ellie's face poised above his glass of Cel-Ray tonic, asking to hear more, always hear more about the lives other people
led, she could not resist.

"You'd probably hear anyway," she said softly.

"Hear what, doll?" She could almost see his ears stiffen.

"Hear what Nick did with the money he took with him to
Mississippi?"

"He bribed a guard of course."

"How did you know?" she asked.

"That's what everybody does—or tries to do—the moment
they get locked up. You want another chopped liver? I'm
gonna get an order of blintzes. They're great here." Ellie
waved at the waitress who winked at him and came over.
When he had ordered, he said, "What did Nick's guard do for
the money? By the way, how much *was* it?"

"Well, he took fifty dollars with him but he came back with
fifteen of it; thirty-five bucks," she said, "for a number of
services."

"Such as?" Ellie was so interested he was almost taking
notes.

"The first thing he bought was a call to *The New York Times*
bureau in Atlanta. Then he got himself a pillowcase and a
clean blanket. He was also slipped a slice of real ham for
dinner. But best of all—and this is what really kills me—the
guard let him out twelve hours earlier than the others. You see,
Nick had found out somehow that the judge who was going to
try their case was a cousin of his college roommate."

"Come on, what's the joke?"

"No, Ellie, listen to this. Nick figured he might be able to
talk to this man, you know, sort of spread the gospel in a
civilized manner. So he bribed the guard to let him out and he
went and found this judge and took him to lunch in the town's
only hotel where they ate porterhouse and drank lager and
talked for hours—mostly, I suspect, about mutual enthusiasms
and very little about why Nick was there in the first place."

"How can you be sure?"

"Because later, when Nick was describing this little scene, he told me that the judge was one of those men who are paranoid about Negroes. Rational, maybe, in every other respect but paranoid about what's referred to as mongrelizing the race and so on. You know the type. It's best not to get anywhere near the touchy subject with people like that because they'll only dig their heels in harder. Anyway, apparently Nick's being who he is and all, the others in the group thought he did just fine to try and didn't begrudge him his few extra hours of freedom—or his pillowcase. I myself think his performance was sickening."

"And I think, Sophie, you're being just a little hard on Nick," Ellie said, wiping his glistening lips. "Going down there wasn't the easiest thing for him, either."

"Ellie, the only thing I see is that we can't agree about this. You either do something or you don't. You can't be somewhat jailed for your principles any more than you can be a little pregnant."

Ellie shrugged. "Kid," he said gently, "the whole world's a little nutty and that's what keeps the reader going; just to find out what nutty things are going to happen next. For example, dig this: your friend Margo the maniac is going to marry that art critic whatshisname, Ginkgo."

"What?"

"Margo's going to get married on Sunday, like all good Jewish girls. According to the horse herself it was a whirlwind romance." Ellie looked, for a moment, as if he were holding a mouthful of slightly high egg yolk in his mouth with no place to spit.

"Now, why, I wonder, did she tell you and not me?"

" 'Cause with you, doll, she might feel sheepish. With me she wants to rub my nose in it or stick out her tongue like a little girl."

"He's twice her age," Sophie gasped. The pieces and people of Sophie's world were being shaken in a cup like a pair of dice and poured out in peculiar, shocking combinations.

"She'll do all right with Ginkgo," Ellie told her. "He'll look after her, tell her when she's putting on too much weight,

(226)

criticize her work before it's finished, teach her about serving filet of beef to his rich collector friends, buy her even maybe a fur coat, and dress her properly for once—for an artist, her taste in clothes is vile. She'll profit from living with someone like him; she needs his kind of arrogant support. I, for one, think she'll be much happier with Ginkgo than *she* thinks she'll be. And then, Margo's probably gonna have several years of merry widowhood—which never hurt a chick like her. Gives them a kind of desperate dignity. Why, she'll be almost irresistible as a widow."

Sophie drooped and Ellie went on:

"Don't, doll, don't look so down in the mouth. Not everyone wants to marry the handsome young prince and live happily ever after. Marriage isn't like that. *You* of all people should know that." There were things he wasn't saying out loud but she heard them nonetheless.

"I'll call Margo myself. She didn't invite you to the wedding, did she?"

"Good heavens, girl, Margo may be impulsive but if she can pull herself together sufficiently to become Mrs. Ginkgo, then she's still got enough sense not to invite me to her wedding. After all, she's convinced Ginkgo that she stabbed me in self-defense."

"And he believes that?"

"He's got to, doll, for his own self-protection."

As things turned out, not even Sophie was invited to Margo's wedding. The engaged couple squeezed into Ginkgo's Triumph with their new cowhide luggage and drove away from the city until they reached a town whose best motel offered them large clean towels and a private refrigerator. They spent the night there and were married the following morning. The place was just west of Pittsburgh. After the marriage was legalized, they got in Ginkgo's car again and drove clear across the country to San Francisco, where Ginkgo sat on an exhibition jury for $350. It was in all respects a successful trip and Margo discovered that, as she wrote to Sophie on a postcard from Denver, "Marriage helps you sit still," which message, though cryptic, Sophie understood.

Nick did not venture farther south than Maryland again. He had accomplished, however, even more than he had set out to do. His one journey's sequel was an example of the expert galvanizing of the public's opinion. There were, for example, the television programs during which, seated on a director's chair, Nick took turns listening and describing, in raw and cold-blooded details, the trip itself, the rationale behind it, and, especially, the hazards in store for those still to go. Sophie would watch his doll-sized figure on her screen at home, trying desperately to separate the words from the man whose mouth had issued them and reproaching herself at the same time for questioning their validity. They performed a real function; they persuaded. And if they did not, in some cases, persuade, at least they moved.

"Look, kid," Ellie told her one day, after the usual complaint, "Nick means what he says; he's no crap artist. But stop trying to make him 100 per cent saint. Just accept it. The man's as complex as the rest of us—no more, no less."

"Ellie, you simply don't know what Nick's really like. He means it but he's a bastard." Sophie was utterly frustrated, in the way that some people can see shapes and patterns in their lives and yet be helpless to alter anything. "Not a bastard, just terribly terribly difficult and destructive." The temptation to create a public scene nibbled at the edge of her consciousness. She considered calling her old therapist, a man of seventy-five with a reputation as notoriously white as his hair, to complain and argue, but she dismissed the impulse as weak though she secretly suspected she was a coward. Sophie felt split down the middle.

It was still agreeable enough to go out with him—to parties or receptions—and hear him crediting "those brave kids" as he called them, generosity glistening like oil on a swimmer's skin. Then she would go home with him and have to listen to him accusing her of not opening her mouth enough (or too much), of flirting with someone (a fantasy on his part; she was far too unhappy to flirt), of yawning through the meal, of, in short, making a poor impression.

"You ought to think about pulling yourself together," he said.

"Oh, for heaven's sake, Nick, you sound so flatulent." It grew easier and easier for her to say what she was thinking; the consequences seemed less dreadful than they had even in the recent past.

"And you sound as if you were deliberately avoiding the subject." Why is the subject always me or you, she wondered.

"Nick, I've . . . something's got to give." It was out at last.

"I don't know what you mean." Nick removed one shoe and inserted a hinged shoe tree into it. He took off the other shoe, treed it, and placed both exactly parallel on the floor of his closet.

"We're not getting along the way we should any more."

"Who's to say how we should? If you ask me, there's been no appreciable change in our relationship since we came back from our honeymoon. Have you been talking to your mother?"

"Of course I've been talking to my mother. But not about you. I don't talk about you to Mama."

"Why, Sophie," he said, smirking, "I didn't know I was such a threat to your old lady."

"Don't flatter yourself, Nick," Sophie came back. "It's my barrenness, as she refers to it, that keeps me from discussing you with her. Mama blames *you* for it." Sophie watched her husband preparing himself for bed and was amazed at how detached she felt by his performance. The play was tedious and she wanted to leave. Even his nakedness was boring.

"You're too tense," Nick said, turning the conversation on its bottom and then spinning it so the sparks hit her and not him. "You won't conceive until you permit yourself to loosen up. Your ova exist in a prison of tissue as impregnable as a concrete wall."

And as Sophie listened to his medical advice—which was no more than just another accusation—the notion that a year earlier had occurred to Margo with unhappy clarity suddenly struck Sophie, the wife, bit into her like a tack left on the seat. She jumped up and flew onto the stage: "I'm beginning to doubt seriously whether I *ought* to have your baby, Nick: it would probably be as monstrous as you are! Look at your precious Robby!" The notion was as stunning as any she had ever entertained. Sophie's past and present coincided, created a terrific explosion, and collapsed in a shuddering of tears and unintelligible sounds.

Nick remained calm. He climbed into bed as if nothing at all had taken place.

"Can't you say anything real to me?" Sophie cried.

"How can I possibly talk to you at all when you act like a child and start shrieking and crying? You're in no condition to discuss anything. Look how you drag Robby into this. Just what the hell has he got to do with it?" She suspected her speech had startled him, but not into revealing anything. He would retreat further from a threat as threatening as divorce.

"Oh God, the man's daft," she said, amazed at how little it mattered now. She went into the bathroom and gazed at her image, which was fuzzy with emotion. Thank God you're in shock, she told it, or you might do something to be sorry about.

10

Amy invited Nick and Sophie for dinner. Nick had a speaking engagement so Sophie went alone, assuming Nick would have got out of going in any case. He didn't much care for people younger than twenty-five unless they were working for CORE or SNCC. In fact, more and more frequently now, Sophie and Nick drifted to different engagements, tacitly avoiding, both of them, the circumstances which might arouse her to tears or anger. The night Sophie was invited to Stuart's and Amy's for dinner, she had come home from work late and very tired. Without bothering to take off her dress, she had flopped on the double bed and fallen asleep. In her dream, a particularly vivid and poignant one, scraps of her childhood floated up and bobbed around, provoking her. Actual scenes were reproduced for her inspection, including one particularly terrifying moment when her father had dropped a yapping dog into her crib while she was sitting in it, and the face of her mother, hanging by the edge, a mask of impotent fright.

When Sophie woke up it was late; darkness had found all the cracks in the apartment, and for a minute she did not know what time it was or what day. She rose groggily and felt her way to the bathroom where she washed quickly and decided it was too late to change. She found a string of red glass beads and, fixing the clasp, shuddered at their iciness as they hit the flesh of her throat. She looked once more at her reflection (it was getting to be a habit—as if she were checking to make sure she was still there) and saw a kind of spinsterish chill in her features.

Stuart and Amy lived in the closest thing to a ghetto the New World has produced. To Sophie, as she walked the two blocks from the subway, it seemed very much a home that she might have wanted. Maybe I'm a throwback, she thought, wondering if Nick had ever tasted a knish or the air inside a synagogue on Friday night, though of course he was as thoroughly a semitophile as it was possible to get without converting: his best friend was a Jew, and his wife. The idea that he might have married her in order to tell his OK anti-Jew jokes was as appalling as it was sudden, and she dismissed it as a symptom of her own anxiety.

Sophie found the place with some difficulty for few of the houses seemed to be numbered. Stuart's apartment was three flights up in a peeling and cracking five-story house, so like its sisters on the block that even the smell of garlic and faulty drains were identical. She was breathless after the short climb and had to pause on the dark landing before she was able to ring the bell and apologize for being late.

Amy had dressed for Sophie. The skin of her forehead and cheeks was scrubbed shiny. The girl wore no makeup except black eyeliner, which had the paradoxical effect of suggesting at the same time startled innocence and confident sophistication. She wore a simple, beltless black wool jersey dress with a beautiful star-shaped silver pin on the slope of one breast. If she had had any more style, it would have seemed insolence.

"We got married last month," Amy beamed at Sophie.

They sat. Stuart said, "Would you like some beer? I'm sorry that's all we have."

Sophie recognized that they were still stumbling around in the unfamiliar territory which belonged, by rights, to accomplished hosts and hostesses. Amy brought out a plate of crackers and Italian cheese and passed it. They lived, it appeared, in two rooms and a kitchen. The place reeked of love and paint, both equally strong.

Amy chattered about, of all things, her family. A brother was in the army, in Georgia. "He says he can't bring himself to use his pass. What he sees makes him sick, he says."

"Danny's a very sensitive guy," Stuart said. "He better learn not to brood about everything he sees or he'll lose his marbles."

"How will shutting his eyes do any good, or change anything?" Amy wanted to know.

"Danny's got to exist on his own terms. Right? He's also got to live in the world. Somehow he's going to have to square it with himself."

"But what about the things that make him sick? They'd make *you* sick too if you were there."

"How much he does about those things depends on how strong a stomach he develops. And you can't do that by sitting around on your prat and reading *Remembrance of Things Past* all day and all night." Stuart's dialogue with Amy excluded Sophie; they had forgotten her. She took the opportunity to think about herself and Nick; but the thoughts made her queasy so she stopped. She was finally aware that the one real bona fide mistake she had made in her life—marrying Nicholas Brean—was immense, its consequences innumerable and lasting, its implications almost too much to be asked to bear. Sitting with these two, one of whom she had never laid eyes on before, was like sitting in front of a mirror that told you not what you saw but what you ought to see.

She stared openly at Stuart, who was her consolation. His

handsome features had thickened slightly just as his meta-
phorical skin had. He looked his age; he acted older. Whatever
he would do to his credit would be to her credit as well.

"I'd like to give you two a wedding present," Sophie said.
"Something beautiful or something useful. It probably won't
be both."

Amy and Stuart looked at one another, considering the offer.
Amy said, "That's awfully nice of you, Mrs. Brean."

"Please don't call me that—I'm Sophie," she said. And
silently begged Dr. Strauss to forgive her. "I'm breaking all the
rules," she explained, "but—you understand—I have to."

"We do need a large sharp knife," Stuart said, shy of
admitting it.

"They're so expensive," Amy said. "I saw one in Macy's
yesterday for twelve dollars." Sophie saw that Stuart was
embarrassed for his wife but would say nothing, trusting that
she would learn, in time, when to keep her mouth shut.

"If you really would like a knife, I'd love to get one for you.
So you chose the useful. I think I would, too." She looked at
Amy's dress and decided the girl was pregnant, though she
could see no real clue. There was, however, something about
the way she stood, exaggerating the sway of her slight back
and the thrust of her hips, something that was a dead give-
away. Stuart moved closer to his wife on the couch and took
her hand. They are lovely, thought Sophie; they have created a
dream and have stepped right into it. Amy pulled her hand
away reluctantly. "I have to put the fish in the oven," she told
Stuart. She left the room and they were alone together.

"I'm sorry it can't be steak," Stuart apologized. He was
obviously suffering from being left in the same room with his
former therapist; it was as simple as that.

She was *not* studying him; she would like him to be aware of
that. If she could never be his friend, at least she could try to
make herself available to him in other ways.

"I love fish," she told him. "I wouldn't eat it when I was little
but I grew up. I don't know many children who like fish."

"Maybe that's because it's so easy to imagine them all slimy and slithering through the water. I never liked it much either, until Amy started cooking for me. What I hated most was gefilte fish. Man, the way my mother used to serve it was really vile. She always made me eat at least two bites so I used to smear it up with red horse-radish and swallow it with a mouthful of water so I didn't have to taste it. Amy wants to learn Jewish cooking, but *I'm* not going to teach her; she's going to have to find herself another teacher. Don't tell her, but I wouldn't care if I never had another bite of Jewish food in my whole life." He was visibly relaxing. He poured himself another beer and offered more to Sophie.

"My husband would agree with you," she told him, wondering when they were going to talk about Stuart. She waited, suppressing impatience, and lit another cigarette.

"It's too bad," Stuart said, "that he couldn't come tonight. Amy bought enough for six. Don't tell her I said so, but she seems to have trouble with quantities."

"It took me four years to learn just how much food to get," Sophie said. "It's usually a matter of guesswork anyway because you never can tell how hungry your guests will be." They continued to look past one another. She could hardly blame him. "Nick said to tell you how sorry he was he couldn't make it tonight," she lied. "He had to give a talk."

"Oh," Amy said, coming back to set the round table in the corner with Salvation Army silverware, "we understand." Sophie suspected that Amy was trying to thank her for something—though she could not imagine what—and was reluctant to come out with it. She retired once more to the kitchen where the dinner was waiting for her final touches.

"Stuart . . ." Sophie began and then found suddenly that she was shy.

"Yes?" he said, his eyes finding hers for the first time all evening.

She held his response in her mind, for a moment, like a blessing. "Will you show me some of your work?"

"Sure," he said, sighing. "If you really want to see it. After we eat, if that's OK with you."

"Fine," she told him. "That will be fine." It shouldn't be so difficult to talk to him, she thought. They were waiting one another out, but for what? Could she praise him openly without losing something precious? "I think you have done beautifully, even without seeing your work," she ventured at last. "I'm more pleased than I can possibly tell you."

It wasn't quite right; it was like the time she had called his drawing beautiful when she meant strong. She saw him flush. He said, without acknowledging the clumsy compliment, "We think Amy is pregnant. We're pretty sure, in fact."

"I guessed," Sophie said. "But are you trying to make me believe that's why you got married? Should I believe it?"

His expression—uncharacteristically sheepish—told her she did indeed understand him. It buoyed her. "That's *not* why, is it?" she insisted.

"No," he admitted, his eyes down. "We're really hung up on each other."

Amy came back and sat down next to her husband again, close, so that their flanks touched and their hands. She looked as if she had been working hard in the kitchen. She did not bother to suppress a sigh of fatigue. The shine on her skin had been replaced by a pretty blush of heat.

"I don't like it when we're apart for even a few hours," the girl told Sophie proudly. "I guess I'm terribly spoiled."

Amy wanted to find out about Nick. "I admire Dr. Brean," she said. "There aren't many people Stuart and I see, that is of *your* generation, who we'd want to think of as models," she said. "I guess I really was sort of disappointed that he couldn't come tonight."

"He had a speech to make in Washington," Sophie said. "There'll be other times," she added a little wistfully.

"He's taken sides, hasn't he?" Amy pursued her.

"Yes, he has. All his free time—and some of it that's not so free—he's been working with civil-rights groups."

"You must be proud," Amy said. *Proud* was obviously a word she used only once every two or three years.

"Of course I am," Sophie said. "But I don't get to see much

of him these days. He's an absentee husband a lot of the time."

Stuart said something about the price men had to pay for being heroes. Sophie wondered if Stuart had caught on. She remembered that he possessed the neurotic's uncanny sense of smelling out fraud.

She would never uncover anything intimate for Amy and Stuart to inspect, no matter how close they might become. She could no more tell Stuart her troubles than she could her mother or Dr. Strauss or Margo (busy being a bride and collecting other people's pictures). Ellie, of course, listened. But she could not wholly trust Ellie. He was a writer before all. He might listen with sympathetic eyes, but he also might go and write it all down as soon as they parted. He had warned her himself, one boozy moment. "Watch out for writers, doll; they're a bunch of sneaky bastards." Oh, Ellie, she thought, there are so many things wrong. How do you get so many women?

A buzzer went off in the kitchen and Amy jumped up again. "I can see why you're hung up on her," Sophie said to Stuart.

He said nothing to that. "I'll go see if she needs some help."

"Can I do something?" Sophie asked.

"Oh no," Stuart said. "But thanks. It's much too small in there. The two of us can hardly fit as it is. Why don't you just take it easy for a few minutes? I'm sure dinner'll be ready soon." He followed his wife.

Sophie was given tacit permission to snoop. She had rules about such things. You could not open anything that was shut: drawers, doors, envelopes, boxes, refrigerators, closets, cabinets. Everything else was fair game: letters left lying about, books, pictures, family artifacts, all smells, sights, suggestions, implications, bathtub rings, shaving equipment, the clues to the rhythms and substance of other lives. You could tell more from a woman's stockpile of cosmetics than from her table manners or even her publicly expressed opinions. The rooms Sophie examined now were grubby, she discovered, in ways that were not immediately evident. Cigarette ash, for one thing, lay over the table tops; fine and filmy, it might have been there for weeks. The backs of the wooden chairs were gummy; the curtains, an inexpensive burlapy material, were streaked with tears of sooty New York grime. The couch cover had nebulous stains; the floor under her shoes felt sandy, indicating that it had not been vacuumed for quite a while. Yet all around was evidence of a sincere effort to clean up, probably for her sake. Cushions had been plumped into fat symmetry and neatly arranged; the small rectangle of purple oriental rug was swept clean; things had been generally straightened or put out of sight, for nothing irrelevant could be seen. No old socks or newspapers, empty glasses, the remains of a snack; no paper bags, cleaner's bills, unfilled prescriptions, envelopes; no contorted paint tubes or unread advertising circulars. With no difficulty Sophie could imagine drawers or closets stuffed with some or all of these things. There were stuffers, and there were sorters and Sophie figured Amy to be a stuffer—which was fine as long as she was married to a stuffer.

The squalor had, for Sophie, an inverted but unmistakable glamor. For she had little patience with compulsive scrubbers and sweepers and scourers. They were as unsympathetic as hypochondriacs and, in fact, shared some of the hypochondriac's morbid and wasteful preoccupations. She knew people —too many—who could not hand you a drink without a coaster to slide underneath it, who never ran out of toilet paper or toothpaste or shampoo, and who neglected, in the process, the strained cries for help from the people who shared their lives. And she knew few, like this couple, to whom order had as little importance as the name of the baby just born to the couple two houses down the street.

Sophie looked at a painting on the bedroom wall and would have recognized it as a Prince even without its small, black, cornered signature. She could have, if called upon, described this picture as restrained thrashing, as if the swimmer were tiring critically. The colors were bright and clear, almost fierce. The message, however, was somewhat garbled, and at once Sophie recognized that Stuart was preparing himself to make a decisive compromise. Poor thing, she sighed, it happens to the best of us.

"Soup's on," Stuart said, coming up behind her. Sophie sat between them like the mother. In front of her lay a shallow white bowl of inky borsch with a white lump of sour cream like an island of shaving soap. "Lovely," she said, not aware until now that she was hungry at all. The food seemed to have the same ungluing effect on her that gin usually had. She felt almost giddy over the large haddock lying in its tub of hot sour cream. An experienced cook would never have ventured to use sour cream twice within the same meal, but Amy, without knowing what she was doing, had brought it along as a kind of leitmotiv. When dessert arrived and it was pears with an imported cream cheese, Sophie thought, she's seen it right through to the end, and knew that if Amy lacked the imagination to be wholly various, at least her coherence was admirable. The cheese was delicious.

Unaccustomed to feeding company, Amy was solicitous to the point of sweetness. There was a certain amount of clattering between courses, and Sophie would have preferred to help. It would have brought her closer to Amy; if not in reality at least physically, it would have made her one of them instead of the outsider, but they refused to let her get up. When, toward the end of dinner, Sophie had to use the bathroom, she encountered, as she rose with a polite murmur, a double cry of protest until she explained exactly what she was doing. In the bathroom a curious question occurred to her: why have they asked me here? The giddiness was now giving way to insecurity. She looked at her hair in the mirror above the sink and it was dowdy; it was looped and curled, altogether too "fixed." Amy's blonde hair hung straight and unadorned, though brushed to a shimmer. There *is* a difference, she thought, but I'm hardly an old lady. Sophie worried about the difference, standing in the tiny bathroom among the old-fashioned fixtures nobody had bothered to modernize: the tub on squat bowlegs; the toilet with its huge overhanging tank; faded and scuffed linoleum on the floor; and grime in the corners that could not be reached by any ordinary cleaning method. The difference had crept up on her in spite of the fact that every day she saw girls only slightly younger than Amy in her office, and what she had read as rebellion might be simply *that* difference, not age exactly, but a style, a cleaner style and more direct. She touched her hair and decided to cut it short. When she came out of the bathroom Amy had cleared the table.

"May I see the pictures now?" Sophie asked Stuart.

"They're all over the place," he told her. "I'll go get them." He acted as if she were prying, but justifiably, like a doctor taking a medical history. He submitted but his willingness had an edge to it, which Sophie deliberately overlooked because she wanted to see his work. She stood as he showed them one by one, like a gallery owner, saying nothing. These paintings transmitted their messages in the same way that the one hanging on the wall had, as if there were a great deal of static between sender and receiver. He looked at her just once, and in his eyes she detected a desperate resignation, very like a muzzled dog's. When he had shown her the final picture Stuart said, "I'm thinking of going out and finding a real job."

Sophie laughed with nervous relief. "You can probably use the money," she said.

"It's not what you think," he protested. "It's because of the baby. It makes Amy nervous; she keeps asking me what we're going to feed it. I told her the tit was good for at least six months, but she says in that case, *she's* got to eat more. So I'm going to work."

"What do you call all this?" she asked, indicating the paintings.

He shrugged. "Anybody can slap a paintbrush around a canvas."

"Stuart," Sophie began soberly, "I'm no longer your therapist so you don't really have to listen. But I hope you don't object. After I've finished, you can disregard it if it doesn't make sense to you."

He shook his head as if he were not sure he wanted to hear anything from anybody. After all, he had spent irretrievable time convincing himself he had only one mother and, at that, one whose usefulness had long been outlived.

"Remember," she said, smiling, "I'm not your mother."

He laughed and relaxed. Amy was somewhere in back of them.

"This all sounds so ominous," Sophie said. "All I'm really trying to say is this: if you decide to quit art school and get a full-time job, make sure you know *why* you're doing it. Otherwise you may wake up some morning when you're forty-five and realize you've been running in the wrong race—if you'll forgive an unforgivably square metaphor. And you know, you won't be able to start all over again, not unless you're a Gauguin." She stopped, surprised at the ardor of her moralizing. If anyone had talked to her like that when she was Stuart's age, she would have dismissed him as either crazy or a meddler.

Stuart looked thoughtful, taking in about half of what she implied. Sophie felt the room heat suddenly and start tilting. She sat down without acknowledging her vertigo and pretended, while trying to keep from passing out, to inspect something on her instep. The blood gradually filled her head once more. She sighed, sucking in gulps of reluctant air.

Stuart was silent, still speculating and discarding. "Amy says I could be first-rate."

"What do *you* think?" Sophie said, trying not to sound as if she were gasping.

"I'm not sure," he admitted. "But you can't live on maybe. At least not when there's a baby around the corner." It was melodramatic, but he'd made his point. "You don't have to give up painting," Sophie said, beginning queasily to revive.

"Sunday painters are worse than the tourists with their cameras who come down here to gawk at the quaint little Hebrews in their natural habitat." Stuart nearly spat on the floor.

"You don't have to be a Sunday painter," Sophie said. "You can get up early and paint before you leave for work. Or at night. I have a friend who writes. He never even *looks* at his typewriter until eleven at night."

"Painters can't work at night; they need daylight. At least my kind of painter."

"Well, the mornings then." She did not like the niggling tone of their conversation. "In any case, that's really beside the point. What's relevant is that if you're a painter you'll paint; if you're not, you won't. It's a perfectly normal compulsion, just like any other." She was reciting a lesson that no one believed until he could test it for himself, like a remedy for toothache.

"It's so easy to say that," Stuart said.

"Are you worried about turning out to be just like everyone else?"

He stared at her, mute, afraid to talk.

"You won't, you know; you're Stuart. You're you." Sophie nearly choked over the words. Her creature, Stuart, had surpassed her—and he wasn't even aware of his feat. He could "carry on"; she would have to start all over again at the beginning.

Amy came up then. "Aren't they neat?" she said, indicating the canvases.

"He keeps improving," Sophie said. And then, on an impulse, she added, "I think I'd like to buy one. If they're for sale?"

Amy and Stuart were startled, just as Sophie was startled by her offer. "How much is this one?"

Stuart's face twisted. "You don't have to do that," he said.

"I know I don't have to. I *want* to."

"That one's called 'Oedipus Three,' " Amy said.

"That was my joke!" Stuart was upset. "It's untitled. Why do painters feel they have to stick a name on something abstract? Aren't there millions of particles of feeling and thought that can't be labeled? Why does a picture have to have a name? It's not a dog, for Christ's sake. This one you want is untitled. It's seventy-five bucks."

"I think you're underestimating your market value," Sophie said, "but I won't argue." She told them she would mail them a check in the morning. Stuart put the paintings away, all but the one Sophie had bought, and the three sat again, in the same pattern they had formed before dinner. Sophie looked at Amy's body and envied it and thought, with an immense sadness because it was composed of so much truth: I may never have one. At the same time she was struck by the agonizing reality that she was happier away from Nick than with him, a reality she had resisted much as you do the certain knowledge that your child is a thief or your best friend a liar, a truth so unpalatable as to be regurgitated the moment it is swallowed, so disastrous as to invite a lasting cloud of depression to come and stay at your house until they bury you.

I have to start all over again she cried in the silence of her solitude, wondering why it had taken her so long to admit a mistake so grotesque. It is because we are in love with what we do, she decided, and we cannot bear to think our choice is as bad as we're afraid it might be.

Amy and Stuart, lulled by dinner and the quiet, the satisfaction of eating and entertaining, the pleasure they felt at having Sophie there—for after all they looked on her, too, as a model though she was not aware of the intensity of their gratitude—stared at one another with open lust. They wanted her to leave so that they could go to bed and make love.

Sophie sensed something and got up to go.

The couple saw her to the door, standing hip to hip and swaying slightly in their anticipation. She thought (as she thanked them, the picture gripped in one hand), they are just where they ought to be. I have no desire to disturb them. The moment when the dream ends will come but it would be cruel to force it.

"Good night," she said softly. "It was a lovely evening. The food was delicious—I'm afraid I ate too much of it." Then she added, "I think you're both terribly lucky." It was a concept Sophie, like all good mind doctors, was extremely skeptical about. People generally create their own luck; it does not happen to them.

On the way home Sophie had one further thought which

seemed to matter: some people don't think about getting married; they just get married, entering with no more thought than a monkey might into what she remembered Marianne Moore had called "this crystal-fine experiment, this amalgamation which can never be more than an interesting possibility."

And at last she began to comprehend a little more about Nick's concern, his intensely personal, bleeding concern for those deprived by society of mercy: it was all very well as long as the sufferers remained as abstract as the gray dolls hopping around the television screen; but as soon as Nick was confronted by the *reality* of human need—as in her case or his first wife's or Robby's or anybody's—he could be as cruel as the rest of them. No—crueler. And was it always like that with the reformers and champions? She hoped to God not and was not sure.

As Sophie lay, later, in the half-warm bed that smelled like Nick, she recognized this tiny mound of truth, distilled like a precious powder from the partial truths and accidents of her life, and she stared at it with mournful clarity: she might ultimately have adjusted to living with Nick (in spite of his vanities and barbaric habits) if he had been willing to let marriage be a game that did not have to be a winner. Ellie was right: Nick needed a contest. Well, she didn't feel like being the perpetual contestant. She wanted her work to mean something more to Nick than the source of a sour-grapes joke; she wanted to do certain things at her own speed, in her own way. She wanted, in short, a balance that meant harmony, not misery. I don't want to fight for the rest of my life, she sighed. I haven't the stomach for it.

The next morning Sophie was gripped by an attack of morning sickness so severe that after she vomited her breakfast, a small blob of blood, a crimson punctuation mark, followed; the whole nauseating experience queering any attempt she might make to leave Nick with prudence, indeed.

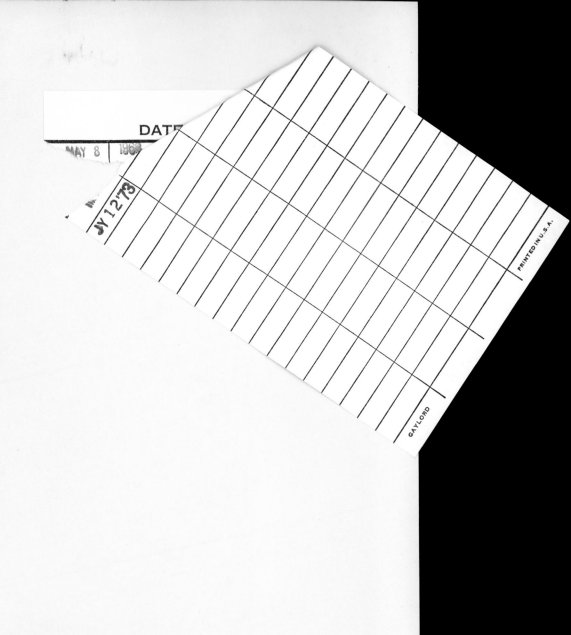